Dark Harbor House

Dark Harbor House

A Novel

by
Tom DeMarco

Down East Books
Camden / Maine

1   3   5   4   2

Down East Books
P.O. Box 679, Camden, ME 04843
BOOK ORDERS: 1-800-685-7962

LIBRARY OF CONGRESS CATALOGING-IN-PUBLICATION DATA

DeMarco, Tom.
    Dark Harbor House : a novel / by Tom DeMarco
        p.   cm.
    ISBN 0-89272-511-7
    1. Islesboro Island (Me.)—Fiction. I. Title.
    PS3554.E449 D37 2000
    813'.54—dc21
                                        00-60114

Contents

To Justin Kodner,
my favorite storyteller

Cast of Characters

IN AND AROUND DARK HARBOR HOUSE IN THE 1890S

Norbert Chance, builder and original owner of Dark Harbor House

Jeannie Isobel, religious charismatic and leader of the Gideon Compact

Dorothea (Haydée) Benton, religious charismatic and leader of the Zion Benton Community

W. K. Kellog, inventor of the cornflake

Dr. Orin G. Ralston, inventor of Wheat Chex and Rice Chex, original owner of North Star House

Charles William Post, inventor of Postum and Post Toasties

Ephram Whittier, lobsterman and mechanic

1

Mr. Collyer

"Portland." The mahogany and fabric-covered box above Liam's head was speaking. "Portland Station next. Portland! Portland, Portland, Portland. Next will be Portland Station. Portland Station is next. The next stop is . . . Portland!" A hiss and then relative quiet.

Liam yawned, waking slowly. Outside there was still the thin rain that had been following all the way from Boston. He knew it was there, though the window was fogged so thickly that he couldn't actually see. He stretched in his seat and yawned again. For want of anything better to do, he rubbed his hand on the window's surface, clearing a small circle. The view revealed nothing more than what he'd been able to see through the clouded glass: mist, a swath of pine trees not too far from the track, now and again a bit of cleared field. There was a good deal of mud. No sign yet of the outskirts of a city or town. The train rattled past an unmarked platform piled high with shiny metal canisters. "Milk," he said, apparently to himself; there was no one else riding in the car.

He looked down at his nails, considering whether ad-

1

ditional buffing would add to the general air of elegance or take him across the line into obsessiveness. Above all, not to be obsessive. Elegance, but casually achieved, was the goal. He turned the polished top of one cordovan loafer this way and that to reflect the light from the window.

The top crease of his linen trousers was in fairly good shape. The bottom crease, of course, would be a shambles; there was no avoiding that. And there would be at least a few of those sharp wrinkles that marked the crotch, almost like signposts pointing inward. Damned linen. You'd think they could invent something better than that, some kind of newfangled synthetic fabric that wouldn't wrinkle at all. Of course, he could have worn different trousers for the journey, then changed at the last minute into the linen to arrive looking fresh. There were risks in that, however. Arriving *perfectly* fresh might seem suspicious. If anyone suspected that he had changed to make a Grand Entrance, then the Grand Entrance would be spoiled. Better perhaps to arrive looking ever so slightly mussed.

A perfect exterior, in any case, would be out of keeping with his mood of deep, abiding melancholy. Liam sighed deeply. The sound of the sigh, as he considered it, was not quite what he'd had in mind. It wasn't precisely the sigh of deep, abiding melancholy, more like a sigh of exasperation or even a swallowed belch. He sighed again, this time slightly less emphatically. Much better. Now there was melancholy for you. He tried sighing a few times through the nose alone. Also acceptable, provided that he could avoid the slight liquid gurgle. He was still nursing the last of a summer cold.

Yawning again, he ferreted about in his jacket pocket until he found Marjorie Forsythe's letter and unfolded it in his lap. His hostess had written in a slightly childish scrawl, in her characteristic green ink.

2

My Dear Liam,

We're all so pleased that you can be with us again this summer at Dark Harbor House. We are looking forward to another season of gay times and good company. Of course, it won't be fancy, you know. As usual we are stony broke. But we'll somehow make do.

The contingent of young people is shaping up nicely. There will be yourself, Clark and Sissy, of course, three friends of Sissy's from school, including (I know you'll be pleased to hear this) the lovely Laura B., plus Clark's roommate from Amherst, Evan Mayberry, Bruno Somebody-Or-Other, whom Sissy met at Yale, and a certain Miss Groton from Smith (I've misplaced her first name).

If we put flags up in front of DHH the way the Plaza does for foreigners, then we could have the flags of Cornell (yourself), Radcliffe (Sissy, Laura, and Angela Pickering), Smith (Miss Groton), Amherst (Clark and Evan), and Yale (Bruno).

Among the old fogies, there'll be Yrs. Truly and the Colonel, and Mrs. (Grace) Hollerith, Andrew's great-aunt. (And a very awesome grand lady she is—she certainly terrifies me. Do remind me to tell you about Aunt Grace at our wedding!!!) More of the elderly set: Monsignor Leary, who was at prep school with Andrew ages ago, Mr. Collyer again (sorry about that), and Scarlet.

Falling into neither category (college age or fogey) is our celebrity guest of the summer, Gabriella Lake, who was on Broadway this fall and evidently will be again next season, we hear,

3

doing the lead in the new Clayton Lewis play, *Ravishing Beauty.* She is that.

Tyndall will meet you with the boat in Rockland. Keep an eye out for Mr. Collyer, who should be on your same train from Portland Station.

XXX,

Marjorie

Yes, by all means, keep an eye out for Mr. Collyer. How kind of Marjorie to have warned him. Of course Mr. Collyer would not be traveling Club in any case, not inclined to dig into his trust funds to pay anything beyond the barest minimum. Liam had splurged on a Club ticket for himself, allowing, along with the other benefits thereof, a comfortable degree of separation from old Mr. Collyer.

Liam leaned back in the leather seat, trying to conjure up an image of "the lovely Laura B." Blond hair, intriguingly blue eyes, almost like the eyes of a Siamese cat, radiant smile, a certain healthy amount of girlish bosom pushing pleasantly upward, long legs, and fascinating, long-fingered hands. He could see each of the pieces of the puzzle, but not the whole. The whole was somehow more than the sum of the parts. And the whole, for the moment, was eluding him.

"Ah, Laura. So good to see you again," he practiced, offering a hand to the empty seat opposite. "Ah, Laura. *So* good to see you again." "Ah, Laura,[significant pause] how lovely to see you again." Or perhaps, "How truly lovely . . ." Best to get it down now, because he might well become flustered at the moment. It wouldn't be the first time Laura had gotten to him. "Laura. What splendid luck to have another summer together." No, that would imply that she ought to feel lucky to be with him for another summer. "What splendid luck for me that we should again have the opportunity of being . . ." No, no, no. ". . . that we again should . . ." "Aren't

4

I the lucky fellow to have the opportunity that our presence together in this lovely setting might provide that we should actually . . ." Yrggh, a double subjunctive; she would probably collapse in giggles. Stay away from the subjunctive; keep it simple. "Ah, Laura." Just that. Steady eye contact, deep focus, looking right into her. Let her see just a touch of the melancholy. "Ah, Laura." He listened critically to the tone of his words. Maybe a bit softer. "Ahhh, Laura."

The train had slowed, clattering into a covered area with platforms on both sides. "Ahhh, Laura. Together again." Liam checked his watch. He had twenty minutes to change to the Maine Central. Portland Station had but two tracks, side by side—the Boston and Maine on one side and the Maine Central on the other. It would be a matter of a minute at most to make the transfer. So he would just take his time and make the change at the last minute, while the final call was being given. That way there would be no chance of encountering Mr. Collyer on the platform. "Ah, Laura. This *is* a pleasure." The train lurched to a stop. The loudspeaker above was droning again. Laura would be seated, he thought, as he approached. She would be looking up at him, smiling prettily. When she offered her hand, it would be palm down, not sideways the way some girls do. And so his hand, when it reached for hers, should be turned up, slightly cupped. She would say, very simply, "Liam," and then he would say . . . What would he say? "Ah, Laura, I trust you have been w—"

"Well, here you are, Liam. What luck." A round little man with a bow tie was standing above him. Liam looked up, gaping, his hand still extended toward the seat in front of him. The little man maneuvered around to seize the hand and shake it vigorously. "Good to see you, Liam. I thought it might be best to find you here, rather than chance a meeting on the platform."

"Oh, Mr. Collyer. Um, I trust you have been well."

Mr. Collyer was nodding. "Quite, quite." He had a young woman in tow, whom he now pulled forward to introduce.

"Mademoiselle, this is Mr. Liam Dwyer. *Monsieur Dwyer est un étudiant à une de nos grandes universités.* This young lady, Liam, is traveling quite on her own in this foreign land. I've saved her from having to manage the natives all by herself." Mr. Collyer turned back to the woman to fill her in: *"J'explique seulement à Liam comment je vous ai encontrée."*

"Mademoiselle. Charmed, I'm sure." Liam took the young woman's hand.

"I don't think she understands all that much, Liam," Mr. Collyer said in an undertone. "Possibly nothing at all."

"I . . . ," the woman began to say.

Mr. Collyer waved his hand breezily. "But that's no great problem, is it? We're here to help, my dear, Liam and I. We're here to help. Now, the first thing to do is to move ourselves over to the other train and find three nice seats together."

"I am afraid, Mr. Collyer, that as much as I would enjoy being with you for this next stage of the journey, still, as it happens—"

"Hmm? Oh, Liam, you're saying something, aren't you? Hold on a minute. I need to turn on my contraption." He fumbled in his vest pocket. *"Je fais marcher le gizmo,"* he explained to the woman, *"pour mieux entendre . . .* There. Switch on. Yes, Liam, you were saying?" Mr. Collyer held the little instrument out toward Liam, its wires disappearing into his shirt front.

Liam spoke directly into the box. "As much as I would like the three of us to be together—"

"Yes." Mr. Collyer snapped off the switch and put away the hearing aid. "Of course. Three nice seats together. Now, if you would each give me your ticket. *Votre billet, Mademoi-*

selle." He pointed to his own ticket and urged her with his other hand. "And yours, Liam. Have you got your ticket?"

The woman, rolling her eyes, took a ticket out of her purse and gave it to Mr. Collyer.

"*Merçi.* And yours, Liam? Let me see."

Liam reluctantly surrendered his ticket.

"Let me see, let me see, now. What have we got here? Oh, this will work out nicely. A piece of luck. You've each got a club ticket, which gives you the pick of the whole train. You can sit just anywhere. And my ticket is for the Smoker, so we'll just settle in there. Come along. Don't forget your jacket, Liam." With the butt of his cane, he tapped Liam's neatly folded white jacket on the overhead rack. "Come along. Here we go." Mr. Collyer swept the woman toward the front of the car and started forward behind her with the three tickets. "Stick with me now. Come along."

"*Voilà, une vache.*" Mr. Collyer interrupted himself to point out the window. "I'm just telling her there's a cow out there. Quite a few of them in this part of Maine. *Les vaches partout.* But where was I? What was I saying?"

"About Colonel Forsythe."

"Hm?"

Liam shrugged.

"Well, whatever it was... Oh, yes. About Andrew's father, also a colonel. All very confusing, but we're up to that, aren't we, Liam? Colonel Andrew Forsythe was the father of Colonel Andrew Forsythe, not junior and senior, mind you, though I never could figure out just why not. The elder Forsythe, now departed, made his money on the short side of the market. This was all before the income tax—or at least before the tax was anything other than a token.

"You remember, don't you, Liam, that when the tax was first passed, the country was on the brink of rebellion. Peo-

7

ple were not about to put up with it, I should say not. No one was for it. We had a meeting at the New York Yacht Club with practically the entire membership present, and I would have said that night that the tax just couldn't be passed. I mean, there was not a single vote for it, not one in the entire hall. If we had voted. We didn't, of course—vote on it, I mean. The vote, unfortunately, took place somewhere else, possibly in Congress. More's the pity. And so we had the tax, in spite of the objection of the New York Yacht Club."

Liam suppressed a sigh.

"Well, it was not too long after that when the Colonel's father took a huge position short of RCA. *Encore une vache, Mademoiselle. Voilà,*" Mr. Collyer said, pointing at another cow. The woman nodded glumly. "As luck would have it, that was the break in the market, and so he cleaned up a boodle. Not that he didn't have one long before that—a boodle, I mean. He had several of them, scads of money. Not clear what Andrew the present has done to let all that fortune get away, but he has. The father was short of RCA, and Andrew is just short of money." Mr. Collyer chuckled. "Still, though, he does put on a fine show of a summer. I imagine we'll be taken care of in the usual style, and want for nothing. Though it may rain occasionally through the roof in the east wing, no doubt, and you never can be too careful underfoot, what with things giving way every here and there and no one to fix them but Mr. Jervis and his wife. Why, in the old Colonel's day, there was a staff of twenty looking after the place. And even with the twenty, they were falling behind. I can't imagine what it would take to put Dark Harbor House into proper shape again. But in the old Colonel's day, and I was there for much of it, we had an approximation, I might say, to civilized life. An approximation, but still . . ." He spoke through a yawn. His voice carried on, mumbling a bit, as his eyes were closing. "Still there were the niceties . . . niceties . . . approximation . . ."

Mr. Collyer, Liam knew from last summer, was now within one minute of being sound asleep. And because he heard almost nothing, awake or asleep, nothing was going to wake him up. The little man slowly let his chin down onto his chest, his glasses sliding forward slightly. Liam turned to the young woman.

"I gather you're not French at all."

"No. I'm from Bangor." She spit out the words.

"Oh."

"My name is French."

"And because you have a French name, he assumed—"

"No, my name is French. Elaine French."

"I see. Well, he means no harm."

"He attached himself to me in New York," she said bitterly. "I've come the whole way—"

"Sorry to hear it. Really."

"I brought a lovely book to read. I was looking forward to a bit of peace and quiet."

"I understand. Well, he's out for a while now."

The woman stood up. "Listen, I'm going to take my nice seat in the club car. Tell your friend I got off at Pemaquid or something. Tell him I was met by the prince of Monaco, who's summering there. Or maybe the king of Sweden."

"I don't think Sweden has a king, actually."

"Oh, it does. Trust me."

She made her way forward toward the club car. Liam stared after her sadly.

Mr. Tyndall was waiting for them on the platform at the Rockland depot.

"Mr. Collyer. Mr. Dwyer."

"Mr. Tyndall." Liam shook his hand democratically. Tyn-

dall was the Colonel's full-time household employee, during
the winters in Connecticut and summers in Maine. "Trust
you've had a good year."

"Oh, very good."

"The Colonel and Marjorie doing well, are they?"

"Quite well."

"And the *Nepenthe*? I understand we'll be going out
to the island in *Nepenthe*. Got her all polished up, have you?"

"Oh, yes. The engines, however—"

"Oh, dear. Always a bit iffy, I remember. But we are
going out in the cruiser, is that right?"

"Oh, yes."

"That's good. A perfect day for it. Looking forward to feeling the spray on my face. A little sun would be nice, but at
least we've got a calm day. Don't know that Mr. Collyer
would be up to a sea. I, of course, have a strong stomach."

Tyndall saw to the loading of Liam's two bags and Mr.
Collyer's nine onto the porter's wagon. Liam wondered how
all the baggage was going to fit in the boat, which was long,
but not long on storage space.

They headed out of the station and down toward
the docks.

"Love that air," Liam said enthusiastically, breathing in.
"Wonderful salt air."

"Mmm," Mr. Tyndall said. "Salt and sardine, I'm afraid."

"Oh, yes. The sardine factory. Well, the world needs sardines, I guess."

"Yes. Elsewhere would be better, though."

"Jobs, Tyndall. We have to think about jobs. People hereabouts need some sort of work. There has to be something
for them."

"Perhaps."

"I'm sure of it. And sardines . . . well, I guess that's what
there is."

"Apparently."

They were approaching the docks. "There she is, the *Nepenthe.*" Liam suppressed an urge to run forward to see the sleek craft. "She looks splendid."

About thirty feet long, *Nepenthe* was stem to stern varnished mahogany. She had a flush deck with three open cockpits, each one with a wide, bright red upholstered seat. There was a windshield in front of the forward cockpit. A thick black steering wheel was set there into the middle of the dash with a half-dozen chrome-bezeled dials arrayed on either side of the wheel. From the flagstaff on her stern, a ragged American ensign—red, gray, and blue—drooped in the still air.

"Splendid," Liam went on. "This is going to be a treat." He ran his hand fondly along the windshield's chrome frame, even more thickly encrusted than last year with salt and corrosion. At the small staff beside the windshield there was a yellow pennant, which Liam pulled back to admire its ornate device. "Ah, yes, and here we have the Colonel's private signal, all shipshape: check. American ensign: check. What else? Um . . . am I wrong about this, Mr. Tyndall, or does she seem to be ever so slightly down by the bow?"

"She is. Or, more precisely, up by the stern. It's the engines, as I said."

"The engines?"

"Out, I'm afraid. At the shop. We put some concrete blocks in their place for ballast, but, as you can see, the weight is not quite as it should be."

"The engines are out?"

"Unfortunately."

"But then how . . . ?"

Tyndall nodded farther down the dock to where an old-fashioned green-and-white lobster boat was tied up. "Mr. Jervis in the *Nellie B.*" There was a stout line leading down from the stanchion on the afterdeck of the *Nellie B.* to the bow of the *Nepenthe.*

"Oh." Liam said.

"If you please, gentlemen." Tyndall motioned them toward the forward cockpit of the *Nepenthe.* "I'll keep Mr. Jervis company in the towboat with the bags. Do make yourselves comfortable."

2

Jeremiah

The slow procession of lobster boat and polished mahogany express cruiser under tow threaded its way up the lee of Seven Hundred Acre Island and through Gilkey Narrows to the town of Dark Harbor on the island of Islesboro. There was no town to see, at least not from the water, only a jaunty fleet of sailboats and yachts of all sizes lying at anchor in front of an array of bright green lawns. The lawns ran down from the ridge of Ames Hill, each one proceeding from its own massive house down to the bay. There were, Liam knew, twenty-four fine houses that made up the town, plus the usual assortment of not-so-fine houses. The fine houses all had names. As the boat approached, Liam could pick out North Star, Penobscot, Nokomis, Eggemoggin, Norumbega, and, largest of them all, Dark Harbor House.

Dark Harbor House had the distinction that even its outbuildings were named. Nearest to the water was East House, a two-story fieldstone manor with green-painted wooden porches On the other side of the main house were Jeremiah, looking somewhat the worse for wear, and

Gideon. The four houses together had more than a hundred rooms.

An oval lawn lay in the center of the four houses, opening up toward the west. At the foot of the lawn a pier made of massive granite blocks extended a good hundred and twenty feet out from the seawall. Mr. Jervis steered the *Nellie B.* up to the pier, where Clark Forsythe was waiting to take *Nepenthe*'s line.

"Clark, old man," said Liam as he stepped off.

"Hey, Liam."

"Great to be back to Dark Harbor House." Clark was busy with the line. Liam rubbed his hands together, looked around for something to do, another line to tie down perhaps. "Oh, Mr. Collyer. Here, let me help."

"Thank you, Liam. Well, Clark, my good fellow. Isn't this jolly?"

"Welcome, Mr. C. Welcome back, sir. Good trip?"

"No, I didn't have to steer at all. Liam took care of that."

"No, I meant your train trip."

"We just followed the other boat all the way."

Clark nodded soberly.

As soon as Mr. Collyer was on his way up the pier, Liam headed back toward Clark. "Well, what a pleasure to be here. Really. Can't tell you how I'm looking forward to another Dark Harbor summer. Looking forward to spending a bit of time with you, Clark." He thought he had just the right touch there of gruffness and manly affection. "I'll be fascinated to find out what you've been up to all year."

"Right. Well, we'll have the rest of today and, of course, this evening."

"Hmm?"

"I'm away tomorrow morning, haven't you heard? Didn't Marjorie tell you in her note?"

"Away, you say?"

"To the continent, old man. My Aunt Arabella has proposed to show me about the ruins. She's the well-to-do side of the family. Usually it's my cousin Compton who shares in her beneficence. But this year, I got the nod. Haven't the foggiest idea why. The Colonel says it's too good a chance to pass up, though."

"You're not going to be here?" There was a small squeak in Liam's voice.

"Off on the *Mauritania* Wednesday afternoon with Auntie Arabella. Afraid you're in charge here, Liam. I look to you to play the host in my absence."

"Host? Me?"

"Well, someone's got to be responsible. Keep the Colonel on the straight and narrow, make sure the girls don't get bored, keep Compton and Sissy apart—they can't stand each other. That sort of thing. I won't ask you to look out for Scarlet; that would be a bit much."

"Compton?"

"Yes. He'll be here. Since he got passed by for the continent this summer, poor fellow had nowhere to go. You'll like him. He's at Bowdoin. An SAE, I believe. Or maybe it's Theta Delta Chi. Anyway, some preppy house or other. Compton's a real tweed."

"Well, I'm crushed that you won't be—"

"No one's sorrier than I am, old man. Believe me. Tromping about with my less than sprightly chaperone, looking at significant craters where significant churches used to be . . . I don't suppose there will be a lot of nightlife. Oh, say, Arthur," he called up to Mr. Jervis, who was just off-loading the last of the bags. "Don't disappear quite yet. We'll be needing your services for one more shuttle run." Clark turned back to Liam. "Mayberry, my roommate, came in this morning by yacht. The black schooner. You passed her on the way in." He gestured out to an enormous dark-colored hull in the harbor. "She's the *Hiawatha*. Arthur Curtis James, you know. Friend of the family. Quite the splendiferous thing, *Hiawatha*. I hope you'll have a chance to get out on her when she comes back to claim Mayberry. His family is off for a cruise down east and then a stop with friends in Seal Harbor. What do you think of that, eh? A hundred and sixty feet if she's an inch."

"Oh."

"Evan has just run out to return her launch. I am to follow with Mr. Jervis and the *Nellie B.* to bring him back. Not as elegant as one might wish, but it beats a swim."

"I see."

"Well, run along and get yourself salted away. You'll find a blackboard inside the door that shows all the room assignments."

"I'll want to pay my respects to your mother."

"She's off with the girls on a flower-picking expedition or some such thing. I don't doubt they'll be having a swim on the way back. Sissy told me I had to keep all the fellows away from the pond, and you know what that means." He wiggled one eyebrow. "Modern young ladies."

"I can imagine."

"They'll be back by dinner, though. The Colonel is down at Jeremiah, haggling with a local builder. There's some thought we may try to save the roof before it falls in. All depends on the finances, which are beyond my understanding. Probably beyond the Colonel's as well. And certainly beyond anybody's power to do much about."

"I'll stop down at Jeremiah then and pay my respects to him."

"By the time you're back, I'll be just arriving with Evan. This is his first time here. So he'll have to have a grand tour. The Colonel is itching to take him about and show him whatever is still standing. You never know what that will be.

A little less every day. And, of course, tell the story that goes with each brick and block."

"I remember."

"Oh, and there's Scarlet up on the porch. So you might as well get that over with on your way past.

Liam looked up toward the main house in time to see Mr. Collyer bend over a frail woman, holding out his hearing aid toward her. She waved him away in disgust.

"Scarlet. Yes, I suppose I should."

Miss Virginia (Scarlet) Forsythe was the Colonel's older sister, a woman of sixty or sixty-five. She spent much of her time in a wheelchair, Liam remembered, but then might stand up at any odd moment and walk perfectly ably wherever she wanted to go. No one had ever offered him a clue about the wheelchair, which, in any case, he felt more comfortable ignoring. Not as easy to ignore, however, were Scarlet's other oddities.

"Back from the war, are you, young man?"

"Well, no. I was a bit young for the war. Only seventeen when it ended, actually. Afraid I missed my chance to—"

"Just don't tell me any war stories. I am fed up to the gills with war stories." She waggled a bony hand at the level of her gills. "Don't tell me about the trenches, don't tell me about the gas. I've heard it all."

"I wasn't going to. I'm Liam Dwyer, Miss Scarlet. You remember, from last summer?"

"Heard it all over and over again. The Chemin des Dames, the bloody fields of the Marne, the drive out from Paris in taxis to relieve General What's-his-name—some wop name or other—the damned pilots with their silk scarves—"

"Um, that was the other war, I think."

"What?"

17

"The other war."

"Another war? Of course there was another war. There is always another one. This was the big one I was talking about. The world war."

"The first one."

"The millionth one. There have been wars ever since ever. But don't tell me about them. Don't. I am fed up."

"Okay, I won't then."

"If you lined up all the young men who came back to tell me of their exploits in the wars, well . . ." She rolled her eyes. "The line would go back as far as that little island off to hell and gone." She pointed vaguely out toward a scattering of islands in the bay. "That's how far the line would go. This was when I was your age. An endless line full of soldiers, each one eager to tell me of the 'horror of it all,' of 'man's inhumanity to man,' and about how shattered they were by the experience of war. And it was my invariable experience that all the talk about how shattered they were was just a prelude to getting a hand in my pants."

"Excuse me?"

"A hand in the pants!" she repeated, raising her voice. "I suppose they're still doing such things. I mean, there must be some things that don't change."

"Well, I suppose—"

"It was, I believe, the whole reason for war. To talk about and to give them the opportunity. I think evolution planned it that way. Evolution with her giant preoccupation with knocking up young girls."

"Really. I don't think evolution . . ." Liam looked around uneasily to see if anyone else might be listening.

"A whore, evolution, a perfect slut. And a panderer to boot."

"I am a great believer in the theory of evolution."

"Some theory! Who needs a theory? This is fact. No

18

question in my mind about evolution. She dreamed up the whole idea of war so boys could tell you how shattered they were while all the time they were having a little exploration under your petticoats. Not that I begrudged them, mind you. It would have been okay, but if only they could have spared me the ghastly prelude. Where is my useless brother?"

Liam blinked at the change of subject. "The Colonel? Down at Jeremiah, I think. I mean, your brother is down at Jeremiah."

"Serves him right," she said emphatically.

What serves him right? Liam wondered. He waited, curious as to what more she might offer, but the conversation was evidently over. Scarlet was turned away toward the sea, muttering to herself. Liam tiptoed down the length of the porch and made his way over to Jeremiah.

"Colonel? Hallo. Anybody up there? It's Liam."

A somewhat surprised face was suddenly visible at one attic window. "Liam? Oh, Liam, my boy. We're up here. All the way up in the attic."

Liam made his way carefully up over the dicey stairs. Colonel Forsythe was waiting for him on the top landing, beaming down. His strawberry blond hair was still without a streak of gray. He had apple cheeks and an easy grin. "All the way up. Watch your step. Do watch your step. Anything that looks like an abyss, walk around it."

Liam was sticking to the inner side of the stairs, as the outer part was more problematic. The far banister promised little support, leaning alarmingly as it did into the open space that descended all the way to the basement. The ground floor was rotted away near the foot of the stairs. Above the Colonel's head at the top of the stairs, Liam could see open sky and clouds through the roof.

19

"Liam. Here's our fine fellow. How's my boy?" Liam held out his hand, but the Colonel passed it by for a hug. "And your mother?"

"Fine, sir. Doing fine."

"Well, that's excellent. Excellent. School?"

"Very good."

"Good. School is good. Health?"

"Perfect, I guess."

"Perfect health. Who could ask for anything more? And . . . and . . . what else? Oh, meet Mr. Hopkins. Evander Hopkins, Liam Dwyer."

"Mr. Hopkins."

"Good to meet you."

Mr. Hopkins was a tall man with something of a paunch. He wore a tool belt under his waist, and in it he carried what looked like twenty pounds of tools. There was a long measuring tape spread out on the floor at his feet.

The Colonel filled Liam in:"We're thinking of saving the roof, though, as you can see, much of it is beyond saving."

"Replacing the roof is what we're thinking of," said Mr. Hopkins.

"Now, Andy. No need to get carried away. There's a lot here that can be saved."

"Save yourself the bother and start fresh."

"It doesn't have to be perfect, mind you. We must be prepared to make compromises."

"It's the compromises we made last summer and the summer before that have given us this view." Mr. Hopkins nodded through the wide opening in the roof.

"And a wonderful view it is. Come here, Liam. Have a look. What an oversight to have had a roof here at all to interrupt this view. You can see the whole island, almost. Do have a look. All of Islesboro spread out beneath us. What a view."

Liam stepped tentatively over the fallen slates to see. The Camden Hills were visible to the west across the bight of Penobscot Bay that separated them from the mainland. He could see the northern tip of the island to his right and the southern tip to his left. In the immediate foreground were Seven Hundred Acre Island and Spruce Island, two low-lying barriers that formed the outer part of Gilkey Narrows.

"More rot over here, Colonel," Mr. Hopkins said behind them. "Quite a lot of it."

"Oh, dear. Excuse me just a second, Liam. Another of my fingers seems to be required for the dike."

The Colonel went back to his conversation with Mr. Hopkins. As they began talking about money, Liam made his way over to the east side of the attic to give the Colonel some privacy and to look out through a small gable window at the outer reaches of the bay. From this vantage point, he could see nothing higher than Jeremiah's roof anywhere on the island except for the tall, slightly bent spire on the top of Dark Harbor House. All the way across the water to the east were other largish islands. He knew that somewhere out there were Swans Island and Deer Isle and Mount Desert and Butter Island, but as to which was which, he had no idea.

The gray skies that had prevailed over their endless crossing in *Nepenthe* were broken now, and a late-afternoon sun was glinting through. Liam thought of Laura and the other girls, who might this very moment be bathing—in the altogether, evidently. He wondered where the pond was from here. The roof of Jeremiah, he seemed to remember, was visible from the pond, so it was just possible that . . . He traced the path with his eyes from the back of Gideon, on out through the little stand of white pine, and across the clearing. From there the pond would be . . .

"Come along, Liam. Let's see if we can't get ourselves back down without loss of life or limb."

21

"Oh, yes. Coming." He left the little window to follow the Colonel.

"Watch this step here most of all. I put the flowerpot there to keep people off the rotten part. Once you go through, there's nothing to stop you all the way down to the cistern."

"Splash."

"More like *thud,* on the rock bottom."

"But no one really uses the steps, isn't that right? I mean, Jeremiah is closed up, except for repairs."

"Well, this part is. But the wing is still fairly much intact. And there is one very elegant bedroom there, the Post bedroom, where Mr. Collyer likes to put up. It was built for C. W. Post, you know."

"Post Toasties?"

"The very same. A frequent guest at Dark Harbor House in its prime."

"I didn't know that."

"A great friend of our Norbert." Norbert, Liam knew, was Norbert Chance, the industrialist who had built Dark Harbor House and its companion buildings starting in the 1880s. "They went way back, a grand old friendship. But Post wouldn't stay in the main house as a matter of principle."

"Why was that?"

"Because the main house was where another one of Norbert's friends used to stay, Will Kellogg."

"W. K.?"

"Himself."

"Cornflakes?"

"The same. Post hated Kellogg, and Kellogg hated Post. Detested each other. They wouldn't stay in the same house."

As they stepped out onto the lawn, they were passed by Mr. Jervis, struggling under the weight of Mr. Collyer's baggage, on his way up to the Post bedroom. The Colonel stepped away from the building, drawing Liam along with him, then turned back to look at the sad spectacle of the roof line.

"Poor old Jeremiah. She's the oldest of the outbuildings, you know. Her first stones were laid in 1882. She was built quickly—and none too well—to provide 'camping out' accommodations for Norbert and his household staff of about thirty while the main house went up. Now, as to the name Jeremiah, there's a bit of a story."

"I suspected there would be."

"Always a story. Each one of the outbuildings, you see, marks a stage in Norbert's religious life."

"His religious life?"

"Oh, yes. Jeremiah comes from his earliest stage. He was, at that time, a Millerite. The Millerites, followers of William Miller, were millenarianists."

"End-of-the-world types."

"Exactly. They were all Millerites, Norbert and C. W. and Will Kellogg. That's what they had in common."

"Ah."

"Jeremiah means something to the Millerites, but I haven't the slightest idea what. Something to do with blood and thunder, I suspect."

"Uh-huh."

"Gideon House was next." The Colonel gestured toward the somewhat more prosperous looking stone building immediately opposite. "Gideon dates from the time Norbert fell under the spell of the beautiful Jeannie Isobel and her Gideon Compact. In fact, he built Gideon for Jeannie. The compact made their summer headquarters here, the entire colony guests of Mr. Chance. Much of the island in those years was a summer revivalist camp. People came from all over to bask in the glow of Jeannie and her Gideons."

"I remember that." There had been wonderful stories

about Jeannie and her followers related during Liam's stay the previous summer.

"On a good year there might be seventy or even a hundred Gideons staying right here on the grounds, most of them youngsters—about your age or even younger. Boys and girls."

"A huge summer house party."

"Well, a party in fact only. In principle, it was a spiritual retreat."

"Aha."

"The young gentlemen, the 'Acolytes,' put up in Gideon House. It was a kind of dormitory. Jeannie and her 'Angels' stayed in the main house—all very proper."

"Only it wasn't so proper." Liam remembered there were hints of scandal associated with Jeannie's Gideons. At the very least, there had been a certain amount of nighttime traipsing back and forth between Gideon and Dark Harbor House.

"Not perfect. But then who is perfect? The theory, one supposes, was that young people who were sufficiently infused with spirituality would be immune to the baser temptations. So no real chaperoning would be required. That was the theory." The Colonel shrugged.

Liam waited, hoping for more.

But the Colonel turned to face the last of the great outbuildings surrounding the lawn. "East House marks Norbert's final stage. It dates from the time he chucked it all. Throughout his life, religion had been his most essential influence. But at the end, after the great fiasco—when Jeannie disappeared in disgrace, Post was dead, and Kellogg was estranged—Norbert turned away from religion. He built East House as a cinema."

"A cinema? I thought it was a theater."

"A cinema. The stage is there only for the warm-up act.

24

In those days there was always some live entertainment before the film. The magic lantern of moving pictures had only
just been invented. Norbert was captivated by it. So it became, at least to my mind, his final religion. He showed films
here—the whole island was invited—films that couldn't be
seen anywhere else in Maine: *Martyrs of the Alamo,* with
Douglas Fairbanks; the first *Adventures of Jesse James*;
Tilly's Punctured Romance with Marie Dresser; and the films
of Richard Bartlemess. All these were silent, of course. This
was long before sound, long before Chaplin and Lloyd and
Griffith and the Gish sisters."

"So East House was originally—"

"A chapel of film. Anyway, that's how I think of it."

3

Jeannie Isobel

The Colonel stayed behind with Mr. Hopkins as Liam headed toward the pier again to look for Clark and Evan. Seated with her back toward him at the end of the pier was a young woman who Liam at first thought might be one of the guests, possibly Laura. But as he approached he saw it was only Jody, the Colonel's youngest child. She was barely thirteen. She turned as Liam approached, squinting a bit through her large, black-framed eyeglasses. She had her mother's wide, dark eyes.

"Well, Jody."

"Hi, Liam." She was not a pretty child, except when she smiled. But then she was almost always smiling. "Welcome, and all that. They've got you in Lancelot this year. That's a step up. It's got its own bath. I think that makes you the guest of honor. Except for Miss Lake, of course. She's going to be in Gawaine. Gawaine has a huge bed you can jump on. It's made of iron."

"Oh."

"How have you been?"

"Not too great, just between us." Liam sat down on the pier beside her. "If I had to characterize my mood," he confided, "I think it would be one of deep, abiding melancholy."

"Yuck."

"'In sooth, I know not why I am so sad.'"

"That's Shakespeare. *The Merchant of Venice*, Act One, Scene One. Antonio: 'In sooth, I know not why I am so sad / It wearies me; you say it wearies you / But how I caught it, found it, or came by it / What stuff 'tis made of / Whereof it is born, I am to learn / And such a want-wit sadness makes of me / That I have much ado to know myself.'"

"Yes. Just like that. Deep, abiding melancholy."

"Well, we'll have to get you patched up. The Colonel says that bad moods are often brought on by a stoppage—you know—of the plumbing."

"Jody!"

"I'm not saying that in your case, Liam. That's only what the Colonel says. But if I were you, I would take particular care to eat lots of roughage."

"Gee, thanks."

"Marjorie's gone off with the girls, for a picnic and a swim. I wasn't invited." She made a face.

"Oh, well."

"Laura's here, you know. She's in Guenevere, across the corridor from me. I'm in Childeric this year. It leaks a bit, but there's a nice window overlooking the bay. Marjorie says the rooms that leak aren't to be given out to the guests."

"Laura's in Guenevere?"

"And you're in Lancelot. Isn't it fate? I expect so. I poked into Guenevere after she had unpacked, to look at her stuff." A naughty smile.

"Really, Jody."

"Well, how else am I to learn? I think Laura is spiffing. I want to be just like her, only still like myself at the same time, only grown-up, if that's all possible. And tall. Nobody takes you seriously when you're a squirt."

"You're not a squirt. Hardly."

"Oops, sorry."

"I'm not the least bit sensitive about my height."

"No, I shouldn't think so. Anyway, she's got a black dress that's barely below the knee. A cocktail dress. It comes down to my ankles, but on Laura, you know, as tall as she is, it's going to be a shocker. And cut down almost to the navel in front."

"I'm sure it's not cut down to the navel. That would not be like Laura."

"Well, on me it goes down to the navel. And you should see her underthings—"

"Please. A little respect."

"Oops. I forgot. I'm talking about the woman you love."

"Well, a woman I like."

Jody pointed out toward the water. "Here's Clark coming back with Evan. There's not a lot to like about Evan. Aren't I awful? But there isn't. I think they have an asshole machine at Amherst and they put him through. Oops, I'm not supposed to say that word. They didn't have to do Clark, of course; he was born that way."

Liam stood up to catch the bow line of the *Nellie B.*

Colonel Forsythe was holding forth in front of the giant fireplace in the central sitting room. "Each room has a fireplace. There are no exceptions in the main house, not even one. And the fireplaces are all equipped, as you can see, with the most elaborate brass andirons. Now, remember that it was in brass manufacture that Mr. Chance made his fortune."

"The Chance Brass Company," Evan parroted back what he had just learned.

"Just so. And, we suppose, the fireplaces were a kind of

showplace for the andirons. As we move to more modern rooms, you'll see that the andirons become more and more ornate. Some would say rococo."

"Some would say bizarre," Clark offered.

"Each room has its own brass nameplate. You can imagine that we keep Mrs. Jervis busy almost full-time just polishing the brass. I hate to think what our annual Brass-O bill must be."

"This room is called Inverness." Evan was reading from the brass plate, nearly four feet wide, over the door.

"Inverness, yes. And through here, Xanadu." They were passing into the main dining room, with its vaulted ceiling of ebony beams inlaid with ivory. "And the library, across the corridor, Biscay. And the smoking room, Aragon, and the music room, Navarre. Et cetera. One suspects that the names were merely an excuse to justify the nameplates. They are all made of brass, a full two inches thick. We needed to take down one of the plates from the doorway of Savoy when we were doing repairs. I had hopes that Clark and I could support the thing while Mr. Jervis undid the bolts. But fortunately my daughter, Jody, did some calculations before we started. Three hundred and fifty pounds. We ended up needing Tyndall to help."

Evan whistled. "Three hundred and fifty pounds? My gawd."

Navarre, which they came to next, was in a sorry state. The painted canvas was peeling in several places, one piece hanging almost to the floor.

Evan was most appreciative. "Now this is my style!" The walls were painted with a harem scene featuring young women in various stages of bathing, playing, and reclining—all of them nude.

"Howard Chandler Christie, in his early harem stage. Came to visit Norbert one summer and stayed on, boozing and painting until he was finally sent packing a year later. Claimed he painted from memory, but there is reason to believe that a few of the Angels were enlisted."

A raucous laugh from Evan. Liam began to think that Jody might be right about Evan and the Amherst machine.

The Colonel pointed up to one of the nymphs, sprawled bottom-up over a book. "The purple birthmark here on this thigh was unfortunately found to be quite like a birthmark on the thigh of a certain young lady who was thought to be here for spiritual enlightening. And although I say 'thigh,' you can see that the mark was rather high on the thigh, actually more the fanny. Positioned in almost exactly the same place, I understand, on the young lady in question."

Significant smirks passed between Clark and Evan.

"We have a restorer looking at doing some work here," Colonel Forsythe said with a sigh, "pending only the funds. As you can imagine—"

"But a national treasure, I suspect," Evan said. "I mean, Howard Shandie Whateverhisnamewas. We're talking national treasure."

"Mmm. A national treasure, no doubt. Now, come along this way. We'll take the back stairs to the second floor and look at some of the bedrooms." The Colonel led them out of the music room and up a long oak staircase.

"We'll begin with Charlemagne, which was Norbert's own suite, occupied by Mrs. Forsythe and me just now. I'll show you only the main room, as Marjorie has hung her washing in the bath."

"Wow! What a room," Evan exclaimed.

"Notice the andirons here."

"Dogs. They look like greyhounds."

"Whippets, I think. When we get to your room, Evan— you're in Duncan—you'll see that the andirons are carved figures of monks."

31

"The man was obsessed with andirons."

"Actually he had other obsessions. We'll just have a peek into the east wing next. This is where the Angels had their rooms. We've respected that convention through to the present. Sissy and Jody and Angela and Laura and Lizzie are all putting up here for the summer—all the young ladies, in fact, except Gabriella. We hope to have her in Gawaine, which was the room that Jeannie Isobel had for her own. Gawaine is *hors du combat* for the moment, I'm afraid. We're pushing forward with the repairs in time, I hope, for Gabriella's arrival. Now let's have a look into Cleopatra."

Liam hesitated at the door. "Um, isn't this the girls' john?" he asked.

"Precisely. The girls, however, are all off on a picnic, so we won't worry about disturbing anyone. I will just knock, though. Hello? Hello? No, no one here. Come along, gentlemen." He ushered them in.

Liam had never looked inside Cleopatra before. "Oh, my," he said as he entered. The room was as big as Savoy, an enormous expanse of tile and marble and walnut paneling.

"Now you see one of Norbert's other obsessions. Remember he was, first and foremost, a plumber. He went on to make brass fittings, principally plumbing fittings, but at the beginning he was a simple plumber."

"You can see," Clark added, "he must have had ideas all his life about finally building bathrooms the way they ought to be built, an ambition he realized here. All the baths in Dark Harbor House are wonderful, though none quite as grand as Cleopatra."

The center of the room was taken up by a giant tub, as big as a small swimming pool. There were showers and dressing rooms at the sides, and mirrors and sinks. The Colonel nodded toward the far wall, where a low banquette filled the area under a high frosted window. On top of the banquette were the polished mahogany lids of four toilet seats, side by side.

"Friendly."

"Well, you must remember that this wing was a dormitory. On any given summer there might be twenty to thirty Angels housed here."

"Do you think they bathed together in the tub?" Liam wanted to know.

"I do," the Colonel said gravely. "I'm quite sure of it. There are even some records. We've been able to accumulate diaries of some of the residents. People write down the most surprising things in their diaries. They often forget to mention earthshaking events—the outbreaks of wars, for example, the things you'd be most interested to learn about—but they note the trivia. Some of the Angels recorded in detail just who was bathing with whom and what was said and who scrubbed whatever part of whomever else."

"Actually, that *is* what I was most interested to learn about," Clark said.

"Well, we have it all. Your little sister has accumulated quite a collection, the makings of an extensive history of Dark Harbor House and its denizens."

"There seems to be some pattern to the room names," Evan said as they made their way out. "But I'm not sure I've got it yet."

"Something of a pattern, though not entirely consistent. Names from the Middle Ages are bedrooms for the most part. Earlier and mythological names such as Zeus, Medea, Cleopatra, and Ulysses are baths. The place names are common rooms."

"The kitchens are all named after metals," Clark added. "Manganese, Molybdenum, Copper, Zinc."

"Then there are some we can't figure out. There's a storeroom named McKinley, the only name from contemporary politics. On the third floor there is one little room named Phil."

★彡

They descended the main staircase, comprising two grand, curved flights meeting at a landing halfway down and continuing to the ground floor. On the landing, Colonel Forsythe turned them about to face the wall behind them.

"A new addition since your last visit, Liam." The Colonel lifted one hand toward a life-sized oil portrait of a tall young woman in a white satin gown.

"Wow, some babe!" Evan offered.

"Our own Jeannie Isobel."

Liam gaped. He had never seen a picture of Jeannie before. From the stories, he had imagined her plain and Sunday-schoolish, with a lumpy shape and a slightly disapproving expression. After all, she was supposed to be a preacher, wasn't she? Instead the figure in the painting was ravishing. Her hair was long and auburn, and her skin a golden tan. The artist had expended considerable talent on the glistening gown and its highlights, which gave a voluptuous dimension to the shapely body underneath. Jeannie was grinning at the artist (and now at Liam). Her expression wasn't a smile but a full, engaging grin. Her brown eyes were merry and full of mischief.

"She is...exquisite," Liam managed after a moment.

"She is. She was. We know that the portrait was originally painted to hang here, but it disappeared for nearly fifty years. Now it's back, a gift to Dark Harbor House from an anonymous benefactor. What do you think?"

"I think hurrah for anonymous benefactors."

Evan looked befuddled. "Tell me again who she was, this Jeannie."

"Today we would call her a charismatic," Colonel Forsythe informed him. "The leader of a religious group—a kind of cult—called the compact, or the Gideon Compact. They believed . . . well, who really knows what they believed? It's all very complex. Mostly they believed in Jeannie Isobel."

"I can see why." Liam couldn't tear his eyes away.

"She was rather spiritual, wasn't she?"

"She was delicious."

4

The Monsignor

ᴬᴺᴼᴹᴸᴬ ᴬᴺᴼᴹᴸᴬ ᴬᴺᴼᴹᴸᴬ ᴬᴺᴼᴹᴸᴬ ᴬᴺᴼᴹᴸᴬ ᴬᴺᴼᴹᴸᴬ ᴬᴺᴼᴹᴸᴬ ᴬᴺᴼᴹᴸᴬ ᴬᴺᴼᴹᴸᴬ ᴬᴺᴼᴹᴸᴬ ᴬᴺᴼᴹᴸᴬ ᴬᴺᴼᴹᴸᴬ

A h, Laura." Liam with his hand out, palm up, slightly cupped, steady eye contact. Damned Mayberry was right behind him—waiting to be introduced, no doubt—but still, Liam was determined to have this one moment in its fullness.

Laura looked up. "Oh, Liam, you're just in time to resolve our question."

He dropped his hand. "I am?"

"We were wondering about the tides, how they precess."

"Precess?" He had no idea what she was talking about.

"Yes. The time of the tide moves from day to day by an hour or so. Only we can't agree on whether it moves forward or back. Or by how much. I was sure you would know."

"It moves? The tide isn't at the same time every day?"

"Heavens, no," she laughed. Laura turned to Mayberry, smiling. "Evan, you must know, man of the sea that you are."

"Fifty-two minutes a day," Evan answered confidently. "Fifty-two minutes, four seconds. Later each day."

Laura nodded, confirming. "That's about what I thought, Lizzie. As I was saying, about an hour later each day. So our low tide tomorrow ought to be around three."

"I gather that you and Evan know each other?" Liam asked a little bitterly.

"Oh, yes. From the Christmas Cotillion. Sissy arranged it all. This is Lizzie Groton from Smith College. Liam Dwyer and Evan Mayberry."

A chunky girl in an overly tight, gray silk dress and black patent leather shoes. Dark hair, a bit greasy. "Howdjadoo," she said.

Evan stepped around Liam to take Lizzie's hand. He bowed over it, one eye on Laura. "Fräulein."

A giggle from the fräulein.

"Be careful of Evan, Lizzie. He's quite the charmer. Oh, here's Angela, everybody. Angela Pickering." Angela must have come down right behind them.

Liam noted with dismay that she was even taller than Laura. He sat down abruptly beside Lizzie.

Evan bowed over Angela's hand. "Signorina."

"Oh, Italian. My day is made. Really. You can't imagine." She batted her lashes becomingly.

"Angela, that's Liam over there."

Liam had to get up again.

Laura commanded their attention. "I was just telling Lizzie, everybody, that Marjorie wants us to get the pool all mucked out tomorrow. It's a saltwater pool, down by the shore. When the tide comes in, it flows over the pool wall and fills it up. But it's still all gunked up from the winter. So Marjorie has suggested that we pump out the residue and spruce things up during tomorrow's low tide. The actual mucking out promises to be quite disgusting, so it's boys, I guess." She laughed her silvery laugh. "We girls will

observe and give instruction. I'm going to wear a spotless little white sundress and carry a parasol."

"I do have to be careful of my back, though," Evan said
somberly.

"Well, it's you and Clark then, Liam."

"And I'll be gone," Clark said. "Off on the first ferry of the
morning."

"Oh. Well, we'll give you ever so much moral support,
Liam." The silvery laugh again. "Why, here's Marjorie."

Evan snapped to attention. "My dear Mrs. Forsythe. You
do look lovely this evening." He bowed low over her hand.
Marjorie was in bright horizontal stripes, making her look
even wider than usual, but very cheerful.

"Well, don't we all?" said Marjorie. "All in our finery, and
aren't we a splendid-looking dinner party? Good evening,
everybody. Hi, Liam. Welcome back to Dark Harbor House.
I heard you got in this afternoon. Sorry about the *Nepenthe.*"

"It was fine, really," said Liam.

"Still doing the poetry then?" asked Marjorie. "Going to
be the lyric Irish bard, as you were thinking last year?"

"Well, no. I'm inclined more toward fine arts these days."
Liam had rehearsed this. "Time someone did something
about the mess in American fine arts."

"Oh, that's good." It was exactly what she had said last
year about his potential career as a poet. "That's just what's
needed. And you can still be Irish and poetic on the side.
Now, who's missing? Jody. Well, she's always late. Sissy? Mr.
Collyer? And where ever is Andrew?"

They milled about in front of Inverness's giant fireplace,
waiting for the rest of the party to assemble. When the
Colonel arrived, he had a middle-aged gentleman with him:
ruddy face, gray crew-cut hair, wearing a clerical collar.
Colonel Forsythe did the introduction.

"This is Monsignor Leary, everyone. Bill Leary, an old friend from school days. Bill, this is—"

The Monsignor held up his hand, interrupting. "A pleasure, ladies and gentlemen. Hello. Good to meet you all. I'm sure we'll get acquainted." He turned back to the Colonel. "Now, Andrew, what do you suppose we've got on for tonight? Something good, I hope. Another one of Mrs. Jervis's special meals? Oh..." His eyes had lit on Laura. "And what's your name, young lady?"

"Laura Beauchalet, Monsignor." Laura curtsied slightly. "Awfully pleased to meet you."

The Monsignor took her hand and tucked it under his arm. "Well, one presumes our hostess has had the foresight to seat us together. If not, we can change the little cards around. Now, why don't we go in?" He led Laura, blushing slightly, toward the arched doorway into Xanadu. Evan took Angela's arm and followed. Liam felt a hand slip under his elbow. He looked over to see Lizzie at his side. "Why, thank you," she said.

"No, I don't think we're going to see a Pax Americana, not at all." Monsignor Leary raised his voice slightly as he spoke, stopping conversation around the table. "I believe I can say that with some authority." He turned away from Laura to look expectantly at Colonel Forsythe.

"Yes, I think you probably can, Bill," said the Colonel, nodding. "What the Monsignor has been too modest to mention, Laura, is that he is in the midst of a most extraordinary project. He is writing a book."

"Oh, do tell." Laura opened her blue eyes wide.

"Yes, well." The Monsignor shrugged dismissively. "A little project of mine. But it does give some, shall we say, insight." He waited to be drawn out.

Laura was obliging. "Well, I think we'd all be interested, Monsignor. Really."

"Oh, I don't know."

"Oh, please."

"Yes, do let them in on the secret, Monsignor," Marjorie urged him. "I think you'll find our young people a very bright and fascinated audience."

"Well..." The Monsignor looked dubious. "If you do think—"

"Oh, yes."

"Well, I could..." He paused, looking down meaningfully at Evan and Angela, who were whispering to each other. After a moment, they went quiet and looked up toward him. "Yes, well, a little project of mine. A lifetime of effort, really. It is—how shall I say this?—a kind of history book. Just that." He looked as if he weren't going to say more. His eyes were on the Colonel.

"A history book, but with a twist," the Colonel said. "The Monsignor's book is to be a history of the future."

"How *fascinating*," Laura exclaimed.

"It's quite scientific, actually. Not a speculation, mind you. One can say fairly precisely what the future holds, at least in broad terms. This is the field of study known as psycho-history."

"Psycho-history?"

"Yes. You see, the events of the future cannot ever be divorced from those of the past. For example, once the Roman Empire had allowed itself to fall into moral degeneration, its future was effectively determined. Through the science of psycho-history, I could have told you from about the time of Pope Innocent that the sack of Rome was at hand. I could have told you that quite easily."

"Could you, really?" Laura seemed to be entranced.

"Oh, yes. Not the exact date, of course, but plus or minus a few years."

"How extraordinary."

"And this recent war, another perfect example, was pretty much determined by the foolishness of the League of Nations." The Monsignor paused to chuckle. "You don't have to be a professional psycho-historian to see that."

"I suppose not," Laura said. "Was it just the outbreak of the war that was determined, though, or the entire progression of the war?"

"The entire progression," Monsignor Leary answered emphatically. "Any amateur psycho-historian could have set it out for you as of about 1934. Again, without perfect precision as to dates and such details. No, the science is not quite *that* exact. But as to the general unfolding of events—the Balkans, the entry into Poland, the French caving in as they did, North Africa, the Battle of Britain—it was all in the cards. So, you see, just as one could have predicted the fall of Rome or World War II, so too one can now look forward in time. The difference of course is that you can go to a library and check out a history of past events, but so far, you can't check out a history of the future. I intend to change that."

"What's he talking about?" Mr. Collyer asked.

"The future," Marjorie shouted into his ear. "He's looking into it."

"Someone ought to."

"But don't keep us in suspense, Monsignor," Laura implored. "Tell us what the future holds."

Tyndall and the Jervis girl were clearing the last of the plates. Monsignor Leary waited, frowning, for the clatter to finish.

"The future," he said at last. "Well, I can tell you one thing about it right off. The Depression is going to be back."

"Oh, how depressing," Marjorie said.

"History will look back at the fifties, I expect, as a great depression that makes the old Great Depression seem like a picnic." He looked around at them in apparent satisfaction. "You're going to see Ph.D.s selling apples again on street corners everywhere. And by that I mean *everywhere*. Even right here in Dark Harbor, I predict."

"Of course, there aren't any street corners in Dark Harbor," Liam pointed out, "there being no streets to speak of."

The Monsignor ignored him. "The Depression, you see, never really ended. Oh, we thought it had ended, but that was just the war. The war drove it underground. But it's still here, gnawing away at our vitals."

Evan was looking very serious. "Then you don't think, Monsignor Leary, that the current American boom is going to continue?"

"No, my boy. I'm quite sure of it. We're just coasting along at the moment, propelled by the vitality of a much earlier time. A vitality, I might say, that has been absent now for most of a generation. No, I don't see an American boom on the horizon, at least not a *North* American boom."

"You have more optimism, then, for the south?"

"Oh, yes. South and Central America. That's where the future lies."

"And Europe?" Clark asked.

"Pfeu!" The Monsignor shook his head in apparent disgust. "No, don't look to Europe to save us. Europe, I'm afraid, is kaput. Europe and the States."

"And just why is that, Monsignor?" Laura asked. "I mean, how do you know that?"

"Well, there is quite an extensive analysis required, my dear. I won't bore you with that. You have to look at a number of different factors, all integrated into a meaningful whole through the use of higher mathematics."

"But just give us the flavor of the thing, Monsignor.

What, for example, is the chief factor that ensures the decline and fall of America—or North America, at least?"

"The shackling of capital." Monsignor Leary smiled grimly. "That alone would be enough to guarantee that the Depression will be back by 1950 at the latest. The shackling of capital."

"Oh."

"Europe, of course, with its hopeless infatuation with all things socialistical, is on a fast track to oblivion. By about the year 1980, we will think of Europe as we think of Africa today: that is, as a great, trackless emptiness with no culture to speak of and useful only as a provider of natural resources."

Angela raised one eyebrow. "Europe with no culture?"

"None. You see, culture cannot exist without population. Without population, there is simply no culture. I'm sure you can see that."

"Seems reasonable," she allowed. "But don't they have some population? Admittedly a bit depleted, but one assumes they know what to do about that."

"Hear, hear," agreed Evan.

"On the contrary. Now you begin to see just how complex psycho-history can be. It is precisely that, not knowing what to do about declining population, that will be Europe's undoing. And to what could we attribute Europe's breakdown, an entire continent seeming to forget the very mechanics of procreation?"

"Beats me," Scarlet said.

"To rampant atheism. You see, the act of procreation is, quite simply, a glorying of Almighty God. Without faith in such a god, the act seems pointless."

"Now, wait a minute," Evan objected.

Monsignor Leary shut him up with a glare. "A pointless act, an offense to dignity and hygiene."

"Oh, I don't know . . ." Marjorie was smiling.

Liam was unable to stay silent. "Wait a minute. Wait a minute. You think we reproduce only because of our religion?"

"I do. That's what gives the act its purpose. We merely lend ourselves to the intentions of One whose mind transcends all."

"What about the lower animals, then?"

"What about them?"

"Do you think they reproduce only because of *their* religion?"

The Monsignor sighed deeply. "My boy, the lower animals have no free will. They reproduce because that is what is required of them—nothing more, nothing less. They do it without pleasure; it's merely a task, like pulling a wagon or giving milk."

"I have my doubts about that."

"Atheism is inevitably accompanied by a declining birthrate," said the Monsignor. "Take the example of France, a country in which religion has ebbed to the present disastrous low tide. And look at the population. Fifty million at the turn of the century and today barely thirty million."

"Two wars, of course, have taken their toll," Liam pointed out.

Again the dismissive wave. "Nothing. A few deaths along the way. It isn't the drain that leads to today's low ebb, but the fact that the faucet has been turned off."

"Ah, the French faucet," Scarlet said. "I remember it well."

Laura was distressed at the thought of another bad depression. "But what about Asia? What about the Japanese, for example? What with all we're investing to bring them back to economic health, can't we expect something in return from them? Rather like parents who invest in their children and then the children help them out in their old age? They're saying that Japan is going to be a force to be reckoned with in the future."

"No, my dear, don't you believe them. The only people of note in the Pacific theater are the Filipinos. The Japanese are not going to be significant players. The Japs have no head for business. Those people can't even make toys that hold together until Christmas night. They certainly aren't competent to make cars and engines—not that there would be anyone to buy them, even if they could make them."

"No one to buy airplane engines?" Liam challenged. "I thought the demand for airplane engines was nearly infinite."

The Monsignor was ready to concede a small point. "For the moment. For the moment. I don't imagine the airplane industry will be with us for very long, however."

"What?"

"A few years at most. No, you look back at the *Hindenburg* disaster, and you'll see the future laid out for you as plainly as though you were a prominent psycho-historian like myself. One disaster of those proportions, and the era will be over in a flash. One of these fat airplanes is going to fall out of the sky with fifty or a hundred deaths and you will never hear of airplanes again. No, my friends, the railroad is with us for posterity."

"I love trains," Marjorie said. "It's just as well with me."

Laura had her hand on the Monsignor's arm. "But let's go back to what you said about the decline of North America. Why is South America going to be different?"

"South and *Central* America, I said. Don't forget the Central."

"What do South and Central America have that we don't?"

"Leadership," the Monsignor said simply. "They have it and we don't. So they will prosper, and we will not."

46

Liam shook his head. "Where is this Central American leadership going to come from?"

"Cuba." Monsignor smacked his palm on the table. "From Cuba. Cuba is the sole remaining vestige of sanity in the Americas—the last refuge of right thinking and progress, and the last ray of hope for all of us. Cuba in this part of the world and the Philippines in the Pacific."

"Cuba is full of spics," Scarlet said. "So are the Philippines, for that matter. Wall-to-wall spics."

Sissy was shocked. "Spaniards, Aunt Scarlet. Puh-leese. We have modern sensitivities here. We are very modern young people."

"Spics, Spaniards, what's the difference?"

"*Spic* is a pejorative, that's the difference."

"So is *Spaniard.*"

"*Spaniard* is a pejorative?"

"Of course it is. The suffix *-ard* is pejorative, as in *coward* and *braggard* and *drunkard* and *dullard.*"

"I never knew that."

"Cuba and the Philippines," the Monsignor said, raising his voice to regain control, "they are the future."

"I have to say," Liam sputtered, "this sounds highly dubious to me."

"You're not going to be very happy in the future then, my boy. It's not going to work out as you had hoped."

"Tell, us, please, what leads you to make these, may I say, rather questionable predictions."

"CAMBRAG analysis," said the Monsignor with a gesture of finality.

"What?"

"CAMBRAG. It's an acronym. Stands for Capital, Authority, Management, Birthrate, Religion, Access, and Grace."

A long silence around the table.

"Well, it does explain one thing," Jody allowed, "about

how several Catholic countries are expected to prosper. What with authority, birthrate, religion, and grace. Gives the Catholics a certain leg up."

"There is a natural advantage to being Catholic," the Monsignor agreed. "There always has been."

Liam was having trouble containing himself. "So we have the emergence of the great Cuban–Filipino axis to look forward to. Then what?"

"That brings us to the end of the twentieth century, with Cuba and the Philippines locking arms—on behalf of all of the civilized world—against the monolithic empire of the Soviets. Good against evil, capitalism against communism, freedom and liberty against oppression." The Monsignor's voice rang from the paneled walls of Xanadu. Then the sound died out, and there was complete silence.

At last Laura spoke up. "Oh, don't leave us there, Monsignor. Don't leave us in suspense. How does it come out?"

"That, my friends, will be the subject of Volume Two."

5

Modern Sophistication

L iam had taken his journal and pen out to one of the lawn chairs to think deep thoughts and capture them in verse. Whatever deep thought came to him, he decided, he would write it down in the poetic form called a villanelle. He had only just learned about the villanelle: a fixed scheme of four or five tercets followed by a final quatrain, relying on but two rhymes. He wrote the rhyme scheme down the left side of the page: A-B-A / B-A-B / A-B-A / B-A-B / A-B-A-B. Byron, it was said, could write Latin with one hand while he wrote Greek with the other. If Byron could do that, then Liam Dwyer could certainly dash off a villanelle on any appropriately meaningful theme that suggested itself. He settled back to wait for the meaningful theme.

What came instead was a short snooze. Liam started awake at the sound of his own snoring. He looked around to see if anyone had heard. Not a soul nearby, thank goodness for that. No one on the tennis courts or by the pool or along the seawall. Then he caught sight of Colonel Forsythe, barely recognizable from this distance, taking in the view from Jeremiah's new attic gable. Liam set off up the lawn to join him.

"Ah, Liam. Come help me drink in this lovely morning." The Colonel slid sideways on the still unpainted sill to make a space for Liam. There was no window in place yet. Mr. Hopkins and his crew had completed only the framing. There was tar paper overhead where the roof slate had not yet been laid. "What do you think of our new gable? Wasn't it a stroke of luck that the roof fell in at just this spot, to let us know where the view needed to be opened up?"

Liam looked around, admiring the workmanship.

"I come up here often," the Colonel told him. "It's where I think my deep thoughts."

"Ah," Liam said, seating himself carefully on the sill, his legs dangling out over the lawns below.

"I find peace here when I'm troubled." Colonel Forsythe swept his left arm out over the lower part of the island and the bay, sparkling sleepily in the morning sun. "And when I'm too peaceful, too complacent, I find some tension here as well." He gestured with his other arm toward the mainland. There was a black cloud clinging to the hills above the little town of Northport.

The Colonel nodded toward the dark patch of sky. "That's Temple Heights, where the storm is brewing." He tapped out his pipe against his khaki pants leg. "There is no love lost between Temple Heights and Dark Harbor, you know."

"Oh?"

"Or at least I feel that. Do you ever get the sense that places can have antagonism for each other? An honest-to-god antipathy?"

"Oh, I don't know." Liam strove for the noncommittal. You never could tell where the Colonel was headed.

"I think of England glaring across the channel at France,

or Russia sticking out its tongue at Japan. Places that just don't like each other. Not the people, but the places."

"Well, England and France have a long history of bad blood," noted Liam. "As do Russia and Japan. I mean, the people do. Whereas Temple Heights and Dark Harbor—"

"Had only one little war between them."

"War? War?"

"Oh, yes. A war," said the Colonel. "The people around here know it as the Great Zucchini War. A pitched battle, with the Gideons against . . . well, against their opposite numbers from Temple Heights. My daughter, Jody, knows all about it. We'll have to get her to tell the whole story. But it had all the standard trappings of war: betrayal, saber rattling, ultimatums, sneak attack, counterattack, fatalities— or at least one fatality—the flush of victory for one side, and for the other the bitterness of defeat."

"There really was a war here? The Gideons were attacked?" Liam still suspected that his leg was being pulled.

"They were, indeed, attacked. Ages ago. What's left now is only the brooding tension between these two places. It's still there, though. You can feel it."

Liam stared out toward Temple Heights. It certainly did seem to be brooding this morning. "Um, I know you said that it's Jody who's got the details. But, since you've whetted my appetite, couldn't you just sketch in the broad outlines of the war? I mean, who—?"

Colonel Forsythe laughed easily and clapped an arm around Liam's shoulder. "Why is it, do you suppose, that the old are patient, while the young, who have so much longer to live, can't seem to wait for anything? Why do you suppose that is, Liam?"

Liam thought it over. "I guess I don't know the answer to that one, sir."

☙

"I think I could forgive almost anything except a lack of sophistication," Laura was saying. "It really is the only fatal flaw."

"I do agree with you on that, Laura," Compton Forsythe weighed in heavily. "I find the idiot enthusiams of the unsophisticated to be particularly trying." An exasperated shake of the patrician head, causing a thick patrician lock of hair to tumble onto his forehead. Compton pushed it back into place with a manicured hand.

Sissy gagged. "Oh, Compton. You are such a snob. You're bringing out the very worst in Laura. I never heard her talk like this till you arrived."

"No, Sissy, it's not Compton. It is what I really, really believe. A certain degree of sophistication is, I think, a requirement. Really."

The girls were dressed for archery in long blue skirts and striped blouses. Liam had on a pair of powder gray trousers and a white sweater trimmed in red and blue, probably more appropriate for tennis. He honestly had no idea what one was supposed to wear for archery. Compton, he was relieved to see, had on a nearly identical sweater.

"The film last night," Laura went on, "just as an example, was *so* unsophisticated. The sentiments were positively maudlin. I can't think who would have appreciated it. And Ronald Coleman...well, I think that Ronald Coleman is simply not my cup of tea."

"Nice to have a film, though," Liam said. It's very festive. And it is a venerable tradition, films shown in East House. The Colonel told me—"

"Still, though, a better selection of film might have...but I'm not criticizing anyone, Sissy. I'm really not."

Sissy shrugged. "The Colonel gets these films on the cheap from the theater in Camden. They rent by the week but are open only six days. So whatever they have in Camden gets picked up by Mr. Jervis, and we 'borrow' it for the extra day. The Colonel has some sort of an arrangement. But we have to take what the theater manager chooses for—"

"A rather unsophisticated clientele," Laura finished. "That's just what I was saying. Now, I don't mean to be critical of your father at all, Sissy. I adore Andrew. He is a perfect sweetheart, and I appreciate his little program of films. It's just that we need to maintain our standards. If something is unsophisticated, let us simply note that and go on. We can have a little laugh about it. There is no need to be unkind, only scrupulously honest."

"Laura's right," Compton said, nodding. "We have to have our own standards, which in many cases are far beyond the level that one might encounter—"

"We do have to keep our standards," Laura interrupted, "and by that I mean particularly among ourselves."

Angela, standing off to the side, was taking no part in the conversation. "Here goes me, everyone. Just you watch." She loosed her arrow, and it slid with a satisfying *twang* into the tin disk that Liam had hung over the bull's-eye.

"Very nice, Angela. That will be hard to beat." Compton took up his arrow.

"You'll have to split mine in two, I think, to beat that shot."

Laura ignored them. "We need to maintain a certain standard of sophistication, and supply gentle reminders to each other when it is not upheld." She looked reprovingly at Liam.

"Uh-oh."

"Well, I was just thinking of you getting all blushy when the Colonel mentioned that he gave you boys a guided tour of Cleopatra. I think that was so unsophisticated. Really, what was there to be embarrassed about? For a sophisticated person, I mean."

53

"It is just a john," Liam said, agreeably.

"And it is not a *john*," Laura shot back at him. "That's the kind of talk that we can dispense with forthwith. I propose we simply ban all childish euphemisms from our talk. That should be the rule in our company."

"Hear, hear," Compton agreed.

"So if it's not a john, what are we supposed to call it?" asked Liam.

"Cleopatra is the ladies' bath. Just that. We call a thing by exactly what it is," Laura told him.

"Ah," said Angela, "the 'ladies' bath.' That's calling a spade a spade. No euphemisms for this crowd."

"Precisely. And while we're still doing you, Liam, just think of your reaction when the Colonel offered us a brandy last evening. You looked so shocked. I could practically hear you thinking, Oh dear, what if Mummy should find out?" Laura laughed mirthlessly. "I mean, we're not children, are we?"

"Well, you have to remember that I *am* Irish," Liam said with what he hoped was a certain ominous note.

"Irish? Does that matter?"

"The Irish have a terrible problem with their whiskey. It's something I have to keep in mind." He tried to look tragic.

Laura laughed again. "Oh, I hardly think you're going to become a drunkard, Liam. One little taste of brandy."

"Really, Laura, you shouldn't be so hard on Liam," Sissy put an arm around Liam, comforting him. "The poor boy is crushed."

"I was not in the slightest unkind. It's just that Liam does need some special attention from time to time. I think of it as a particular responsibility of mine. He has no sister, you know. I am taking him on as I would a little brother."

"I'm the same age as you, actually."

"Girls mature more quickly, as we all know. They grow

ahead of their brothers from puberty, and maintain that difference until about the age of—"

"Ninety," Angela finished for her.

"And it's not just Liam either who can be tiresome." Laura had turned toward Compton.

"Uh-oh," Compton said, lowering his bow. His arrow had gone wide of the mark.

"Well, you went all 'aw shucks' when I mentioned that we girls had had a swim au naturel." That, too, showed a lack of sophistication."

"Bad Compton." Angela waggled a finger at him. "'Aw shucks'-ing like that. Really."

"Well, what could be more natural than swimming as we did? If you think about it, swimming au naturel is perfectly—"

"Naturel?" Liam offered.

"Precisely. Why, it's swimming with suits on that is unnatural, if anything is."

"Now this is getting interesting." Compton affected a leer. "Are you suggesting—?"

Laura stamped her foot in exasperation. "I'm not suggesting anything. Only that we try not to be so dreadfully awed by things that are so utterly natural. That's all. Try to show a little...a little..."

"Sophistication?"

"Yes. Thank you, Liam."

Compton pointed toward the target. "Say, it's your turn, Laura. Aren't you going to shoot?"

Very deliberately, Laura began to unstring her bow. "No, I don't think I shall. I find archery rather boring, actually."

"Oh, me too," Compton agreed, also unstringing his bow. "Nothing but a game, really, and games are for kids, aren't they?"

"Just 'cause you missed by a country mile," Sissy said.

"Sweet of you to have noticed, Sissy *dear.*"

Laura shook her head at them. "That's another thing, this babyish squabbling between you two." She linked one arm through Compton's and the other through Sissy's and began to draw them away. "Time for a little chat, I think, about mature interaction. Come along, Angela. I'm going to need your help with these two troublesome children."

Angela rolled her eyes but handed her bow to Liam and followed.

"Be a dear, Liam," Laura tossed back over her shoulder, "and take the gear back up to the gatehouse for us."

Liam, who had not yet taken a turn, was dying to try the bow and arrow. It was something he had never done before. Just as well, he thought, that the others had gone on, because he would look the proper fool until he got the hang of it. He tried to remember just how Angela had stood as she aimed.

His first arrow was no closer to the target than Compton's had been. But the second one, a lucky fluke, landed almost on the piece of tin. He felt a thrill of satisfaction, a positive "idiot enthusiasm." Liam gathered up the four quivers and counted their arrows: twenty altogether. Then he methodically shot off all twenty. Two of them landed on the tin. He retrieved all the arrows and shot them again. This time he made three new holes in the tin.

On the third round, he practiced saying, "I find archery rather boring, actually," on each shot. Or "People are so unsophisticated these days." Or "I find the idiot enthusiams of the unsophisticated to be particularly trying." Ah, another bull's-eye. "Particularly trying ..." "Rather boring ..."

He had never recognized boredom before as an antidote to deficient sophistication, but now that he thought about it, what could be more sophisticated, really, than boredom?

The more excited he became about his new proficiency with the bow, the more he tried to look perfectly bored.

The tin disk had been Colonel Forsythe's suggestion. He found the top of a number-ten can for them in the kitchen. "Put this on the bull's-eye. Then, when you hit it, the tin gives off a sound, a good, solid *thunk*. Makes it a bit more fun." Of course, fun was something else that would need to be sacrificed in the interest of sophistication. Liam rounded up the arrows again and carried them back.

By the end of an hour, he was hitting the can top regularly. The tin circle was full of holes, and Liam was actually becoming a bit bored (there was hope yet for his sophistication). He wondered idly if it would be possible to toss the tin disk into the air and hit it in flight. Might be amusing. Not an idiot enthusiasm, mind you, but mildly amusing. Mild, slightly scornful amusement, he thought, was entirely consistent with mature sophistication.

He got the bow and arrow ready and spun the tin into the air, coaching himself all the while: Now wait for it to come down so the arrow doesn't get lost and . . . now! Liam shot his arrow at the floating target. Pretty close. He went to retrieve the arrow and the can top.

On the third try, the disk spun down in front of him, almost into his arrow, and Liam had to suppress a grin. None of that, now. No grinning; someone might see. He went again to retrieve it. This time he spun the tin higher to give himself more time to set up. There it is . . . sliding down, nicely, right in front, now aim and . . . let go!

The arrow and the disk swooped together as though fate had predestined their meeting, and meet they did with a glorious *klang*.

The can top, pierced with its arrow, fell in a clatter directly at the feet of Mr. Collyer, who had just come around the hedge. He stopped and stared, his mouth wide open. "My word . . ." Mr. Collyer poked at the disk with his cane. Then he leaned to pick it up. The arrow was lodged right in its heart. He looked back admiringly at Liam.

"Why, what an extraordinary shot, my boy."

"Yes, well. It's not as hard as it seems." Liam yawned.

"And look at all these holes!"

Liam unstrung his bow. "I find archery rather boring, actually."

"What's that?"

"Boring," Liam shouted.

"People are so unsophisticated these days," Liam observed. He was sitting alone with Marjorie on the flagstone terrace. A small regatta of sailing boats was making its way in front of them along the Narrows.

Marjorie smiled her pleasant, easy smile. "You know, I've begun to notice that whenever someone says 'these days,' they're almost invariably telling you something that's been true simply forever. Why, just this morning, Monsignor Leary was talking about 'the problem of poverty these days.'" She did a credible imitation of the Monsignor's voice. "As though there hadn't always been a problem of poverty. And people are always saying, 'What with the crime we have these days,' as though there hadn't always been crime. Or, they say, 'The politics these days.' Now, that's just plain silly. Politics has always been politics. Always the same."

"So you think people have always been unsophisticated?"

"Well, it does follow, doesn't it? If we're unsophisticated today, how much more unsophisticated we must have been, say, a thousand years ago."

"I suppose so."

"So don't be too down on our time. I doubt that history

will mark this particular era as a nadir of sophistication. Not that I'm competent to project what history will record. For that I would have need of—"

"Leary's Bleary Theory."

"You're hard, Liam. Very hard for your years."

"But not sophisticated."

"That comes with age. It is unfortunately irreversible, however. When you've got it, you might wish you could go back to an earlier time."

"To the idiot enthusiasms of youth?"

Marjorie sighed deeply. "That sounds so lovely."

"Oh, I don't know."

"But you seem like a mature young man. I haven't noticed you—"

"Gaping. Blushing. Enthusing. Gushing."

"Not so awful."

"I'm afraid it's my Irish nature that does me in."

"Oh?"

"The characteristics of the Irish, you know."

"Well, you're half Italian, I happen to know. Your mother—"

Liam brushed aside her objection. "The Irish passion is incompatible with modern sophistication. And I am almost powerless to overcome my Irish nature."

"An Irish nature makes you—?"

"Passionate, gloomy, alcoholic, pugnacious."

Marjorie laughed delightedly. "Why, Liam. You are none of those things. Pugnacious? Goodness no. And gloomy?"

"I feel in the grip of a deep, abiding melancholy," he said sadly.

"Oh, that's bound to be your digestion."

"It is not!"

"I have something you must take before bedtime. We'll have you fixed up in no time at all."

6

Purple

The last of the full-summer guests arrived that evening just before sunset. She was the New York actress, Gabriella Lake. The manner of her coming had set the others to buzzing all day, in spite of their great sophistication: She arrived in a silver floatplane. She had taken off from New York Harbor and flown directly—"non-stop," as they were saying now—to Dark Harbor. The Forsythes and their guests were lined up on the front lawn as the plane made its final approach and taxied up to the stone dock. They could see her through the windshield sitting beside the pilot. A leather flight helmet was pulled down over her long blonde hair.

Liam and Sissy grabbed onto the wingtip and pulled the plane into position so that the Colonel could open Gabriella's door directly onto the dock. "She is very dramatic," Sissy whispered into Liam's ear as soon as the engines had gone quiet. "For an actress, entrance is everything. Pay attention to her first line. I'll bet it'll be a corker."

The Colonel took the actress's hand as she stepped out of the plane. Bowing slightly, he said, "Welcome, my dear Gabriella."

She smiled wanly at him. "Bathroom, please," she said.

"She is almost *too* beautiful," Liam ventured over breakfast the next morning. The new guest was sleeping late. "Beauty needs to be flawed in some way so that..." Well, he wasn't too sure what. "Laura is beautiful too, of course, the lovely Laura, prettier than anyone really needs to be. But Miss Lake is...well, something else. We need new words for her."

"She is quite something," Colonel Forsythe agreed. "But the difference in years is important here. At twenty, Laura is mostly just showing her genes; what we see is what she was born with. But give her a few years to find herself. At twenty-six, on the other hand, Gabriella is showing us the person inside. She knows who she is, and it radiates from within."

"I never thought of that. You don't find, then, that a woman's beauty is at its peak of perfection at twenty?"

"Oh, no. Her prettiness, perhaps, is at its peak. But the beauty is still to come. Our young ladies here this summer all affect a certain detached calm. But Gabriella, you will see, has a perfectly unaffected calm. She is entirely at peace with herself. And that is the source of her beauty."

"Why, Andrew, I do believe you are smitten," Marjorie chided him.

"Quite right, my dear. I am. I have been for years. I am smitten with a certain young woman named Marjorie— Marjorie Pickering, as she was then known. She was twenty-seven when I first set eyes on her, and she has transformed my days and nights ever since. In Gabriella I see a reminder of that earlier breathtaking peacefulness and beauty."

Marjorie looked over at Liam. "There, Liam, is Irish for you. That is the Forsythe Irish. No melancholy, no gloom, just pure blarney."

Laura too had skipped breakfast. Liam found her in mid-morning, taking the sun near the man-made tidal swimming pool at the water's edge. There was an excellent book on the tides in the Colonel's library, and Liam had brushed up on the baffling mechanisms of rising and falling water levels. This might be the moment to let Laura know that such mysteries were no mystery to him, in spite of his less-than-impressive showing the first evening.

"The tide is ebbing, I see. It's only at the peak high tide, of course, when the water actually floods into the pool through this little door, which is called a tide gate. That's why the water warms up so nicely between one high tide and the next. You can see that the man who designed this pool had a savvy grasp of how the tides—"

"Oh, Liam. It's you."

"Uh-huh." He sat down beside her on the wall, already warm in the morning sun. "At the season of the apogee, or extreme low tide—"

"This was where she did her baptisms, you know. Jeannie Isobel."

"She did?"

"Yes. I've been thinking about that. She would dunk them here when it was warm and sunny, as it is today. The Monsignor was telling me all about it last night at dinner. The Colonel seems to have given him the scoop on Jeannie."

"Oh."

"Mr. Chance had the pool built just for Jeannie, for her to conduct the ceremony. She and the Angels and Acolytes would come down here each evening when the weather was hospitable and have a nice splash. It didn't matter that you'd been done before. Jeannie felt that you could never be baptized too many times. The Monsignor said that her baptisms were a cause celebre in those days. In religious circles, I mean."

"You mean because people got rebaptized?"

"Well, that of course. But, even more because she baptized in salt water. The rest of the religious world was shocked."

"Oh."

"And they attacked her. There were tracts written and campaigns mounted to stamp out the evil of saltwater baptism. It was considered a heresy. They tried to use it to destroy her."

"Jody says that everybody hated Jeannie except the people who loved her."

"Nobody was on the fence about Jeannie. You were either for her or totally against her."

"I think I would have been for her. Not so much on religious grounds, mind you, but because she seems to have been an original. And not as gloomy as the other Holy Rollers." The picture over the main stairs had been enough to make a fan out of Liam.

"Nothing gloomy about Jeannie. It might have been better for her if there had been."

"Oh?"

"Well, it may have been her sense of fun that got her in trouble. She did get in terrible trouble, you know. Had to leave Dark Harbor under a cloud. That's the other thing the Monsignor was telling me—it wasn't just the matter of salt water but one of the other particulars of the way the baptisms were performed. At least in the Dark Harbor years."

"What particular?"

Laura looked at him sternly. "Now, I'm not saying this is true, Liam, only that it's a rumor. Nobody's quite sure. I shouldn't even be telling you."

"Only you're going to." He waited a moment. "Aren't you?"

Laura was smiling naughtily, making him wait. "The rumor is that they did the baptisms in the nude." She affected her silvery laugh, but she was blushing a bit too.

"Oh."

"Angels and Acolytes together."

"Oh."

"Nobody knows. But some people think that. It was a rumor. Of course, I don't believe it myself. Are you shocked?"

"Of course not. Nothing to be shocked about."

"Well." She paused. "There is an earthy aspect to it, though, isn't there?"

"Earthy."

"Nothing *we* can't handle. Only, I must say, I might not have shared that little fact with just anyone. I can't see myself mentioning it to Evan, for example, or Compton. I do feel ever so much more relaxed with you, Liam, than with . . . others."

"You do?"

"Uh-huh. I think it's because we are . . ." A shy sideward glance.

"We are?"

"I think we are."

Liam stared at her. He waited a long moment. Laura smiled back at him sweetly. She seemed, maddeningly, to have completed her thought.

"Um, we are what?" he asked at last.

Laura stared off up the lawn, frowning slightly. "Now, where could that Angela be? My, these late sleepers at Dark Harbor House. I think I shall rouse her. We can't let a whole morning go by without some serious girl talk."

She lifted herself up and headed toward the main house, leaving Liam alone with the nude Angels and Acolytes frolicking in their pool.

Jody was the authority on all matters of local history. Liam set out to find her. She would be able to tell him whether it was true about the baptisms. It would be just like the Monsignor to have gotten it all wrong. Of course, Liam would have to put the matter to Jody in some way that left out awkward words such as "nude" and all mention of indelicacy or impropriety of any kind. So how should one ask the question? A classical allusion, perhaps? How exactly does one convey "buck naked" with an erudite reference to the classics? Perhaps something would come to him.

He found Jody in the Biscay library. She was popping with excitement. He'd been able to hear her shrieks and giggles all the way from the front porch. Gabriella was standing beside her, trying to suppress a grin.

"Liam, you have to see this," Jody bubbled over. "We've made the most fascinating discovery." She had evidently broken her glasses and the bridge had been repaired with white adhesive tape. She seemed completely unaware of her odd appearance. In her hand was an oversized magnifying glass, which she waved energetically. "I wrote to Gabriella and asked her to bring me a book by Jillian Winthrop from a bookseller in New York. And she did. And I read it. It explains everything, and even the dates match. Can you believe it?"

Gabriella gave a low, almost manly chuckle at Liam's side. "Back up a little, sweetie. Liam is looking lost."

"Oops. I got ahead of myself." Jody made a visible effort to calm herself. "Jillian was one of the Gideon girls who were here in the early 1900s—in 1903 to be exact. Now she lives in Greenwich Village and dresses in tweeds and trousers and smokes little black cigars and writes books."

"A bohemian." Liam knew all about bohemians.

"A bohemian." Picking up a volume bound in brown and silver, Jody explained, "This book—the one Gabriella bought for me, I mean *procured* for me—tells about being here that summer and how she..." Jody blushed. "Well, it tells everything. Which clears up the puzzle of the hand-holding."

"Hand-holding." Liam was lost again.

Gabriella took the magnifying glass from Jody's hand and passed it to Liam. "On the composite photo. This is the picture that the group had taken the summer of 1903." She pointed him toward the wide-framed photo hanging over Biscay's fireplace. It was a posed group portrait with some fifty people, most of them in their teens and twenties. All were dressed in white choir robes, holding open sheets of music. The front porches and terraces of Dark Harbor House were visible up the lawn behind them.

Gabriella took Liam's hand and drew him onto the ottoman that was pushed into position in front of the fireplace. "The picture was supposed to show the spirituality and lofty ideals of the Gideons. Now, see if you can find any faces in the crowd that seem to be less lofty in their demeanor and perhaps a bit more lusty."

Liam focused on the picture. The first person his eyes lit on was Jeannie herself, now familiar from the painting. She looked both lofty and lusty, if that was possible. She was smiling and staring directly into the camera. Almost all the others were looking heavenward with their mouths formed into an "O"; they seemed to be singing. He scanned slowly from left to right. At the far end of the front row were one Acolyte and one Angel who weren't singing and weren't looking where the photographer had directed. They had eyes only for each other. They were pressing up against each other and laughing. Sure enough, they were holding hands.

"That's Jillian and her special friend, Grant," Jody told him. "Now, look in the lower right-hand corner for the date when the photo was taken."

"August 20, 1903," he read.

He looked down at Jody who seemed to think he should have grasped some deep significance. "Um, perhaps you better tell me: What is the importance of the date?"

"Well . . ." Her face was becoming pink again. She looked to Gabriella for help, but all she got back was a smirk. "It's important because Jillian, as she explains in her book, gave birth to her 'love child' on May 19, 1904, in Greenwich Village, New York." Jody's voice cracked slightly on the term "love child."

There was a short moment while they all did the math.

Liam thought out loud. "August 20, May 19 . . . it could have been."

"It was, it was. I just know it," Jody exclaimed. "Look at them. Look at their expressions."

Liam looked. He was suddenly aware of the tops of his ears turning red. He stepped down hurriedly and handed the magnifying glass back to Gabriella.

Jody was paging furiously through the little book. "It had to be approximately August 19 that Grant and Jillian were together for"—she found her page and read out loud—"'a night of purple bliss in a deep, soft bed in the love nest that was called Lancelot.'"

"Lancelot?" Liam gulped.

"That was the night before that picture was taken. I'm sure of it."

"Looks that way to me too," Gabriella confirmed. "They've got that dewy look that only lasts for—"

"Did you say Lancelot?" Liam couldn't get past that point.

"Oh, that's your room, isn't it Liam?" Jody looked sympathetic.

Liam made an abrupt exit. He started up toward his room, then remembering the phrase "the love nest that was called Lancelot," he wheeled abruptly on the stairs and headed outdoors to clear his head.

What Liam needed was a good, long walk. To stride out briskly through the pine woods and up the Colonel's blue-

68

berry hill. Put all the craziness behind him. He had half a mind to go all the way around the island while he was at it, mile after cleansing mile. Except, of course, he didn't want to miss lunch.

Liam had vowed to himself to write at least one serious poem each day, and in the two weeks he'd been at Dark Harbor House he hadn't done a thing. Nothing. No wonder, with all the distraction around him. Who could think? You'd have to be a eunuch. Meaningful thought required super-human discipline, at the very least. Serious discipline. Empty the mind of everything except the natural grist for the poet's mill: abstraction. Concentrate on beauty (flawed and unflawed), essence, and truth. Not just truth, mind you, but Truth: Deeply True Truth. Don't let any other thought in. In particular, don't let in "the love nest that was called . . ." Erghhhh. They should have named the damned place "Hormone House."

He went all the way around the property and ended up at the corner by the seawall, where the Forsythe land butted up against North Star's wide lawn. He stood there with the sun on his back, looking out toward Seven Hundred Acre Island. There were lobster boats in the bight, gulls wheeling overhead.

A bright spot here was that the line about Hormone House had possibilities for repartee. He looked around to be sure he was alone before practicing it out loud to judge its effect. "You know, Laura, they might just as well have called it Hormone House." That should be good for a laugh. Or was the "it" in that sentence too obscure? He could imagine Laura saying, " 'It?' What 'it'?" She was so hard on him.

He tried again: "You know, Laura, instead of Dark Harbor House, they might just as well have called it . . ." That was better. Above all, the line had to be delivered in a perfect deadpan. He had to resist his horrible tendency to break out in laughter right in the middle. To which Laura would respond, "What was that, Liam? I missed the part right after you started cackling." Perfect deadpan. A steady, wry delivery: "You know, Laura..."

It wasn't just Dark Harbor House, he realized, that had an earthy history. If places could talk, they'd each have a tale to tell. There had probably been couples in sensual interaction of one sort or another almost everywhere over the years. Right here along this beach, for example. With his artist's sensitivity, he might even be able to hear their stories if he listened closely enough. Or see the aura they had left behind; that was even better. The refined vision of the true artist could look at a place where there had been an erotic act and see its aftermath, a kind of pinkish glow. Or dusty rose color. Or better yet, purple. Yes, glowing purple. He looked up the shoreline toward North Star's secluded little crescent beach, and sure enough he could see, in his mind's eye, a distinct purple glow. Things had happened there, he had no doubt about that.

Liam turned slowly to look down the beach in the other direction. There were spots of purple here and there as far as the eye could see, each one large enough to include an embracing couple. The seawall was crowded with purple areas. The tide pool, as one would expect, was a solid purple, as was the idyllic little path that led from there up through the rose bower and into the woods. Gideon House, the next to come into his line of vision, glowed purple at each and every window, even the one in the laundry. But that was nothing compared to Dark Harbor House itself: The entire structure was enveloped in a massive purple cloud, lit from within and pulsating steadily.

Liam took in the vision for a long moment. He found it oddly comforting.

7

Revelation

~~~~~~

For the Fourth, Colonel Forsythe had ordered a large assortment of fireworks through the mail from a company in North Carolina. The crate arrived in time, lugged in from the ferry dock aboard the *Nellie B.*

"Six hundred one-inch salutes," the Colonel was reading from the enclosed inventory. "One hundred two-inch salutes, fifty cherry bombs, one thousand Chinese firecrackers, sixty skyrockets in assorted colors, one hundred Roman candles, twenty spinning salutes, twenty two-stage rockets, two hundred sparklers, fifty punk sticks, and a grand finale. And here I quote verbatim: It says the grand finale is a 'standing display of the flag, flying in the breeze, in twenty brilliant colors with attendant skyrockets, salutes, high-altitude mortar bombs, sizzlers, multistage rockets, and sound effects.' Well. I think we should invite the whole island to see that. I shall set it off myself in front of the admiring throng."

"Oh, Andrew. Do try not to blow yourself up."

"Thank you, Marjorie, for that sage advice. I wasn't going to give it a thought, and now it will be foremost in my mind."

Evan was busy lifting packages out of the excelsior. "These must be the one-inchers. Wow, there's a ton of them. And these fat little round red ones—"

"Cherry bombs, no doubt. I can't imagine what we'll do with those. For the party, I mean. Still, it does seem a shame to waste them."

"We could set off a few today," Liam suggested. "Just to test them, I mean."

"Quite right, my boy. Quite right. Just to test. Since they won't be of any use at the party, we might as well test all the cherry bombs."

"An exhaustive test," observed Marjorie.

"Exactly, my dear."

"We'll have no doubts about the cherry bombs, then, that they might let us down at a critical moment."

"None whatsoever. Of course, there will be no cherry bombs left by the time of the critical moment."

Jody was looking into the box. "Too bad we can't test the grand finale, though."

"Ah," said the Colonel. "There is always an element of danger with fireworks. There is the danger of blowing your hand off, and then there is the danger of having to face guests who have been invited explicitly for fireworks, and explain to them that the grand finale has been a fizzle. And somehow imply that they ought to go home anyway."

"We'll keep dessert till after the finale," Marjorie suggested. "People always go home after dessert."

Evan spoke with a businesslike air. "But this testing, sir, how shall we go about it?"

"The testing, yes. Well, methodically, of course. To eliminate any possible error of bias, I propose that we divide up the materiel to be tested, and distribute it among as many testers as we can persuade to help. Now, who will volunteer to be a tester?"

Jody jumped up. "Me me me me me me meeeeeeee."

"Yes, that's one. Liam, good. Evan. Compton. Sissy, that makes five. Angela, six. Monsignor, seven. Marjorie, don't blow yourself up now, dear. Marjorie is eight. Lizzie? Lizzie Groton from Smith makes nine. Gabriella ten. And how about the lovely Laura? No? Yes? No?"

"Oh, well."

"Oh, well, indeed. Laura makes eleven."

"Just to help out."

"Of course. And I will be the twelfth. Oh, Tyndall, could we impose upon you as well?"

"Very good, sir."

"That makes thirteen. I presume Mr. Collyer won't be interested. But then again, who knows? Let's make a pile for him, as well. So, Evan and Liam, if you would be so good as to divide the ordnance into fourteen equal piles."

"The whole works?"

"All but the grand finale. That should give us proper confidence when the moment comes to set off the finale in front of our guests. Because we will have tested absolutely everything else. And, of course, we shall have hardened ourselves under fire to the rigors of the task."

As soon as the counting out was done, Sissy stood up, holding her pile in her skirt. "The actual testing, Daddy. How do we do that?"

"Well, by blowing stuff up, of course. Not one another, mind you. You find things that look as though they could benefit from a bit of firecrackering, then you stuff in a salute, light it with your punk, and run. Now, where is my pile? Ah, splendid. Thank you, Liam. I think this might be a good moment to move ourselves out-of-doors. Do be careful, everyone."

After a full day of pranking about with fireworks, most of

the young moderns had headed up to bed early. Even Laura, normally a night owl, said her good nights before eleven. Only Liam was unable to face the prospect of sleep. He was wide awake, his blood still churning from the—let's call a spade a spade—idiot enthusiams of the day.

What a blunder to have joined forces with Jody, of all people. Whatever had possessed him? How could he maintain an attitude of mild, slightly scornful amusement in the face of that mad creativity of hers in matters of demolition? And her infectious giggles. The others had made at least a perfunctory attempt toward calm, detached sophistication between detonations. No doubt that was why they were so exhausted by the end of the day. Whereas he, victim of his Irish passion, had let himself go completely, whooping madly along with Jody. He had even lent himself to her idea of slipping into Inverness to steal Mr. Collyer's pile of fireworks. The combined forces of Jody and Liam had had three times the firepower of any of the others.

But now on sober reflection, there was a price to pay, an inner turmoil. Liam was torn between the vision that Laura had expressed earlier of a perfect, or at least less imperfect, Liam Dwyer on the one hand, and Jody's wacky vision on the other. Part of him wanted to be just what Laura would ask of him. And then there was that other part.

Unaware of what he had missed, Mr. Collyer smiled at Liam benignly across his newspaper. "Another quiet day, Liam. Very quiet. Nice of you to ask. You did ask, didn't you?"

"Oh, sure."

"A quiet day. Perfectly quiet." He lifted his paper again and resumed reading.

⁂

Liam stopped into Biscay to choose a novel from one of its shelves (there was a complete collection there of the works of H. Ryder Haggard), then headed up to his room. At the top landing, he saw a dark shape at the window. The shape muttered something as he approached and came toward him into the light.

"Oh, Monsignor. Good evening, sir. Still awake, I see."

"Ah, my boy. My boy, uh . . . "

"Liam."

"Liam. Of course. I was just looking at the stars. A lovely sight, lovely." He put an arm across Liam's shoulder and led him away from the window toward the little Coventry sitting room off the landing. "And I was . . . waiting for you, actually. I was. I thought we might have a bit of a talk."

"Oh."

"You know, from my years of being a simple parish priest, I retain a keen sense about young folk and their problems. I have a nose for internal turmoil. I am right, aren't I, that you're suffering from internal turmoil?"

Liam had to concede the point. "Well, I guess you could say that."

"Ah, I knew it." He tapped a finger significantly on his nose. "I knew it. Well, tell me all about it, Liam. Just you blurt it out, my friend. Ask me those questions that are burning away inside you. Don't be shy." He sat down on one of the overstuffed chairs and gestured Liam to the one opposite.

Liam sat, as directed. "Questions?"

"Yes. You know, the kind of questions that haunt young people. Questions about man and God. Or man and woman, for that matter. I am prepared to give help in these and other areas. Think of me as a resource, my boy. Think of me as a member of your personal support team. Like a kindly uncle, for example."

"Oh."

"You were wondering . . . ? What were you wondering?"

Liam thought desperately of something he might have

been wondering. Something that Monsignor Leary would feel comfortable commenting upon.

"Um . . . well, now that you mention it, sir, I have been wondering something, a religious question of sorts."

"There we are. I suspected it. Let's hear what you've been wondering."

"Well, I've been wondering about Norbert Chance, the man who built this house and this whole complex, starting with Jeremiah House. The Colonel told me that Mr. Chance built Jeremiah very early on, and gave it that name because of his religious inclinations at the time. I was just wondering what you could deduce from the name, and what it implies about his religion. I mean, what kind of conviction would make you want to name your home Jeremiah?"

"Mmmm. Jeremiah. What frame of mind would have inclined Norbert, then a fairly young man, to name his house after that particular Old Testament prophet? What was his frame of mind?" He let his gaze move up to the ceiling. "Well, I'd say a very dismal frame of mind."

"Dismal."

"Dismal, gloomy, even depressed. The book of *Jeremiah* is a bleak canvas, you know, a presentation of God's darker side. It tells of a God intent on vengeance, unforgiving, and, frankly, cruel."

"Oh."

"Not a pretty picture. Not by human standards, at least. By godly standards, of course, it is perfectly okay."

"And, if I could ask, does anyone still believe in such a god?"

"Oh, yes. Absolutely. I do myself. God is infinitely merciful and infinitely forgiving, but you don't want to cross him. No, sir. That could cost you quite heavily."

"Doesn't that seem . . . almost contradictory?"

A dismissive wave. "Not at all, not at all. God, you see,

is infinitely merciful, but only to those who have seen the error of their ways, recanted, repented, converted, embraced their Savior, and thrown themselves abjectly at His feet. That's when the infinite mercy cuts in."

"Infinite mercy, within limits."

"Exactly. But now let us remember that Norbert was a fundamentalist Christian, originally one of the Millerite sect. So we need to think what Jeremiah might imply in the context of their fundamentalist beliefs. The Reverend Miller was known chiefly for his reading of the New Testament book called *Revelation*."

"*Revelation* is about the Apocalypse, isn't it?"

"It is. Now with this insight, the puzzle suddenly begins to make sense. *Jeremiah* is seen to be a prologue to *Revelation*. Jeremiah tells us of a cruel and vengeful God, and what is revealed in *Revelation* is the *need* for a cruel and vengeful God. We need Him to lead us in the coming conflict."

"Against the Devil."

"Against the anti-Christ. It is the book of *Jeremiah* that introduces us to a warrior God who is steeling Himself for eventual confrontation with the anti-Christ. So Norbert, we might deduce, was thinking apocalyptic thoughts and worrying about the anti-Christ who might already be among us."

"I see."

The Monsignor paused, reflecting on what he had just said and nodding to himself. Liam was looking for an opportunity to make his escape. A long enough pause and he could simply stand up and make his excuses. Just as he was about to rise, the Monsignor coughed slightly and looked up. He spoke very softly. "I must tell you, my boy, I have such worries myself sometimes."

"Hm?"

"The same kind of worries."

"You mean you think—?"

"I do."

"The anti-Christ?

"The anti-Christ."

"Here on Earth?"

"Yes."

"Now?"

"Now."

"Right here in Maine?"

"Well, perhaps not in Maine."

"Someone we know of, though? A public figure?"

"Most assuredly. A very public figure."

"Oh."

The Monsignor tapped his nose again, knowingly. "Now, put yourself in the place of this mythic force of evil. If you were the anti-Christ, Liam, you would take every precaution, wouldn't you, to conceal your true identity."

"I suppose so."

"Whatever people expected you to be, you would present yourself as exactly the opposite."

"Seems sensible."

"Now, all we have to do is examine our expectations to know what the disguise will be. To know how the beast will *not* present itself. Just tell me, my boy, any expectation you might have about the anti-Christ. Anything at all."

"I've really never thought about it."

"Just whatever crosses your mind."

"Well..."

"Go ahead."

"Well, I imagine he—"

"Ah-hah!"

"Hmm?"

"You said 'he.' You expect the anti-Christ to be a he. So, of course, it will not."

"It won't? A woman then?"

"Of course."

"Oh. A woman. How interesting. Um . . . I don't suppose you have any idea what particular woman?"

"I have my suspicions."

A long silence.

"You wouldn't be willing to share your suspicions, would you?"

Monsignor Leary was nodding his head rhythmically back and forth. "You may not be ready for this," he said.

Liam prodded gently. "You think the anti-Christ may be—"

Monsignor Leary muttered something.

"Hmm? I didn't hear."

The Monsignor leaned forward and whispered the name directly into Liam's ear.

"Eleanor Roosevelt."

8

Dr. Ralston

The great stone cistern behind Dark Harbor House was a ruin now. Its cover had fallen in, so the top was open to the rain. One side was crumbling.

"Still holds water, though," the Colonel said. "Just a little less than it used to."

Liam stared up admiringly at the ruin. "It couldn't have been prettier, even in its day," he said. Where the stones had come down from the collapsed side, they formed a pile, now overgrown with ivy that crept up the intact portion of the wall.

"It's a kind of folly," Laura suggested.

"Folly," Liam repeated. He wasn't sure just what the word meant in this context, but its sound was lovely.

"Yes," the Colonel agreed. "Like the great old houses in England with their Capability Brown gardens. Brown built instant ruins for his patrons and spotted them around the parks of their enormous lands, fanciful remnants of a past that had never really existed. He put Greek ruins in the middle of Dorsetshire and Sussex, where no Greek had ever been. But this is an actual ruin. I mean, before it was ruined it was un-ruined, unlike the follies in England. It actually served a purpose."

"Norbert's folly," Liam said out loud, listening to his own voice.

"That it was," the Colonel agreed. "He filled it with spring water from South China, Maine. Brought it in by horse team to Northport, then by barge over to the island. Norbert said it was the purest water in the world. He set great store by pure water. There were special pipes that took the water from here into the kitchens and baths and bedrooms, special plumbing just for drinking water. The pipes were lined with silver to make sure the water stayed pure all the way to its destination. And the inside of the cistern was lined in silver, too. I'm afraid we plundered all of that years ago to pay for the restorations that have kept Dark Harbor House together, or at least somewhat together."

"Drinking water? So much drinking water?" Liam nodded up at the cistern. "Looks as if it would hold a ten-year supply."

"Mmm. You see, Norbert was a hydrolist, an advocate of the school of hydrolism."

"Seven quarts a day they drank." Sissy puffed up her cheeks as though she were about to pop. "Seven quarts each. Not just Norbert himself, but all of his guests. All of the Angels and Acolytes, the poor things."

"They didn't have to, of course," the Colonel said. "But they were his guests. Most of them were poor young people who had never seen such splendor. They weren't about to say no to Norbert's gentle suggestion."

"I've never heard of hydrolism."

"No, it didn't catch on too well. Norbert thought it was the tops, though. Good for what ails you."

"Well, it would flush you out, I guess," Liam allowed.

"That was the idea. Flush you out, and rehydrate all your tissues. There are some tracts on hydrolism in Biscay, all bound up in a scrapbook. Norbert even wrote some of the tracts himself. *Human Hydration and Drainage* was one of his titles."

"Ever the plumber, our Norbert."

"Speaking of plumbing," Sissy pointed up to a pull chain running down from a large metal fitting on the side of the ruin. "The Colonel installed this when Clark and I were little. And he built the slide for us."

The wooden slide ran down to ground level from a platform mounted on the side of the cistern, immediately under the fitting.

"We used to run up to the top and sit down all giggles, then the Colonel"—she reached for the pull chain—"would let out the rainwater in one giant *whoosh*." She pulled down hard on the chain.

There was a momentary gurgling, then a huge gush of water from the spout. Liam and Laura leapt back to avoid the spray.

Sissy was smiling fondly at the Colonel. "We got tumbled down the slide and dumped in a wet and muddy pile at the bottom. It was glorious. How did you know it would be so glorious, Daddy dear?"

"Just seemed as if it might, I guess," the Colonel allowed, chewing on his pipe. "Water and mud have always been big hits with children."

"I think I shall make a sketch," Laura announced after the Colonel and Sissy had started back to Dark Harbor House for a swim. "You see, from here, Liam, the light slants down, thus," she swept a hand grandly toward the folly, "and splashes off the stonework, or *cascades*, I might say."

"It does. Cascades, I mean."

"To the artist, it is this cascading of light that distinguishes a setting of great beauty from what otherwise might be nothing more than a pile of rock. Do you see what I mean? The artist's eye is attuned to this. Sometimes I may sit for hours at a site, just waiting for the light to attain its perfection. Waiting for it to cascade."

"Well, I know just what you mean, Laura. I myself have often—"

"The light is simply perfect now, so I must begin. I shall require perfect silence as I work."

"Oh. Certainly. I'll be quiet as a mouse."

"In addition to silence, I will, of course, need someplace to sit. Someplace along this wall." There was only one sittable spot on the wall, one large, flat capstone. The rest of the wall was in various stages of ruin. Laura walked back and forth along the wall, framing the folly from each angle. Finally she arrived precisely in front of the capstone, not looking at the wall at all but only at the folly. "Yes. This is the spot, I think. The angle is perfect from here." She nodded down at her selected seat and looked back expectantly at Liam.

"Um...Oh! Here, let me put down my jacket."

"Why thank you, Liam. That would be lovely."

Liam folded his jacket into a cushion and placed it onto the dusty stone seat. Laura arranged herself carefully so that her skirts would not be dirtied. She took out her sketch pad and pencil, issuing a contented sigh. "Now, perfect silence, please."

Liam nodded obediently. He seated himself at her feet, studying her as she studied her scene. She crossed her legs, dangling one ankle and a bit of petticoat not a foot away from his nose.

Laura sighted the folly thoughtfully with one eye closed, holding her pencil alongside, first vertically, then horizontally. "Don't you think that the pursuit of beauty is man's real mission on this earth?"

"I do, actually. I—"

She looked at him reprovingly through the corner of her eye.

"Sorry."

"It's just that it's so hard to find the repose one needs while someone is chattering on. A state of repose is essential for any artistic endeavor, you know."

Liam limited himself to another nod.

Laura sighted again with the pencil. "But don't you think, too, that man is meant to do some positive good?" she asked. "I mean, beauty can't be all of the mission, can it? Beauty, after all, is a source of pleasure, and pleasure is so selfish, don't you think? When we pursue beauty, we are pursuing our own ends, not thinking of others at all." She passed her pencil in a few fluid circles over the pad without making contact. "Don't you agree, Liam?"

"Um..."

"Well?"

"Well, I do. Agree."

"With what?"

"With what you said."

"That it is beauty alone that gives meaning to life? Or that beauty is selfish, and meaning comes only from selflessness? I said both." She laughed enchantingly.

Caught. "Beauty is...," Liam began helplessly. He had no idea where that was supposed to lead. He stared at her, trying not to gape. She was so lovely. "You're so lovely, Laura."

She looked down at her pad, lashes fluttering, smiling a tiny smile.

"You are. I just—"

"Selflessness *and* beauty, I think, are the twin poles of our existence."

"I . . ." He stopped himself. Laura had turned her attention to her pad once more. She smiled at him and formed her mouth into a silent "Shh."

Liam leaned back and let his eyes close. He held the image of Laura's "Shh" in his mind, her lips thrust forward, her mouth slightly open.

Liam's own artistic endeavor, an epic poem of sweeping proportions, was stalled. On his first morning at Dark Harbor House, now nearly four weeks ago, he had sketched out the effort. He'd found himself awake at 5 AM with sunlight filtering in through Lancelot's open bay windows. Taking up his journal, he sat at the writing table, the light coming in over his shoulder, and penned the following resolutions:

1. *Arise at 5 ea. day*
2. *Write epic poem of sweeping proportions*
3. *Work 3 creative hrs. ea. morning*
4. *Finish by Sept. 1*
5. *Dedicate to Laura*
6. *Lose weight*

As luck would have it, he had not even once in the ensuing weeks arisen so early. Most mornings, he woke at about eight, the three creative hours having been spent sound asleep. The work was, he rationalized, in a period of gestation, which was necessary for any artistic endeavor. The gestation had not progressed so far that he could even say with assurance what the epic was to be. He had only a vague sense that it would involve some Greeks.

Biscay was a gracious reading room with two wide bay windows. There was a window seat under each window, suitable for one or two readers to position themselves with their backs to the light. In a small nook immediately opposite the window seats were three photographic portraits in gold frames, three turn-of-the-century gentlemen in period dress.

"The cereal kings," Marjorie told them. "Post was the gray-haired one, here in the middle." The center picture showed an elderly man wearing a waistcoat. He was seated, with a book in his lap. "The andiron you see in the corner of the photo is this one here, so we suspect that the picture was taken right in this room. He must have been sitting about where you are, Angela, probably in that red chair. And this is Mr. Kellogg—still alive, I hear." The left-hand picture showed a fortyish fellow in tennis clothes. He was posed on the court, with Dark Harbor House visible in the background.

The third portrait was much more formal. The tall figure who stared out of it was black haired, black eyed, almost ferocious looking. He had a wide mustache that bushed out well beyond the sides of his face. The man stood stiffly, dressed in a dark coat with five buttons down the front. His starched white collar was folded over sharply into two abutting triangles. He had placed his right hand over his stomach and his left on top of a pile of books. Immediately behind him on the wall was a checkerboard, with four squares in each dimension.

"Ralston," Marjorie said.

This was new to Liam. "Wheat Chex? That Ralston?"

"Oh, yes. Wheat Chex and Rice Chex and Shredded Wheat."

"Now wait," said Angela. "Aren't there Ralstons at North Star House, next door? The twins, Teddy and Louise—isn't their name Ralston?"

"Yes. This is their grandfather, Dr. Orin Ralston, the builder of North Star House, and Jeannie's great patron."

"There is some suspicion that he was Jeannie's lover as well," the Colonel added. "In any event, he was the one that supplied the funds for Jeannie and her little community to summer here, and eventually to move here permanently. We think he may have built North Star House for Jeannie. She was his North Star, coming as she did from Canada. The plan was for her to reside only temporarily with Norbert, until North Star was done. Norbert was delighted to have her. Maybe he was in love with Jeannie too. I've always thought that."

"But she never did move into her new house," Sissy said. "Before it was done, she had left forever in disgrace. Dr. Ralston went back to St. Louis, where he'd come from originally. The others went away too. After that, Norbert was alone—an old man, quite alone."

"Where on Earth did they all meet?" Angela asked. "I mean the cereal kings and the religious folk and Norbert the plumber and hydrolist?"

"Battle Creek. They all came from Battle Creek."

"Battle Creek, Michigan? No."

The Colonel nodded. "They did. Mr. Chance was born there in the 1840s. Dr. Ralston came to Battle Creek as a young man to join a local religious sect, the Bentonites, and to run one of the health clinics that made the city so famous. Post arrived there as a patient some years later. He was already a successful businessman, with more success to follow. When he built a fine house for himself in Battle Creek, it was Norbert Chance who installed the plumbing. They became friends. Kellogg was there too, working in another clinic, the Battle Creek sanitarium. Jeannie Isobel went to work for Dr. Ralston as a young girl, barely of age."

"And they all knew each other there?"

"They did. Even the mysterious Haydée. She was from Battle Creek too."

"Who was Hi-ee-day?" Liam asked. This was a name that had never come up before.

"Jeannie's great rival, Haydée Benton," the Colonel told them. "They were all friends at the beginning, part of a community that was formed around the idea of good health and religion and brotherly love. They cared for one another, joined together in wonderful new ventures, and many of them became fabulously wealthy. Then, little by little, they were driven apart by events and circumstances and jealousies and betrayals until, at the end, they were all enemies. Very sad. Very sad."

9

Fourth of July

There were voices coming from Gawaine as Liam started down in the morning. He stopped in to see how the work was progressing. Gabriella had been able to move in, but there was still minor finishing going on. Angela was there, seated prettily in her cotton dress on the top of a stepladder. She was chatting with Mr. Hopkins's son Tim, who had done most of the fine carpentry. Gabriella had evidently gone down already for breakfast.

"Liam, come see what Tim has done now. Look at the carving."

Tim was on a second ladder, applying a light stain to a carved wooden lintel above one of the gabled windows.

Angela pointed. "It was all gone, rotted away, the whole right side, including half of that lovely butterfly."

"It was that and more," Tim allowed. He spoke with a slow, heavy Maine accent that made the word "more" into "mo-ahh."

Liam got closer for a look. "You carved the butterfly?"

"Only the right side, just from where you can see the

joint if you look close. You won't be able to see it, though, when I'm done with the stain."

"I've heard of butterfly joints."

"This is more like a jointed butterfly."

"I see. Did you have one of those little whirring drills to carve with?"

"Tim did it with a jackknife!"

"Ah." Liam clucked over the fine detail. "If I had done that, I would be feeling...well, wonderful. That's how I'd be feeling about now."

"Feels pretty good. It's not quite up to the original, though. The original is done in locust wood. The whole room is locust, but we had to do the repairs in white oak because there's no locust left."

Liam looked around at Gawaine, now almost perfect again. In many ways it was the prettiest of the bedrooms. Most of the others were paneled in dark brown woods, but here the paneling was honey colored; it fairly glowed in the morning light. "But why had so much rotted away?"

A grimace. "The roof, of course," Tim told him. "Always the roof. We had to replace some two hundred slates and re-build the parapet and the rampart."

"You know, I'm not too up on ramparts and parapets. I mean, what are they?"

Tim pointed out the window. "Look there over Childeric's gable. What's falling down is a parapet. In front of it, the part all rotted away is a rampart. That's why Miss Jody has to sleep with her oilskins over the foot of her bed. We're doing Childeric next."

"Oh."

As if on call, Jody appeared at the door. "Mr. Jervis has dumped the hugest fish on the pier. A salmon. It's for the party. Said I was to find two great, burly boys to carry it to the kitchen. And I've chosen you two."

"Well, one and half," Liam allowed. "But I guess we're up to it."

※※◎◇※

"I'm the reason we're having salmon for the Fourth," Jody confided. "You see, it was a tradition in Norbert's time. I discovered it, in my reading and researching. They roasted a whole salmon out doors in a long pit of coals and served it to hundreds of guests. I told the Colonel that we really ought to do it the very same way, only with fewer guests. We ought to do it to keep the tradition. The Colonel usually does what I tell him, if I put my foot down."

"You've got him trained," Liam observed.

"I, of course, always have to do what he tells me, because he is my father."

"Of course."

"We know all about the salmon because it was a sore point among many of the guests. Food was always a sore point in that group. Their letters talk about almost nothing else. If it wasn't food, it was religion. But more food than religion. It sometimes seems that no two of them would eat the same kind of food. They were all faddists of one kind or another."

"So they didn't all eat the salmon?"

"Most of them wouldn't. Dr. Ralston wouldn't eat fish of any kind. Said it was unholy. Mr. Post ate only grains. Will Kellogg wouldn't touch anything with protein in it. He thought protein was a poison. Elihu Root, who was often a guest at Dark Harbor House in those years—"

"The old secretary of state? That Elihu Root?"

"Yes, that's the one. He would eat protein but no carbohydrates. Wouldn't eat any grains at all. He wouldn't sit at the same table with Kellogg or Post. It was mutual. Mr. Root would eat the salmon, but he had to take yogurt as an antidote. Otherwise, he said, the fish toxins would ruin his

93

clear skin. Fletcher, who invented Fletcherizing, was here too most summers."

"Fletcherizing?"

"Chewing everything a jillion times. He ate the salmon but wasn't too happy about it. He said that the fish melted away too quickly to be properly chewed. He was more inclined toward beef. The Gideons would eat fish but not meat. The Bentonites wouldn't eat fish or meat. Norbert himself was rather partial to salmon. I like it too."

"So do I."

They laid the fish out on one of the marble counters in Molybdenum. Mrs. Jervis instructed them how to remove the scales. Liam and Jody were scratching away with metal scrapers while Mrs. J. prepared a basting sauce. Tim had gone with Mr. Jervis to dig the pit.

"Think what it must have been like to put on a dinner for that crowd," Liam said. "Everybody on a different diet, plus separate tables for the ones who hated each other."

"Not just separate tables. Separate dining rooms."

"Didn't they agree on anything? Anything at all?"

"Oh, yes. Coffee. They all agreed on that. Well, with one exception. Most of them agreed that coffee was simply awful for you. They wouldn't touch it. Mr. Chance drank pure hot water in the morning. Mr. Post invented Postum as a coffee substitute. It was a kind of burned molasses. And Mr. Kellogg, he had his own: It was called W. K. Offee. That one was made from burned roots of sassafras and ginseng. Dr. Ralston invented his own version using burned wheat with caramel flavoring. We have some of each of them around here someplace if you'd like to have a taste."

"No thanks."

"You can't buy them anymore, but we never seem to run out of our supply. People taste them once and..."

"I can imagine. But you said there was one exception."

"Jeannie Isobel. She liked her coffee in the morning."

"Number one-sixteen at B-eleven," Colonel Forsythe read from the instructions. "Now, where is number one-sixteen?"

Searching in the excelsior packing material, Laura eventually came up with a blue, pinwheel-like contraption with a long fuse attached. There was a ticket hanging down from it on a string. "One sixteen," she said. She had a bit of pink excelsior in her hair.

Liam had his doubts. "I think that's nine hundred eleven, actually. All of the even numbers so far have been rockets."

"Oh, dear," the Colonel said. "This is complicated."

"That one then, Liam, isn't that one sixteen?" Laura pointed toward a green rocket.

"It is. But so is this one." He held another rocket, also labeled 116. "Or maybe this is Eleven-B."

"Oh, dear," the Colonel said again. "Listen, why don't you two sort this out? I'll come by after you've got the whole thing assembled, and I'll check it for you. Yes, that's the way to do this. I will take on a strictly supervisory role. In fact, I think I should supervise the wine punch that Marjorie is making, as well. Supervise and taste. That is definitely where my talents lie." He wandered off toward the terrace, leaving them to sort out the grand finale alone.

Laura and Liam had erected the scaffolding and had about a third of the various fireworks in place on its framework. Each had a long fuse that had to be cut to a precise length according to the instructions. Laura was reading the directions: "Number one-sixteen, twenty-two inches."

Liam measured and cut the fuse, then affixed the rocket at location Eleven-B on the framework.

"So much for number 116," said Laura, checking it off. "They say that number one-seventeen is a two-stage mortar bomb, colored yellow."

Liam began searching. "I wish you would take me more seriously, Laura. I really do. You always seem to treat me like a child." He kept his eyes averted, looking for a yellow mortar bomb. "Is this it?"

"It is yellow, and it is a mortar bomb, and it is one-seventeen." She handed it back to him. "Thirteen inches. I do take you seriously, Liam dear. Of course, I don't take anything *too* seriously. Or anyone."

"But still—"

"*Toujours gai* is my motto. Boys are here for us to enjoy, like the flowers and the birds. But not to take *too* seriously."

"If only, though, you understood—"

"But I do. Nothing escapes me, really. Nothing like that. That one goes on V-twenty-one. Check. Let's see . . . number one-eighteen: rocket, red and white."

"I'm left feeling—I don't know—a kind of melancholy. I've been feeling it right along."

"Oh, that's not good."

"A deep, abiding melancholy." He paused dramatically. " 'In sooth, I know not why I am so sad.' "

Laura looked honestly distressed. "It sounds like *melancholia dolorosa*. Could it be that?"

"Yes! That's precisely—"

"A kind of gaseous condition—"

"Oh, no!"

"Do you have any gas, could I ask? It usually—"

"No, damn it! This is spiritual melancholy. Deeply spiritual."

"Oh."

"Deeply. I'm sad. Can't anyone understand that?"

"Oh, don't be sad, Liam. I hate it when people are sad." She put down the instruction sheet and pencil. "I hate it. It makes me cry. You wouldn't want that, would you?"

"Well, no. Of course not."

"Then you must turn your sadness right off. Just do it. You must."

"Laura, I can't simply—"

"You have to. Or I shall be reduced to tears."

"But it's my Irish nature."

She put her hands to his cheeks and stared into his eyes. There was, amazingly, the tiny glint of a tear showing in her lashes. "Oh, do it, Liam. Please."

"I . . ."

Laura pulled his head toward her. One hand pushed up into his hair. "There's a little switch. It's up here, but inside. There is. I know there is. You can find it if you try. Look inside, Liam. It's so important. You have to find it—so I needn't cry."

"A switch?"

"A little Bakelite knob, brown. Look for it Liam. Between the cortex and the medulla."

"What the hell is the medulla?"

"Don't fight me, Liam. Hurry. Find the little switch. The sadness switch. Can you see it? Can you?"

"Um . . ."

"You can, I know you can."

"Brown, you say?"

"Yes. That's it. Grab hold of it."

"I think I have it."

"Turn it all the way off. Turn it till it clicks. Oh, please. Hurry."

"There. I think it clicked. It did."

"Oh." He felt her relaxing. She looked behind her to find

the stone bench and lowered herself gratefully onto it. "Oh, that's better." She still had one hand on his arm. "I feel much better. And you must too."

"Well, I do...I think."

Laura shook her head. "We must keep that little switch off, off, off."

Liam sat down beside her. "Laura..." He didn't know what to say next.

She smiled slightly, wiping away her tear. She was so pretty. Her hair was positively golden in the sunshine, and it all swung forward perfectly, just above her shoulders. He wondered, did it grow that way? Or was there some kind of feminine wile that she practiced to make it fluff forward, with not a single hair out of place. And if it was something she did, when on Earth did she ever find time to—

"I suspect you want very much to kiss me, don't you, Liam?"

"Um...I do."

"Well, you may." She closed her eyes and offered her mouth to him.

My god. Liam took a deep breath and kissed her. Then he put his arms around her and kissed her again.

Laura opened her eyes and looked off toward the horizon. "A little firmer with the lips, I think, Liam. It's like a handshake in a way. I mean, it can't be *too* gentle."

"Laura..."

She closed her eyes once more. "Try again. You'll get it eventually."

In the gathering darkness, Colonel Forsythe stood on the lawn in front of the array of folding wooden seats that now held his fifty-plus guests. He gripped a lit sparkler in his hand so people could see him. "Dear friends—"

An exuberant cheer from the throng.

"Welcome, again. Welcome. Everyone get enough to eat?"

Applause.

"There's still plenty of salmon . . . and salad and chicken and wine punch and . . . so forth." He paused to consider. Then raising his voice to the level of the very slightly oratorical: "We are gathered here together . . . Well, you all know why we're gathered here together. Why don't I just light it?"

Cries of "yes" and "let 'er rip" from the guests.

The Colonel held out the tip of his sparkler to the end of the bundle, the twisted-together fuses of more than one thousand individual fireworks. When the flame caught, he hurried back to take his seat in the front row between Marjorie and Liam. "Now if only it doesn't fizzle," he whispered.

An expectant silence.

When the first salutes began, the guests cheered lustily. The rockets went off in clusters, and people responded "Ooooh," and "Aaaah." Little by little the outline appeared in glittering sparklers and gradually began to fill in with red, white, and blue. A stiff silence settled over the group. There was a long pause during which no one spoke.

"Well, it is a flag," Marjorie said at last. "I can see that."

"Yes."

"Definitely a flag."

"Yes."

"It's just not *our* flag."

"No. Regrettably."

"Where did you say you got these fireworks?"

"North Carolina."

"Mmm. That does explain it, I guess. Andrew, I think perhaps you ought to say something." The guests around them had remained silent.

"Oh. Quite right, dear. I suppose I should." The Colonel stood up and lit himself another sparkler.

"Well. As they say of Independence Day, it is . . . a day of independence from not just one thing, but from everything, so to speak. I'm sure someone has said that at one time or another. And, uh, just as we celebrate our independence from the British, and, of course, from the Germans and Japanese, et cetera, so, too, perhaps, we need the occasional reminder that we have also retained our independence from the Confederacy, which we sometimes forget but which has been admirably recalled to us this evening by this, uh, flag." He gestured over his shoulder at the fireworks flag, which was still glowing dully behind him.

"So, happy Independence Day everyone! Marjorie says there will be strawberry shortcake made with good Maine strawberries served on the terrace starting just about now. And I'm going to have some."

10

Bruno Nougat

The arrival of Bruno Nougat at Dark Harbor House changed the complexion of the little society of young moderns. He was a few years older. He was not at Yale, as Marjorie had thought, but employed by a jazz club just off the Yale campus in New Haven. It was there that Sissy had met him. He played marvelous boogie-woogie piano on the slightly-out-of-tune upright in Navarre. He had a deep baritone singing voice. He taught the girls to do exotic Latin dances like the rumba and the samba to band music he'd brought along on "platters," as he called them, played on the Colonel's old Victrola. He was darkly good-looking. Lizzie Groton from Smith declared she found Bruno "mysterious" and "awfully cute." Sissy thought he was "cool." Laura confided to Liam that Bruno was "rather sophisticated." Liam hated him.

"Mrs. Jervis, this is Mr. Bruno Nougat from New Haven," Sissy made the introduction. Liam had been dragged along into the kitchen for moral support. "Bruno, meet Mrs. Jervis, who runs our kitchens for us at Dark Harbor House."

"Mrs. Jervis. Your reputation precedes you. I hear that the food on your table is fit for kings."

"Mmph."

"Bruno has had the best idea, Mrs. Jervis. He has discovered a whole new cuisine that has everyone buzzing in New Haven. I mean, not in the stodgy, civilized parts of New Haven, but in the little clubs and dives. It's frightfully bohemian."

"Comes from Italy. It's called pits-za."

"It's gooey and wonderful. Everybody's eating it in New Haven."

"Everybody."

"Mmph."

"It's quite easy to make, really. Bruno has suggested that we might give it a try. He can tell you exactly how to make it, then we'll have a bohemian night, where we all eat pits-za."

Mrs. Jervis had her doubts. "I don't know," she said.

"Oh, please, Nellie." Sissy hugged her. "We're going to do up the dining room in red-and-white-checkered tablecloths, and bring in the piano and dance. Just candlelight. Can't you see it? We'll all smoke cigarettes. The place will be transformed. It won't be Xanadu anymore at all. It'll be a dive, a real 'joint.' Only we've got to have the pits-za, Nellie, we really do. Oh, say you'll do it."

"Well . . ."

Bruno took over, with his great, soothing voice and dripping charm. "Really just a bread at its heart. I know that won't give you any trouble. You make a kind of flat bread and cover it with cheese and toppings."

"Flat bread."

"You know, one that doesn't rise too much. Like an English muffin."

"Corn bread then. That's flat."

"Okay. I suppose that will work. Now, for the toppings we need green peppers and garlic and—"

"Garlic?"

"Yes, you know, garlic. A kind of white bulb-like thing?"

"Oh, I know what it is. I know about garlic, in theory. But you won't find any. Not in Maine."

"Oh."

"Maine people don't eat garlic. No, sir."

"Well, onion then."

"Onion we got."

"Then we need mushrooms—"

"Mushrooms now, they cost money. Cost a fortune to feed this crowd of hungry mouths with mushrooms."

"Well, we could substitute, I suppose. We could substitute—"

"Cut-up potatoes."

"Okay, potatoes. In little, round pieces."

"You got it."

"Some anchovies—"

"No anchovies. I can give you sardines."

"Okay. So we have the green peppers, the onions, the potatoes, the sardines, and...let's see, we'll need—oh, yes—mozzarella cheese."

"You want foreign cheese? I think I could get you Swiss."

"Good. Then we need tomatoes. A lot of tomatoes."

"The tomatoes are still green and hard as rocks. How about tomato soup?"

"Fine. Now, here's the tricky part. You make the bread in a big, round, flat shape,"—he held out his hands to illustrate—"and you flip it up into the air." He flipped his imaginary bread.

"I flip the bread?"

"Yes, but with a spin."

"I spin the bread?"

"Yes. In the air."

"In the air?"

"Yes. That is evidently quite essential."

"After it's cooked?"

"No, at least I think not. I think it's before. I could be wrong on that."

"Do I spin it after the tomato soup is on it?"

"I guess so."

"And the potatoes and the other stuff?"

"Perhaps those things go on after it's spun."

"If I cooked the cheese on first, then the other stuff would be all glued in. Folks could spin their own, right at the table."

"That probably would be fine."

"Oh, yes." Sissy was delighted. "We'll teach everyone how to spin. Each person will spin his pits-za up into the air and catch it. On his plate, I guess. Then we'll eat it and drink red wine."

Bruno shook Mrs. Jervis's hand gravely. "This moment will go down in history, Mrs. J., I guarantee you. There will someday be a little plaque in front of Dark Harbor House, saying, 'On this spot was made the first pits-za in the State of Maine by Mrs. N. Jervis.' You'll be famous."

Bruno had used the word "tachycardia" in one of his little humorous routines over lunch. Liam had no idea what the word meant, and thus not a clue as to what the point of the joke might be. Still, he had chuckled along with the others at the end. At his first opportunity, with the word still fresh in his mind, he got away by himself to Biscay to look it up. *Tachy-* . . . *tachy-abic* . . . There it was, *tachy-cardia*: rapid heartbeat. Of course. *Tachy-*, meaning rapid; that was the giveaway. Now, what had the joke been? Damn, he'd forgotten. No great loss, though; just another one of Bruno's dumb bits.

As Liam looked up from the dictionary, he realized that he wasn't alone in the library. In the far corner, Scarlet was slouched down, almost lost in one of the wing chairs. A confusion of books lay open across her body, forming a blanket. All but her feet and face were covered. There were tears running down her cheeks.

"Why, Scarlet," Liam said, crossing to her. "Here now. I'm sure there's really nothing—"

"Oh, shut up!" she snapped at him.

"Whatever could it be, Scarlet? Whatever it is . . ."

She looked up angrily. "Did you ever have an intuition? Did you? Did you ever feel one thing even though you thought something else?"

"Um, well, I guess so. Yes." He must have at one time or another.

"Well, trust the feeling, then." She glared.

"Uh . . . feeling." Liam paused, waiting for a feeling to present itself, any feeling. What could this be all about?

"Just trust it. For once."

He lowered himself hesitantly onto the seat, pushing some of the books aside. She was stiff as a board beside him. Feeling very self-conscious, he inserted one arm under the thin old woman's neck and wrapped the other around her. He could feel her tense in his arms. Then, all at once, she softened. She put her face into the crook of his shoulder and began to sob.

"Is this— " he asked.

"Of course," she answered through her sobs.

Liam held her and let her cry, still none the wiser for what it might be about. He looked down at the books for a clue. There was *The Secret Garden, Little Women, Patchwork Girl of Oz, The Railway Children, Wet Magic, Whirligig House,*

The Jungle Book, and several green-and-gold embossed cov-
ers that were almost certainly volumes of *My Book House.*

Scarlet cried and cried into his neck. He could feel her
tears dribbling inside his collar and down onto his chest. He
rocked her gently, murmuring sounds, not words.

Gabriella came into the room and stopped, staring at
them. After a moment she pointed to herself, mouthing the
words silently, "Could I . . . ?"

Liam shook his head slightly, and Gabriella tiptoed out,
closing the door quietly behind her.

There was a soft moaning as Liam continued to rock.
Then a period of stuttering sound. Then just silent shaking.

When Scarlet was still at last, Liam picked up a red
morocco-covered book with no title on its cover. It was open
to a middle section, where he read:

> The Mole was so touched by his kind manner
> of speaking that he could find no voice to an-
> swer him; and he had to brush away a tear or
> two with the back of his paw. But the Rat
> kindly looked in another direction, and
> presently the Mole's spirits revived again. . . .

"I suppose—" Liam began.
"Don't," she muttered into his neck.
He shrugged and looked back down at the text.

> When they got home, the Rat made a bright
> fire in the parlor and planted the Mole in an
> armchair in front of it, having fetched down a
> dressing-gown and slippers for him, and told
> him river stories till supper-time. . . . Supper
> was a most cheerful meal; but very shortly af-
> terwards, a terribly sleepy Mole had to be es-
> corted upstairs by his considerate host, to the

best bedroom, where he soon laid his head on
his pillow in great peace and contentment...

Scarlet was sitting up beside him.

"It's not such a *terrible* place, our world," Liam offered.

"No." A long pause, after which she yawned. Her tears
were gone as mysteriously as they had come. She looked
out the window. He had the sense she might be feeling a
bit bored. Then, almost as an afterthought, she said: "Too
much hatred."

"Hatred?"

"The remains of hatred from the ones who were here before. That woman."

"Who on earth...?"

"In the garden. Full of hatred she was. All those years
ago."

"You don't mean Jeannie?"

"The other one. She came into the garden at night. I can
feel where she was. Came here to do harm." Scarlet shiv-
ered. "Near the shed where nothing will grow, the hatred
came seeping out of her. And anger. Her anger was like lava
in a hot, glowing stream. Pure red rage. Quite red." She
looked away vaguely. "Cherry red." She turned back to him,
picked out a bright red bit of the paisley pattern on his tie,
and showed him. "Red, like that."

Liam stared at her, openmouthed.

Scarlet stood and walked out the French doors to the
terrace without looking back, leaving Liam to pick up
the books.

He was the most damnably talented fellow, Bruno. His imi-
tations of Amos and Andy or Bing Crosby or Baby Snooks
sent the girls into gales of laughter. He could even imper-
sonate old Mr. Collyer to a T.

"Hmmm? Speak into the little box. Speak up." Bruno held out an invisible hearing aid toward a giggling Angela.

"What's he saying?" the real Mr. Collyer wanted to know.

"He may be a bit hard-of-hearing," Marjorie shouted.

"No crime in that. I'm not perfect myself. He ought to have a contraption, though. I've got one. Andrew has put it away for me in the safe so it's not lost."

Bruno looked down at his empty hands. "Why, it's not here. My contraption. Where is it? Oh, that's right, it's in the safe. Can't be too careful these days."

"Can't be too careful these days," Mr. Collyer reminded Marjorie.

The most impressive of Bruno's talents were the musical ones. He seemed to be able to play nearly anything, and play it well.

At the end of the bohemian dinner, he pulled a lutelike instrument from beneath the table and played a long, involved run that stopped all conversation. "Time for strolling minstrels," he announced. He put the lute down briefly to pull a checked napkin out of Jody's lap and tie it as a gypsy bandanna on his head. Then the lute again. Another clever run, each note perfect and clear. His long fingers hovered expertly over the strings.

Bruno played, the fingers moving automatically, while he strolled. "A love song," he announced. "But what's missing? What is the one indispensable ingredient for a love song? Why, a beautiful maiden, of course. Someone to serenade. Who shall it be?" Nervous giggles around the table. He played perfect chords—majors, minors, minor sevenths, augmented minor sevenths—then another dazzling little run. "Let's see. It shall be the lovely . . ." He was looking directly at Laura. "The lovely, the very exquisitely lovely" —he spun suddenly to the next chair—"Lizzie Smith from Groton."

Lizzie squealed. "Oh, no!"

"Yes!" He seized her hand and led her to the head of the table, where there was a little platform with a tall vase on it. Bruno moved the vase and replaced it with a chair. Then he helped Lizzie onto the chair.

"Oh, gawd," she said.

Bruno began with a few slow chords, lovingly strummed, then in that perfect baritone voice, he sang:

> Oh, why have you left
> Your house and your home?
> Oh, why have you left your
> Treasure-oh?
> Why have you left your
> Bonnie baby boy
> To run with the
> Raggle-taggle Gypsies-oh?
> All to run with the
> Raggle-taggle Gypsies?

After the clearing of plates, and putting Xanadu back in order, the company retired as usual to Inverness, where Tyndall had a fire going. The full moon, rising behind Dark Harbor house, cast its silver light onto the lawn, leaving a black silhouette of the building in the foreground. The sky over the Narrows was full of stars.

"What a night," Bruno exclaimed. "What a night for a walk." He lifted Laura's hand from her lap and stood there for a long moment, frozen in time, holding her hand. It seemed that neither one of them could move. Finally Bruno spoke, his voice low and thick with meaning, meant for Laura's ears alone, though all could hear: "What a night to run with the raggle-taggle gypsies."

Laura smiled slightly, looking down into her lap. Then without a word, she stood and allowed herself to be led outside.

11

The Saint of Song

O ur hostess has been regaling me about your . . . psycho-history—isn't that what it's called? I'd love to hear about it." Bruno was all ears. "I'm all ears."

The Monsignor, who had been laughing with the Colonel, became instantly serious. "Psycho-history, yes. The use of rigorous scientific principle and, I might say, some extremely advanced mathematics, to *project*, not to predict, but to *project* the future, as you would project a slide picture onto the wall. As with a slide projection, it can be finely focused and precise to any degree you might desire. The more precise you want it, the more you have to grease up your slide rule. Of course it takes a ton of work."

"I can imagine."

"I'm just now doing the 1980s. When I get back to my grindstone, I'm going to be calculating the results of the 1988 election."

"Oh, my. Who's going to win?"

"Well, of course I don't know that yet, do I? Only the calculation will tell."

"But who will the candidates be? I mean, will they be moneyed people or professional diplomats or generals?"

"Not generals, no. That's one thing you may be sure of. You couldn't get a general elected in this country, I daresay, ever again. No, a general would have about as much chance of getting elected as a—"

"So we can expect it to be the moneyed people, then."

"Exactly. American history through the end of this century will be dominated by the Hunts, the Gettys, the Mellons, the Hearsts, the Carnegies, the Iselins, the Fords. Those are names you're going to be hearing a lot. I expect great things of the Ford family, for example. We'll have a Ford as president, you mark my words, while we're still alive."

"Bruno has another question he's been dying to ask you, Monsignor. Do ask him, Bruno."

"I was going to, Sissy. I was going to. Just waiting to hear about the Fords, which I completely agree with, by the way. Completely. Blood will tell. There is no stopping quality. But here's my question, Monsignor. Fellow I know says there is this new device that sends a movie picture out over the airwaves, so to speak, so you get a picture right on your radio."

"Tel-o-vision," the Monsignor nodded, knowingly.

"That's it, tel-o-vision. This fellow says it's going to be the next big thing."

The Monsignor shook his head. "Nope. A flash in the pan, perhaps, or perhaps not even that. There is no future for tel-o-vision. None. You see, there just isn't the demand for the thing. People might watch for an hour or so on a Saturday evening, but that's about it. What on earth are you going to put on the rest of the time? And who's going to be out there watching? People don't have time for tel-o-vision. And they don't really want to have a picture, anyway. Who wants to look at Jack Benny prancing around, reading his script? It's just going to be another short-lived fad like dowsing sticks or liver pills." He laughed derisively. "In the twenty-first century, historians will someday come across a tel-o-vision box, and they'll be wondering, Now, what on Earth is this dumb thing?"

"I hate and despise Compton. He is a toad. If he doesn't leave Dark Harbor House instantly, I shall have to leave myself."

Compton seemed more flattered than hurt. "Where ever would you go, Sissy?"

"Back to Radcliffe. I'll do the summer term all alone in a garret, like a nun. Or San Francisco. I've never been there."

"I've been there."

"Oooh. Honestly. Couldn't you just strangle him? There's another thing to hate about you. I'm going to have to keep a list. You're totally horrid. Um....What was it like? San Francisco, I mean."

"Beautiful. Full of ships and sailors in uniform and little old Chinese in skullcaps and long tunics."

Sissy turned to her mother. "You see how he is, Marjorie? He tortures me. I think you should pack him up and send him off to New Jersey or someplace."

"Well, it's true," Marjorie said agreeably, "that you two have never gotten on well. Even when you were tots. I remember we had you in the bath together once and, poor Compton, I'm afraid you pulled his little—"

"I ought to do it again. It would serve him right."

"Ahem." The Colonel addressed the group assembled in the reading room on rows of folding chairs. "It is my pleasure this evening to present for your edification and instruction the noted historian and breakfast-cerealogy scholar, Miss Jody Forsythe."

Applause.

"Miss Forsythe has degrees of all sorts—degrees of talent, degrees of charm, and degrees of utter silliness, which she gets from her mother."

"Oh, Daddy."

"The title of tonight's talk is 'From Battle Creek to Dark Harbor and Back: A Tale of Intrigue, Romance, Scandal, Religion, Sex, and Treason.' Ladies and gentlemen, Miss Jody Forsythe."

Polite clapping while Jody stepped up to the dais. As it was too tall for her, Evan came forward with a dictionary for her to stand on.

"Thank you, Evan. Thank you, Colonel." She set her notes on the dais and adjusted her glasses. "The actual title of my talk is, History of Dark Harbor House, Part One. There is some scandal and those other things in it, eventually. Maybe not in Part One. Marjorie says I tend to talk forever, so I have to limit myself to ten minutes because I'm only thirteen, and everybody's got other more grown-up things to do with their evening than listen to some kid rattle on endlessly.

"Actually, it was Liam who suggested I share some of this with you. Thank you, Liam. I have been telling him about what I found out while researching our Norbert and Jeannie Isobel and the others in between swimming and goofing around. So I said I would. Share, I mean. So..." She looked down at her notes.

"Our story begins in Battle Creek, Michigan, at the Zion Benton sanitarium, a fancy-dancy kind of clinic where rich people went to take the cure. The year was 1886. Among the patients that year was a certain Mr. Charles William Post, a businessman. He was suffering from...Well, he was irregular, actually. They all were. It was an epidemic in those days among rich people, because they ate meat and nothing else and got all stopped up. The director of the sanitarium was Dr. Orin Ralston, of North Star's own Ralston family." She nodded to Teddy and Louise, who waved from the back.

"The sanitarium had been founded in 1867 by the Reverend Horace Benton. Benton and the members of his Zion Benton Community were Millerites. That was their religion. They were remnants of the following built by William Miller, the revivalist preacher who had predicted that the world would end by March 21, 1844. They used to think of themselves in those early days as Millenarianists, or End-of-the-Worldists. When nothing happened on March 21, Miller recalculated the scheduled apocalypse for October 22, which turned out to be an equally uneventful day. As you can imagine, after this 'Great Disappointment,' nobody much wanted to join their sect. And they weren't too welcome in any of the places where they had been before, because people have long memories.

"So they migrated, what was left of them, and eventually ended up in Battle Creek. Since End-of-the-World prophecy had not turned out to be such a hot move for the Millerites, they looked around for some new emphasis. Eventually they decided to become radical vegetarians. All that was around 1861. They got a vision from God not to eat meat and not to eat lots of other things. So they didn't. And they started preaching to the rest of the world about healthy vegetarian eating, how it was God's way and, incidentally, a way to get regular and thin. Eventually the group split into three parts: the Adventist Christian Church, the Seventh-Day Adventists, and the Zion Benton Community. They formed three churches, and each one had its own sanitarium.

"One of the nurses at the Zion Benton sanitarium was a girl named Jane Isadore. She was twenty-one years old the summer that Mr. Post arrived. The nurses there were called Angels, because nursing was considered angelic among the Bentonites. Jane really was angelic. She was assigned to Mr. Post when he first arrived, and he was captivated by her. He called her Janie la belle.

"The main thing they did at Zion Benton was to put you

115

on a vegetarian diet. It wasn't only anti-meat but anti- lots of other things as well. You couldn't take any coffee or tea. You couldn't eat sweets. You couldn't smoke or chew gum or dance. All of those things were considered bad for the digestion. The Bentonites had lots of ideas about religion, and the most important of them had to do with digestion. It was a religion of good digestion.

"The trouble with being a vegetarian in those days was that people were such dedicated meat eaters they just had no idea what to eat if meat wasn't allowed. So Dr. Ralston set up a laboratory in the sanitarium where experiments were begun to make meat substitutes and coffee substitutes and chewing gum substitutes. Mr. Post used to spend a lot of time each day in the laboratory, because he was interested and there wasn't much else to do. He was given a little corner of the lab where he worked on perfecting his own coffee alternative. That's where Postum was born.

"The sanitarium got people healthy and slimmed down and everything, but it was a terrible bore. Patients almost never wanted to come back because getting cured was so dull. About the only attraction was the Angels. People really liked them. So Dr. Ralston hit on the idea of having the Angels do some little theatrical pieces to keep people amused. He put Jane Isadore in charge, because she was the prettiest Angel. Only Jane didn't know much about entertainment. She'd never even been to a theater. The nearest thing she had ever seen were the regular revival meetings that were held in the Bentonite Community. Those meetings were run by a woman, Horace Benton's very beautiful daughter, who always dressed in white. Her name was Dorothea Benton, but in the church she was called Haydée.

"So Jane started going to the meetings and approached Haydée and asked if she could become an assistant. She said she felt the call to follow and to eventually become a disciple. Well, Haydée just loved her. Everyone loved her. So Haydée took Jane into her inner circle. Only Jane really wasn't interested in becoming a disciple at all. She was there to learn. She watched everything that Haydée did and copied it all down in notebooks. She listened to her sermons, copied her songs, learned her ways of getting an audience all riled up. Then Jane would go back to the sanitarium and teach what she had learned to the other Angels.

"Meanwhile, Dr. Ralston was building an enormous theater for the sanitarium. Only it wasn't ever called a theater. This was Jane's idea. It was called the Cathedral.

"By the time Mr. Post came back for his second stay— we think he came back because he was so taken by Janie la belle—the Cathedral was ready. It was opened on the night of July 7, 1887. There was a chorus of beautiful Angels, an orchestra, lights, costumes, and an enormous baptismal pool—built by our Norbert, by the way. Most of all there was one exquisitely lovely Angel in the middle of the stage, dressed in a long gown of perfectly white shimmering cloth. She called herself Jeannie Isobel, the Saint of Song.

"The audience was simply bowled over. They couldn't believe what they were seeing. Jeannie Isobel was prettier than Haydée, she spoke better, and she was surrounded by lovely women—unlike Haydée, who would never allow anyone else to be on the stage with her. And when Jeannie opened her mouth to sing, well, we have Mr. Post's word for it." Jody held up a yellowed sheet of letter paper. "He wrote: 'I thought my heart would burst.' When she sang, everyone's heart felt like it would burst.

"But even that wasn't the best. Jeannie had noticed that the audience in the revival meeting always became most attentive when Haydée was baptizing. They always loved to see someone get dunked. Only at most meetings there was no one to dunk, because they'd all been done. Jeannie felt that there must be a better way. So she thought up what she called her Vision. Many years later, she reflected back on the Vision in a letter to Mr. Chance, which we found in one of the big scrapbooks in Biscay. She wrote:

> Sister Haydée was limited by considerations of theology. I, on the other hand, was thinking more of theater. If one baptism was good, I thought, why, more would be better. And most would be best. The most I could think of was to baptize everyone, absolutely everyone, every single night. And so we did. Thus was born the Gideon Principle of Continuing Baptism...

"They baptized everyone, every single night. You need to remember that this was before radio, before moving pictures. There just wasn't anything like the show she was putting on. One by one she lowered the Angels into the baptismal pool while the audience sang along at the tops of their lungs. Then she led the members of the audience forward too, and into the pool. She had no helpers for this part. Every single person was baptized by Jeannie herself. You didn't have to profess or anything in order to get dunked. You just let yourself get led forward by this smiling, lovely woman, and in you went.

"Finally, as a grand finale, while the orchestra played and the lights swirled about the Cathedral, Jeannie called forth selected members of the audience and leaned back into their arms. They carried her into the pool and then out again, soaking wet. She stood with her arms raised up to the rafters with all the lights on her and cried out at the top of her voice, 'Glory be!' Then the room went black, and when the lights came back on again, she was gone."

12

Dropped Silk

How could I leave my husband-oh?
I gave up all for the wonders of love,
And to run with the raggle-taggle gypsies-oh
All to run with the raggle-taggle gypsies.

Sissy and Angela were teaching themselves to sing in harmony. They practiced in Navarre just after breakfast each morning, with Compton accompanying on the piano. This morning, they were doing "Raggle-Taggle Gypsies."

Liam walked past them without even a nod. He saw the Colonel strolling along the seawall, and headed that way to join him for a morning walk. But as he approached, he could hear Colonel Forsythe whistling the same damned song. Liam turned on his heel and headed back toward the house. Jody was down near the tennis court hitting the tetherball, playing by herself. Normally Liam would have wandered over to give her a game, but even at this distance he could hear her panting between hits:

"Why have you left *(thump)* your bonnie baby boy

(thump) / All to run with the raggle *(thump)* taggle *(thump)* *gypsies...*"

He resolved to spend the morning in his own company.

⚜

"Bloomers," Scarlet said.

The Colonel sighed. "Yes, Scarlet dear, but in this context, I think it means—"

"Oh, shut up!" Scarlet rounded on him. "Just shut up."

"Sorry. Didn't mean to offend."

"Every time I look at you, your jaw is flapping." She illustrated with a hand. "Yap, yap, yap."

"Quite so. Quite so," the Colonel allowed agreeably.

"What the article actually says is 'late bloomers,'" Liam clarified. He was reading to Scarlet from the *Camden Herald*, something that usually seemed to please her. "Late bloomers in the sense of people who don't begin to realize their full potential until..."

Scarlet ignored him. "I never could see all the fuss. What is the fuss? Hardly an object of romance: a bit of silk with a waist and two holes for the legs. I could never see what all the fuss was about. What do you think, Marjorie?"

"Hmm? What do I think about what, Scarlet?"

"Bloomers."

"Well, I don't think much about them at all. Not anymore. Now, during the war it was different."

Gabriella looked up from her book. "It certainly was." She sighed. "Weren't those beastly years? In matters bloomerish, I mean."

"I don't think I understand," Liam said. He suspected that the conversation was about to turn sophisticated, and he didn't want to be left out. Not with Laura listening in right beside him.

"Rubber, you see, was in short supply during the war," Marjorie explained. "That's what Gabriella is referring to.

There was very little rubber available for domestic use. Only enough for essential items. And, for some reason, the powers that be decided that ladies' undergarments were not essential items."

Gabriella nodded. "You were supposed to make do," she said. "Mend and repair, repair and mend. Only how do you repair an elastic waistband when there is no elastic available? So, little by little the bloomers stretched out and out and out. In the end they provided very little sustaining power and no comforting assurance whatsoever."

Marjorie made a grim face. "The truth was they could and did come down, all of their own volition, at the most inopportune moments. "

"Usually at a party, when you were trying to be suave," Gabriella said. "The accepted thing to do was to step out and scoop them up into your purse, without even a pause in what you were saying. At the age of nineteen, I found that rather a challenge. I remember the war years as one long agony of suspense about my undies."

"Ah, the problem of dropped silk," said the Colonel with a smile. "I remember it well. It was considered quite the mark of a patriot."

"Of the female patriot," Gabriella agreed. "When it happened, there would always be some idiot, some *male* idiot, to comment about doing one's bit to aid the war effort. I myself could never quite understand how the war effort was aided by thousands of pairs of underpants on any given day, all across the country, fluttering down toward the floor on their own maddening schedules."

"It does take a particularly male logic to see that," Marjorie agreed.

"The waistbands were perfectly adequate during the war," Scarlet sniffed. "Why, when I was a girl—"

"That was the other war, dear," Marjorie observed.

121

"When I was girl," Scarlet raised her voice slightly, "it took a good tug to get them down. And there was always some soldier boy eager to— "

"Here we go again," said the Colonel with a sigh.

Scarlet glared at him. "Always a soldier boy with that on his mind. Obsessed they were with a girl's . . ." She turned toward the window, muttering in irritation. A long silence. Then more muttering.

Suddenly she turned on Liam, her little black eyes flashing in anger. "And they never gave them back," she snapped.

As the final course was being served in Xanadu, Colonel Forsythe rose to announce the evening's film.

"The movie for this week is *Song of the Desert*, with Kathryn Grayson and Gordon MacRae."

Loud groans from all the young moderns.

"*That* old chestnut," the Monsignor muttered at Liam's side.

"We protest," Sissy shouted out. "No more operettas. We just had Jeanette MacDonald."

"Yes, well. Objections noted. Objections noted." The Colonel looked down at the printed handbill. "Cast of thousands, though. Stirring songs and all that. Romance, adventure, wonderful costumes. Foreign locations. I shouldn't wonder you might enjoy it after all." He smiled a bit sheepishly. "I've always had a soft spot for Kathryn Grayson myself."

They all went. Nobody ever missed a film, no matter how unpromising. It was a weekly opportunity to see people from all the other fine houses and some of the townspeople as well, including Tim Hopkins and a few of his chums who always showed up.

Liam sat with Laura and the Ralston twins all the way

in the back. He had gone determined to hate the film, but he found himself charmed anyway. Still, there were appearances to keep up.

"It was so unsophisticated, really. Nearly maudlin," he said to Laura as they made their way back from East House. "What a chestnut."

"Yes. Still..."

"Positively mawkish. I mean, life is just not like that. People don't burst into song at a moment's notice." He chuckled scornfully.

"Still..."

"I really do think that operetta was an aberration of the last century. A positive aberration, something that the modern people of our century...Um, you didn't *enjoy* it, did you, Laura?"

"Well, no, of course not. Only there were moments, you know, when I actually found myself—"

"Mmm. Well, there were a few moments," he allowed.

Laura was thoughtful. "Don't you think sometimes, Liam, that there might be a kind of *higher* sophistication than what we've been considering? I don't know. There might be. A kind of higher sophistication that could even allow..." She stopped on the path, shaking her head.

"That could allow operetta?"

"Well, I wouldn't have thought so. I never would have. Still..."

There was a railed walkway all the way around Dark Harbor House at the level of the second-story gables. Laura often stepped out there in the late evening for a look at the stars just before bed. Liam let himself out onto the walk from the window of Lancelot. He was in his silk pajamas and new maroon dressing coat, looking rather smart, he thought. Laura, when she did come out at this hour, would be in her

123

nightgown and robe. The thought of an evening stroll together for a few moments in such dishabille was only the
tiniest bit shocking. After all, they were not children any
longer. He was considering what to say when he encountered her. Something about the clear night and the stars,
twinkling like . . ." Twinkling like what? He tried to think.

As it turned out, there were no stars. The sky was over-
cast. And there was no Laura. He could see the glow of her
window. It would be less than gentlemanly, he thought, to
go that way. So he headed in the opposite direction, where
all the windows were dark. If he continued all the way
around, he knew he would end up coming back along the
east wing, the Angel's wing, and approach Laura's window
from the other side. By that time she might have decided to
come out after all.

There was a mist coming in off the bay. It rolled up onto
the roof slates like slow, soft surf. He might almost have
been on the rooftops of London, prowling about in a black-
and-white film with Sherlock Holmes and Doctor Watson.
He picked his way along, one hand on the rail. Vaguely
through the mist he could see lights across the yard in Jeremiah: Mr. Collyer, still awake in the Post bedroom.

The layout of the east wing had never been clear to him,
least of all when viewed in pitch black and fog from the outside. The room he was passing now might be Lamorak, he
thought, or perhaps Ethelred. And, of course, he had no
idea who was in which. The only east-wing assignments he
was sure of were Laura in Guenevere (he could see her light
still on, three or four rooms ahead) and Jody in Childeric,
now behind him. Because the rail was broken here, he
moved inward from it, reaching out to steady himself. There
was a window open immediately next to his hand. And from
out of that window came a single word, spoken very softly,
almost with reverence. Liam froze. The word was lost, but

the voice was distinctly male, and the accent...it was Tim. He was there in the dark in someone's room, but whose? A moment later there was Angela's low, throaty laugh. And then, very softly, she said, "Sweetheart."

Liam retreated on tiptoe, all the way back around the roof walk and into his own window. Oh, my, oh my, he thought: Tim and Angela, Angela and Tim. They were just about to, or just after, or perhaps in the middle of...They were. They really were. Now, right now. Right this minute.

He wondered if Angela would look different in the morning. That was a thought. Would she give it all away by blushing helplessly through breakfast or by being so dewy eyed that no one could miss? And when they were together, Tim and Angela, how could they fail to show what had passed between them? It would be evident. They couldn't conceal it. Or maybe they could. Maybe it had been happening for weeks. It might be old hat. Possibly so. Or maybe tonight was the very first moment of...

Imagine, the two of them. Liam tried to think if he had ever known any other couple who were actually making love. To each other. He thought not. Oh, older couples, of course, married couples, but they didn't count. He wondered how he himself would respond when he saw Tim and Angela next. An awful thought that they might be perfectly natural together, and that Liam might give away their secret by blushing helplessly himself. Imagine, though, Tim and Angela, at this very moment.

He stepped into the corridor, far too agitated for sleep, and headed toward the back stairs. On the landing ahead was a dark shape in the window.

"Huh?" The shape turned around, startled.

Liam stopped in his tracks.

"Oh, Liam." The Monsignor came toward him, one arm out. "My boy. I was . . . waiting for you." He turned Liam around and headed him back toward the sitting room. "I had a hunch you might be hoping for another chance to sit down and chat, as our last little talk was so productive. A young man your age, well, it's no secret what a turmoil he can be in. And the reason for that turmoil? Tell me all about it, my boy. Unburden yourself. Troubled, are you? No, don't deny it." He held up a hand. "I well remember. Oh, yes. I was young once too. I can fully understand. What with all these lovely young things about. A source of delight to the elderly eye they are, but to the young male, his blood a-boiling . . ." He smiled understandingly at Liam. "Now, tell me, my boy. That is exactly what's been on your mind, isn't it? In a word, sex."

"No, really. Not at all. If I had anything at all on my mind, I suppose it would be . . ." He groped for something to offer.

"Sins of the flesh," the Monsignor finished for him. He nodded to himself. "Of course. As I suspected." He tapped his finger knowingly on the side of his nose. "I know these things. That's just what would be on your mind. Sins of the flesh."

"No, really . . ."

The Monsignor stopped him with a dismissing gesture. "Why don't I just shut this door to give us a bit of privacy? There we are. Now. Well, let's talk about it, shall we? What could we say about sins of the flesh? A great many things, actually. It is a subject that, in my profession, is all-important. It may be sin to you, but to me, it is bread and butter." He laughed contentedly at his own little joke. "Bread and butter. It is that essential.

"Now, the key, my boy, is not to think of the sin as something that persists only for the time the sinning takes. Oh, no. No, the life of the sin is just beginning. You will find that it comes back again and again to haunt you. It comes back like a . . . like a—"

"Bad clam?" Liam offered.

"Yes. Only worse, if I could say it, far worse. It comes back like an arrow in the side. Sins unmitigated return, each one to haunt you, to twist painfully into your flesh."

"How unpleasant."

"Oh, yes. Unpleasant. And quite unnecessary. You see, there is no need to endure the punishing agony. Sins can be mitigated. They can be forgiven. They can be made to go away, almost as though they had never happened, through the simple matter of Confession."

"Confession."

"Yes. You tell your sin to a fatherly figure who listens with compassion and understanding. And the sin is gone. Gone forever. No twisting arrows required, no pain. You see?"

"Mmm."

"Tell me, my boy. Get it off your chest. You have indulged, haven't you, in impure acts? Impure acts with the opposite sex?"

"No, I haven't. None. Absolutely none. Not a single one. Not even once!" Liam's voice was a wail.

A long, disappointed pause from the Monsignor. "Oh," he said at last.

"Not even once," Liam repeated sadly.

The Monsignor considered for a while. "Well. That is a confession of sorts, I guess."

"It is. I mean, I couldn't feel worse about it if I had . . ."

Monsignor Bill held out a calming hand. "No, nothing to feel bad about in that. Nothing at all." He did, though, seem to feel as badly about it as Liam did. But then he brightened. "The good news is, no sin, no penance. None required. I can absolve you without so much as an Our Father."

"Oh?"

The Monsignor thought for a moment before going on. "You'll have plenty of it, though, before your life is done."

"Sin?"

"No, penance." He nodded soberly. "You see, my boy, life is full of penance. Life *is* penance. That's just what this Vale of Tears is. Nothing more, nothing less. Penance is continuing and continual. The possibility of sin, on the other hand, is something that occurs only rarely. Opportunities are few and far between. You may find that, as in my case, when an occasion for sin does arise, there is already sufficient penance—"

"Like money in the bank?"

"Just so. Just so."

Liam looked over at him. "And so, if you do indulge—"

"Not that I'm suggesting that, mind you. Not that I'm suggesting it would be okay. Sin is always sin. But if you did just happen to. Well..."

"You might still end up with a positive account?"

"Exactly. Exactly."

13

Riffs

While most of the young moderns headed directly back to Dark Harbor House after the film, a small contingent remained behind to watch *Song of the Desert* all the way through again. The small contingent was Sissy and Compton. Compton worked the projector, while Sissy sat down in front with a clipboard and pencil, copying down the words of all the songs and some of the dialogue. As often as needed, Compton would reverse and play back over a short sequence to give Sissy a second or third chance at the words. By about three in the morning they were done.

"We're putting on a musical extravaganza," Sissy explained at breakfast the next day. "It's to be *Song of the Desert* as it's never been done before. A cast of dozens! Local locations! We'll take over East House and invite the whole island. It's going to be smashing."

"*Song of the Desert?*" Liam scoffed. "That old chestnut?"

Sissy nodded enthusiastically. "Oh, can't you just see it? Bruno has agreed to direct. It's going to be wonderful. Everyone's going to have a part. Why don't you try out for the Red Shadow, Liam? I don't doubt you'd make a splendid lead."

That cast a slightly different light on it. "The Red Shadow? Well. The Red Shadow. Do you really think so?"

"Who knows? We're going to ask Gabriella to be our Margot. Won't she be scrumptious?"

"Mmm." Liam was thinking of himself in turban and caftan, singing "Desert Song," toe-to-toe with Gabriella.

"And the Colonel has agreed to sing the part of Margot's father. Compton has pretensions that he might have a singing role too." She giggled. "If you can imagine Compton singing. Pfff."

"Thank you, dear cousin." Compton smiled sweetly at Sissy and stuck out his tongue.

"What is it with those two anyway?" Liam asked Jody after Compton and Sissy had gone off to recruit some of the others. "I've never seen two people with more natural antipathy for each other."

Jody looked at him oddly. "Compton and Sissy adore each other," she said.

"They do?"

"Of course they do."

"But they're always going on—"

"That's just 'going on.' Haven't you noticed that whenever you see one of them, the other is never more than about sixteen inches away?"

"Oh, I see your point." Liam looked up as Gabriella came into the breakfast room. "Well, here's our Margot."

"Margot?"

"Sissy and Compton are mounting a production of the *Song of the Desert.* Everyone's going to take part."

Gabriella laughed. "Oh, rapture. And there's a role for me?"

"We were hoping you'd be Margot. Will you do it?"

"Not on your life." She laughed again.

"Oh," Liam said, feeling miffed on Sissy's behalf. "Too famous for the stage at East House, I guess."

"You have never heard me sing, or you wouldn't ask."

It was true she had a deep, gravelly voice.

"I gather, though, that you're not too keen on amateur theatricals," said Liam.

"On the contrary. Amateur theatricals are the best kind. Because acting is so much more fun than watching. An East House production is my idea of heaven: Anyone in the audience for any given scene is likely to be up on the stage for the next. That's theater for you. It sounds like great fun. Only singing roles and I aren't made for each other."

"So you would be willing to play *Hamlet*, for example, if we put that on?"

"In a minute."

"Well, maybe we should change our plan." Liam saw himself as Hamlet opposite Gabriella's Ophelia. "I think you'd be a stunning Ophelia," he said.

"Not Ophelia. I thought you just promised me the role of Hamlet."

Liam was shocked. "But you couldn't—"

"I could too."

"Oh."

"I could knock them dead as Hamlet, and I will someday."

"Oh."

"Maybe you could be one of the Riff soldiers, Gabriella," Jody proposed. "I'm going to be a Riff. We'll wear robes and get to carry spears. What do you say?"

"I'd like that, Jody. We'll be Riffs together."

Laura was persuaded to try out for the part of Margot. It took all of them to overcome her resistance, but she finally did agree. "Just not to be a spoilsport," she said. "Just so the others of you may have your fun."

"You'll be fine, Laura," Compton assured her. He shoved a typed sheet into her hands with the words to "Desert Song." Bruno played a short introduction, sounding out the melody, then gave Laura a nod. The young moderns gathered around to listen. Laura sang the first few bars correctly enough but so softly that one could barely hear. Then, gaining confidence, she began to sing with more authority. Finally, she opened her throat, and to everyone's surprise, out came a Great Big Voice. It was high and sweet and strong and positively heartbreaking. Liam found his jaw dropping of its own volition. He had to remind himself to close it. Then he had to remind himself to breathe. She sang and sang, gathering more confidence still. Finally, spreading her arms to the audience—no need for the typed script now— she filled the room with her glorious voice.

> Blue heaven and you and I
> And sand kissing a moonlit sky
> The desert breeze whisp'ring a lullaby
> Only stars above you ...
> To see I love you—ooooooooo.

For the last few notes, Bruno stood up from the piano and stepped toward her, filling in the bass part. He took her in his arms. They ended up with their faces only inches apart, staring deeply into each other's eyes and still making perfect harmony. Oh, shit, Liam thought.

When the tryouts were over, it was clear to all that Bruno would be forced to take the role of the Red Shadow. Liam gave it a good try, but he just didn't have the range to sing "The Riff Song." He had to be content with the part of El Sid, the villainous heavy. Tim was to be the Red Shadow's lieutenant, Ali. Gabriella took over the direction, and

Compton the piano. Angela had a lovely voice but no part, so Bruno tinkered a bit with the script and worked in a song from *The Red Mill* to create new parts for Angela, Teddy, and Lizzie.

❧

Between rehearsals, Liam wandered through the common rooms, showing off his sweeping robes and the saber that Marjorie had found for him in the attic. He came upon Colonel Forsythe listening to a baseball game in Inverness.

"The Red Sox," the Colonel said. "Pull up a chair. The Sox and the hated New York Yankees. They're playing in New York."

There was a sharp crack from the radio. "A hit!" the announcer screamed. "It's down the left field line, no, make that the right field line, no, it's a walk. A walk, ball four, and Kinder is on. He's on. Ellis Kinder on first. Kinder on first. Pesky on second. And it's Dom DiMaggio, the little perfesser striding up to the plate. DiMaggio. He strides up. He's striding. He's at the plate, looking out toward center. We know where he'd like to put that ball right now. Oh, yes. Over the fence. Swinging for the fences, he'll be. Yes, sir. Dominic batting three twenty-nine, one for three today, one for three. The crowd is egging him on. The crowd's going mad..."

"Seems exciting," Liam said, sitting down on the opposite side of the radio.

"Oh, yes."

"What a situation, ladies and gentlemen. The crowd on its feet, DiMag' at the plate, the little perfesser. Brother Joe out there in center field, backing way up against the wall. Ol' number twenty-one. And here's the pitch. Here it comes. Coming soon now. Here comes the pitch. And...it's ball one! No, it's a foul ball." Another sharp crack. "Foul ball. Foul. Oh and one. And the crowd rises to its feet."

"Um, what's the score?"

"Thirteen to one, Yankees."

"Oh."

"The tension, ladies and gentlemen, the tension! The crowd is going crazy. And now the pitch. And there it is, the pitch. And the pitch is . . . It's a strike! No, a conference on the mound. No, it's a strike. Strike two. Strike two on little Dominic. A swinging strike. Yes, he did swing. Ready again. Ford on the mound. He stretches, he winds up, he checks his runners, he stretches, he checks, he winds up. Now the pitch! Coming, coming . . ."

"The announcer seems pretty excited."

"He does."

"I guess you have to be there to pick up the excitement, from the crowd and all. I mean, it doesn't seem that thrilling to me. But he's right there, so—"

"Actually, not. The broadcast comes down from Bangor. The announcer is in a studio in Bangor."

"From Bangor? Then how does he know—"

"Telegraph. He has a telegraph right there in front of him. The play-by-play comes over in Morse code."

"Oh."

"You can hear the dots and dashes in the background. Hear them? The little di-da-di-da-da?"

"Oh, yes. And the crack of the bat?"

"Hitting two pieces of wood together, I should imagine. What comes over the line is just the result of each pitch. The announcer has to supply some of the little details on his own."

"Oh." Liam considered. "Well, he does get involved, though, I guess. Connected, as he is, directly to the action."

"Not so directly, as it turns out. The plays comes from the stadium by phone into a studio in New York, where they're keyed in by an operator, then up to Syracuse, and over via Springfield and Worcester, and finally to Bangor.

That's the usual route. So, there's a delay at each relay station while the message is rekeyed. This game, I would guess, is probably over by now."

Another crack of the bat: "A hit! It's a double. No, it's a double play!"

Liam listened politely for a few more minutes. Then he let himself out onto the screened porch.

Marjorie and Lizzie and Evan were sitting there with Monsignor Leary. Liam joined them just as Tyndall was arriving with a squat gray metal bottle on a silver tray.

"Oh, Tyndall," Marjorie said. "Just in time. We are simply being eaten alive." She waved a hand in front of her face. Now that Liam noticed, there were, indeed, a number of mosquitoes in the enclosed area.

"Give us a good, long whoosh," Marjorie ordered.

"Yes, m'am." Tyndall took up the spray bomb and held it at arm's length, pressing the little metal cap on its top.

Marjorie closed her eyes as he sprayed. "Be sure to do our faces, now," she instructed.

Tyndall gave a generous spray directly into each face. When it was his turn to be done, the Monsignor leaned forward and breathed deeply of the mist. "Ah, DDT," he said. "A modern miracle. Amazing how it kills the little buggers but doesn't harm us. Ain't science grand?"

"It is that," Evan agreed. "Though you do wonder about these bug sprays. If the spray gets on the insects and the birds eat the insects, then aren't the birds going to get sick? I suspect so."

"Sick? Absolutely not," the Monsignor snorted. "Preposterous. No chance of that at all. DDT passes directly through the systems of birds and animals *without* deleterious side effects. None whatsoever. Why, it's positively good for them. Gives them a renewed lease on life."

"That's what I meant," Evan clarified.

"So many of these modern concoctions are given a bad name by alarmists—people who just don't know their science. Now, you take uranium, for example. From what you read, you might think that the stuff was actually bad for you."

"Not so?"

"Not so at all. It is, in fact, an essential vitamin. Without uranium in our diet—just a trace mind you, just a trace—without our uranium, we would waste away in a matter of weeks."

"You don't say."

"I do. And it's just as well, by the way, since we're going to be breathing in quite a lot of uranium in the years ahead." He chuckled knowingly.

"The bomb?" Lizzie shuddered.

"Oh, yes. But now don't let that get you all rattled. A few bombs here and there, well, no great cause for alarm. Time will come when they won't even make the news. Think of them as part of the cleansing process. Cleansing. We should do some cleansing in the Soviet Union, I would say. And if the bombs popping off every here and there do throw a little uranium into the air, along with plutonium and zirconium and all those . . . well, so much the better. We can use them all. In moderation, of course."

Lizzie was not too convinced. "I still don't think I want to breathe in all that fallout."

"Oh, I do." Monsignor Leary smiled. "It will save me a fortune in uranium oxide pills."

Liam stared at him. "You don't mean to tell us that you're taking uranium oxide?"

"Oh, yes. Every morning. Take it with my O.J. That's what keeps me so fit. I have noticed a marked difference since I began taking these pills." The Monsignor was leaning over one side of his chair to get into a vest pocket. "Company up in Albany bottles them especially for me. Here we have them. Uranium oxide. Expensive little devils." He held out his hand to show two small capsules, glowing slightly in the subdued light. "Thirty-four cents each. But worth it, mind you. Worth every penny."

On the grand night, the little hall of East House was packed. Liam looked out from the wings, wondering who all the people in the audience might be. Everyone he knew from the island was either on the stage or backstage waiting to go on.

It was Laura's big scene. For the "French Military Marching Song," she was done up in a khaki skirt and one of the Colonel's uniform jackets, complete with an array of medals and ribbons on the chest. She had a huge French tricolor on a staff, another of the treasures unearthed from the attics of Dark Harbor House. With an officer's cap set at an angle on her perfect golden hair, she marched adorably across the little stage, high-stepping and trilling.

> Did you call for soldiers true?
> For gallant fighting men of France?
> We are here to answer yououuuuuu,
>   [high note, held]
> So let the bugle blow Advance.

Compton pounded on the piano, Jody played the trumpet, and Scarlet lent an enthusiastic hand on the cymbals. At the reprise, Bruno and the Riff chorus joined in:

> We are here to answer yououuuuuu,
> So let the bugle blow Advance.

Bruno and Laura ended up in a clinch. Virtually every one of their scenes ended in a clinch. Their eyes were locked as their last perfect notes died away. The curtain came down to thunderous applause. Liam could cheerfully have throttled them both.

Evan and the Colonel were standing together backstage during the change of scene. Evan nodded toward Laura in her military garb. "Your uniform, I understand, Colonel."

"Oh, yes," the Colonel affirmed. "Somehow looks better on Laura, though, than it ever did on me. I was always a bit of a shambles in it."

"And all those medals. Very impressive."

"Well, the medals. Those actually came from the five-and-dime in Camden."

"Still, though, I imagine you did see a bit of action during the war, sir. Didn't you?" Evan's brows were wrinkled in respectful awe.

"Action?"

"Well, combat."

"Not your actual combat, no. Not unless you count games of bridge. I seem to remember a great many games of bridge."

"You did have a position of importance, though, I don't doubt."

"Important? Well, I suppose you could say that. Sort of."

"Something essential."

The Colonel smiled slightly. "I was Limoged for the war, to tell you the truth."

"Sir?"

"Limoged. It comes from the French army term 'Limogé.' The town of Limoges, you see, is in precisely the center of France. It is the place that is farthest from all the borders. So when a totally incompetent officer needs to be put where he can't get the country into any trouble at all, they send him off to Limoges. It's usually accompanied by a promotion. I was made a full colonel at the time of my Limogeing."

"You spent the war away from the front?"

"In Missouri, actually. I was charged with the defense of St. Louis."

"Oh."

"Which, I might add, was a total success."

"Uh-huh." Evan chewed that over for a moment. "But it could have been an important assignment, though, couldn't it? I mean, if it ever came to that?"

"I should say so. Critical."

"It wouldn't do at all to have the wrong person in charge."

"Goodness, no. It was a relief to the powers that be, I'm sure, to know that I was there. We all had to do our part, and my part was to devise a plan for pushing the Hun into the Mississippi, if they ever came. They never did, but we were ready. And while we waited for them, we played a great many games of bridge."

14

The Seventh Proof

Jody was bent over the library table in Biscay where she had all her project material spread out. She looked up as Liam entered.

"Ah, the dedicated cerealogy researcher," he said. "Hard at it, already, first thing in the morning."

"Hi, Liam."

"Ferreting out the sins of the past, are you?"

"A few sins and an enormous amount of verbiage. What are you up to this morning? Something fun?"

"Well, yes. Now that you ask. A birding expedition with Laura. She has asked me especially. It's to be just the two of us." Liam found himself grinning stupidly. He forced his face back into an expression of perfect neutrality. "I mean, just Laura and me, as it happens."

"Won't that be nice."

"Only, Laura, of course, is not known as an early riser."

"No."

"So I thought I might nip in here to look for something to read. It could be hours before she gets up." Liam still had a half-finished volume beside his bed, but the truth was he had exhausted his capacity for H. Ryder Haggard. He ran a finger along the titles of a shelf full of poetry books. "Let's see: Keats, Tennyson, Tagore . . . What will it be?" He turned back to Jody. "You know just about everything that's here, Jody. What could you recommend? I hanker after freshness. A little volume of inspiration for the jaded young aesthete, if you know what I mean." What he meant was something deep—in case he should be seen reading it—but not deadly.

"Does it have to be poetry?"

"Well, no."

"Got just the thing for you, then. Talk about fresh, I guarantee you won't have come across this before."

She handed him a slim booklet with a blue paper cover, tattered on the edges.

"*Hydrolism for Women*," he read, "by Norbert Milous Chance, P.D.H." On the bottom of the title page he learned that P.D.H. stood for Prominent Doctor of Hydrolism.

"Hey, our Norbert was a doctor."

"Of hydrolism, yes."

"Think I'll keep it for a rainy day, though. What else have you got?"

"Well, letters. Mr. Chance saved all his letters. There are some from Jeannie, from Mr. Root, from Charles William Post"—she was flipping through packets of envelopes tied in ribbons—"and from Dr. Ralston. Here's one from Dr. Ralston. He had the best handwriting. Look at these flourishes. This is a good one to start with. It's about the wager." She handed him an elaborately scripted letter.

Liam settled into a window seat with the letter. At the top of the first page was a handsome embossed device: a four-by-four checkerboard of red and white squares. There was a different word printed along each edge of the logo in red lettering: PHYSICAL up the left side, MENTAL across the top, SOCIAL down the right, and RELIGIOUS at the bottom. Underneath this logo, written in Ralston's elegant hand, was the following letter.

December 11, 1901
My Dear Norbert,

I accept. Let no one say that Orin Guy Ralston refused to put his Theories to the test. Please convey this fact on my behalf to my one-time friend, Will Kellogg, with whom I shall have no direct correspondence. As regards the participation of the charlatan, Post, I shall not object even to that. You may inform him on my behalf. Let the best man win.

The terms: One thousand dollars to be paid by each of the losers to a charity of the winner's choice. We all agree to trust you to be our judge. I am much impressed, Norbert, by your plan for determining the result. I have no doubt that your Highly Advanced measuring machines will in fact be able to detect even the slightest change in our man's strength and fitness. And, as you might surmise, the changes are not going to be slight. I predict that at the end of my allotted year, said Ephram Whittier will be a bull of a man, powerful, clean and full of spirit. Your only problem will be getting him to abandon the Regime I have put him on in order to take up that of one of my adversaries in this contest. I also agree to pay to Mr. Whittier the sum of Two Hundred Dollars for his cooperation during the twelvemonth allocated by lot to me.

By the end of this month, I shall have in your hands a complete written description of the Regime. I shouldn't think you will be surprised by my choice of victuals. They will include: good whole Grain and Fiber, lots of farm fresh milk, cheese, butter and Eggs (nature's most perfect food is the Egg—there is simply nothing imperfect in it), black strap Molasses in quantity, an Apple every day that such can be supplied, a special daily Purgative of my own invention, and, of course, all the pure China Lake water the man can be persuaded to imbibe. There shall be no refined white flour products of any sort, or white sugar, no coffee or spirit beverages or tobacco, no tom-fool yoghurt at all, nor meat nor fish (none whatsoever), and most important, no poisonous encrustocates from the beginning of the year to the end.

I shall also supply detailed instructions for Mr. Whittier's spiritual advancement. (I under-stand the poor fellow is unschooled in all matters of Religion.) Too bad that the benefit of his Awakening in this regard may necessarily spill over into the period allotted to my chal-lengers. Still, if a man's soul be won for God, what cause have I to complain?

In this past year, I have come more than ever to appreciate the unsalubrious effects of draughts. A person may pay every heed to good nutrition and spiritual learning and still yet fall victim to cancer or consumptive lung or liver ailment, due to evil humours of air blowing about his person. And so I propose to protect

our Mr. Whittier for my year from these per-
nicious draughts. The most expeditious way to
accomplish this is, I believe, to keep him
indoors for the whole year. That may sound
extreme, but I find it not to be. I myself have
remained indoors now since Sept. 1 and feel far
the better for it. He may put up in North Star
House for the duration. I trust none may cry
foul if I make private arrangements with our
subject to attend to minor carpentry in the
finishing of that structure's interior. He will
need something to do anyway, his prior
occupation being rendered impossible and,
as he will soon understand, unacceptable in
any event.

I hope you have warned poor Whittier
what he may expect from Kellogg and Post:
diets of Malta Vita and Grapenuts, burnt
caramel leavings, milk cultures and clots,
and frequent enemas. I wouldn't trade places
with that unhappy man for the world.

Trusting in the faith of your good health
and disposition, I remain,

Very Truly Yours,
Orin

Liam looked up from the letter. "Jody, what on earth are
'poisonous encrustocates'?"

"Lobsters. Ephram was Dark Harbor's lobsterman. He
had a line of traps that he worked inside Gilkey Narrows."

"Dr. Ralston, I gather, was not too keen on lobster?"

"Nor the others. None of them were. They thought it was
deadly poison. And Ephram ate tons of lobster. That's why
they picked him for their subject. They thought the effects

145

of their various diets would be particularly pronounced on a man who was used to eating so much poison before they arrived to save him."

"Now you've whetted my curiosity. Skip ahead to the climax, please. Whose diet turned out to be the winner?"

"Oh, the contest never did come off, although the three contestants all agreed to it. They had a St. Louis attorney draw up a contract, and they each paid their money into escrow. But nobody thought ahead to ask Ephram."

"Because they were proposing to pay him so much money, I guess. They figured he couldn't possibly refuse?"

"That's just what they figured. It never crossed their minds that he might say no when they finally put the proposition to him."

"And did he?"

"He laughed at them."

Laura pointed suddenly. "Oh, what's that one, Liam? The darling little fellow with the spotted white breast?"

"Wood thrush," Liam said authoritatively. "Definitely a wood thrush." He had seen one just the morning before on a walk with Lizzie, and Lizzie had identified it. Lizzie knew her birds. "Cousin to the robin. Ground feeder. Common from Quebec all the way down to northern Florida." All this from Lizzie too.

"He's adorable. And there's another gull overhead."

"Herring gull."

"I didn't know there were kinds of gulls."

"Oh, yes. Pilot gulls and gray gulls in addition to the more common herring gull." Amazing how much he could recall from a single outing with Lizzie. He congratulated himself on having spent a whole hour with her, though at the time he had been thinking of little else except how to

146

make his escape. "Then there are the sandpipers and terns, often mistaken for gulls, but you *can* tell the difference if you have a sharp eye."

"And you certainly have."

"And, of course, there are loons hereabouts as well. I have great hopes we may spot one today." Lizzie had shown him one yesterday, not too far from where they were heading now.

Laura turned her face abruptly upward and pointed at a dark shape sliding past, visible only for a moment through the trees. "Oh, what was that, Liam? A huge one." She turned to him excitedly.

Liam had not the foggiest idea. Then he heard a high-pitched sound, trailing behind the bird. "Chickadee," he said promptly.

"So big?"

"A big one."

"I would have thought—"

"Didn't you hear it go 'chicka-dee-dee-dee'?"

"It sounded more like 'yi-yi-yi,' and it really was quite big for a chickadee. I thought it might have been a hawk. Chickadees are teensy, aren't they?"

"I believe you're thinking of the Lesser Chickadee. And this was a Greater. At least I think it was. Bit difficult to say on such a brief look."

"Well, I shall note it down as a 'possible Greater Chickadee' sighting." She sat down on a wide granite boulder to write into the Colonel's little logbook. "Oh, this is fun."

"It is."

"I'm so pleased we're having this little moment together, Liam. Really I am."

"You are?"

"I am. Aren't you?"

147

"Oh, yes! I mean, yes. Enormously pleased. I am. Well, that just goes without saying, Laura. Though I'm happy to say it. I mean, if you like to hear that."

"I do."

"Gee, Laura..."

"Yes, Liam?" She looked up at him expectantly.

His mind went suddenly blank.

"Yes, Liam?"

"Enormously pleased..."

She patted the rock surface at her side.

"Oh." He sat obediently.

"There is something rather sweet between us, isn't there, Liam? A kind of wholesome affection."

"Well, I like to think—"

"A wholesome affection. Of course, you do sometimes make me cross, what with your ways."

"Ways?"

"But that's just boys, I suppose. Boys have got the most exasperating ways. On the whole, though, I think you're quite the nicest young man I have set my eyes on—since breakfast." She giggled.

"You're hard, Laura."

"I am. I'm terrible. Just terrible." Very deliberately she closed her eyes, offering her slightly pouting lips.

Liam hesitated for a second. Could she possibly mean for him to...? Maybe she was just resting. Laura opened one eye a thin crack and looked at him through its lashes. Then she closed it again. Liam took her in his arms and kissed her, trying for firmness.

When the kiss was done, she opened her eyes and smiled slightly. "Yes," she said. "Well, I think we might carry on a bit, don't you think? Look for that loon." She stood up, smoothing her skirts.

"Oh. Sure." He got to his feet.

148

"The guidebook, Liam."

"Oh, right. Got it."

"I think we should head down toward the pool, don't you? There's an enchanting walk from the pool through the woods. I think there is something lovely about boys and girls and woods, don't you?"

"Well, yes. I think...yes, let's do that. Woods."

"Right along through here, then." She bent down under some overhanging pine boughs and strode out onto the main lawn.

Liam followed somewhat dazedly. "Coming. Wait up."

It was deliciously secluded on the path, sometimes almost dark, sometimes brilliant in dancing pools of sunlight. The only problem was that the trail was so narrow they couldn't walk abreast, and Laura was striding ahead purposefully. At last she paused at a junction in the path, waiting for Liam to catch up. There was a soft, thumping sound, as though someone were pounding on the forest floor. Laura turned to him and took his hand. She smiled, encouraging him. The pounding sound was getting closer. Liam took one step nearer Laura, then stopped, catching sight of something moving toward them rapidly from ahead on the path.

Laura turned to look, still holding Liam's hand in her own. "Why, it's Bruno. Fancy seeing you here, Bruno," she said. "I didn't know you ran this way in the mornings. Bruno is a track man, you know, Liam. An ex–track man, that is."

Bruno was in gray sweat clothes, complete with hood. The shirt was wet under the arms and down the middle. He stopped in front of them, panting, deliberately ignoring their clasped hands. "Well, you two," he said.

"We've been out birding," Liam offered. He would like to have released his hand from Laura's, but she didn't seem inclined to give it back.

"Liam is a *super* birder," Laura gushed. "Bruno, you wouldn't believe. He just identified a Greater Chickadee."

"A Greater Chickadee. You don't say. I *am* impressed."

"Well, it might have been." Liam frowned. "We only caught a glimpse. It might have been something else," he finished weakly.

"Oh, a Greater Chickadee *or* something else. I see." Smug son of a bitch.

"And Bruno, we saw a bald eagle," Laura added.

"You did? Now that is impressive."

"You might just see it too, if you hurry. Down by the sea-wall. Oh, do go ahead, Bruno. We'd like so much for you to see it." She pointed down along the path they had just come up. "Go right along, Bruno, or you'll miss it. Go ahead."

Bruno made a face. But he did start down in the direction she had indicated. They watched his back until he was gone.

"You know, Laura," Liam said, "I didn't see a bald eagle."

"Neither did I." Laura giggled.

"Oh. Oh. Well, shall we . . . ?" Liam started to draw her along the path in the direction from which Bruno had appeared. It looked even more inviting ahead.

But Laura dropped his hand. "You know, I think I've had enough walking for today, Liam, thank you very much. What say we head back to Dark Harbor House and see who else is around?" With that she struck off on the side path back toward the lawn.

Because the dinner bell was delayed somewhat, Monsignor Leary had himself a captive audience in Inverness. On the thin pretext provided by a question from Lizzie, he had launched into one of his prepared "little talks," a sermon entitled "Six Proofs of God's Existence." In an earlier incarnation it had been his pamphlet "Questions Young People

Most Often Ask: A Humble Priest Gives the Answers," published by the archdiocese of New York. And before that it had been an A-minus term paper for his course in apologetics at Fordham.

"Now, the sixth proof comes at the question from an entirely different angle."

"Oh, good," Liam muttered.

The Monsignor kept his voice up so that all could hear—and to suppress any side conversations. "This one is called the Ontological Proof. Ontology, you will remember, is the branch of philosophy pertaining to existence per se, or as such. The natural nature of nature. Clear? Well, the ontological argument, which is also called Anselm's Proof, after Archbishop Anselm of Canterbury—"

Liam looked up. "That's not the Anselm, is it, who figures in the story of Abelard and Héloïse?"

"Oh, Abelard and Héloïse. I do adore love stories," Laura said. She smiled contentedly and gave the Monsignor her complete attention.

"Not exactly a love story, my dear." The Monsignor raised a bony finger. "Abelard and Héloïse is more precisely a *lust* story. But yes, Liam, that is the same Anselm. He was one of our philosopher saints."

Laura was perplexed. "I don't remember an Anselm from the story. Where did he come in?"

"He provided the ending. The grisly ending," Liam told her.

"Was there a grisly ending?" She seemed disappointed. "I always supposed they went on to live happily ever after."

Liam shook his head. "Anselm's response to the love of Abelard and Héloïse was to have Peter Abelard castrated."

Laura winced.

"I do think we might avoid that word," the Monsignor reproved. "Ladies present, I mean."

151

"Is there some other way to say it?"

"Let us say that Anselm took steps to relieve Father Abelard of his . . . temptations."

"The steps being to hire some thugs to remove said temptations with carving knives after jumping him in a dark alley?"

"Well, more or less. More or less. These were difficult times, you must remember. Perhaps a bit more finesse might have been preferred. Still and all, Abelard was a priest, and he was sinning grievously. The saintly Anselm had to move decisively—to stop that sort of thing in the bud."

"The *saintly* Anselm?" Liam sputtered.

Monsignor Leary raised his voice slightly. "But saving poor Abelard's soul is not what Anselm is most noted for. No, he is most noted for the Ontological Proof, as I was saying. Now the Ontological Proof, as Anselm first stated it, is derived from first cause, from the definition of perfection. God is, as we know, all-perfect. But does He exist? Well, Anselm said, wouldn't it be an imperfection for Him not to exist? Since He is all-perfect, He cannot possibly not exist. Q.E.D., God does exist."

The Monsignor picked up the Colonel's pipe from the table and held it in one hand. The other hand he held out, empty. "To illustrate, consider these two pipes I hold in my two hands. They are both perfect pipes, I tell you, but which one is the most perfect?"

"More perfect," Liam said.

The Monsignor nodded approvingly. "Exactly right, Liam. This one." He held up the pipe-bearing hand. "This other one," he held up the empty hand, "although perfect in all other ways, suffers from the evident imperfection of non-existence. It therefore cannot be the all-perfect pipe. So, as we see, God too must exist. He simply has no choice in the matter. Existence is proved ipso facto in a simple turn of logic that has left all mankind awed by its elegance for lo these thousand years since Anselm first shared with us the fruit of his marvelous mind." The Monsignor smiled around the room. "Any questions?"

A heavy silence.

"Anything at all?"

At last Scarlet spoke up from the far corner: "That's it, then? Those are the six proofs?"

"All six."

"I have a seventh."

"Well." The Monsignor laughed condescendingly. "How fascinating. Do let us hear it. We are all ears."

"My proof is that there can't be so many things wrong with this world without it being somebody's fault."

"Mmm." The Monsignor frowned. "Not a proof for everyone, mind you. Still, if it helps you sustain your faith..."

It was the considered opinion of the French statesman Talleyrand—he explained this to Scarlet in a dream one night—that France had a natural right to govern the islands along the east coast of Africa: Madagascar, Zanzibar, and the Comoros. It was the French, after all, he told her earnestly, who had first brought civilization to the region.

Because Talleyrand was a known bender of the truth, Scarlet checked his facts the following morning in Jody's encyclopedia. Sure enough, Talleyrand had it all wrong; it had been the Portuguese who discovered the islands. The French hadn't arrived for another century. Scarlet chided Talleyrand when he visited again on another night, in another dream. "It was the Portuguese who civilized those islands," she told him, "not the French."

"Portuguese?" the sallow little man scoffed. "Portuguese? You call them civilized?"

Talleyrand was not the only historical figure to visit Scarlet's dreams. She often had General Gordon of Khartoum in her bedroom, elaborating upon his grand plan, or Mirabeau or Pizarro, or Hadrian and one time even Ike. She kept a notebook by her bed to keep track of their appearances and to copy down their more preposterous assertions.

The most frequent dream visitors of all were two women who had figured prominently in the history of Dark Harbor House. They were seated now in the two chairs at the foot of Scarlet's bed, glaring at each other. Both were dressed in white. Scarlet was dressed in nothing at all. The night being uncharacteristically hot, she was lying quite nude, not even covered with a sheet. Just as well, she giggled to herself, that it wasn't proper old Mirabeau who had come this night.

Though the room was in total darkness, the two young women seemed to be bathed in light coming down from above. Haydée was the taller of the two. Her lanky frame was awkwardly angular, but her face, even under its cloud of anger, was astonishingly beautiful. And those eyes: they were luminescent, almost gold in color.

"'Thy right hand, O Lord,'" she quoted, "'glorious in power...'"

Jeannie sighed. "Here we go again. Honestly dear, couldn't we strive for a little lighter tone for such a lovely summer night?"

"'Thy right hand, O Lord, *shatters* the enemy.'" She turned her glare again on Jeannie. "I am His right hand."

"She isn't always like this," Jeannie explained to Scarlet, "only most of the time."

"I am His right hand," Haydée said again.

"Golly, who then is the enemy?" Jeannie asked in feigned innocence.

"You!" Haydée leveled an accusing finger at her.

Jeannie smiled charmingly and put a hand to her

breast. "Me?" She batted her eyes. "Dear little me?" She looked down modestly as though just chosen Queen of the May. Jeannie's body was almost the opposite of Haydée's; it was everywhere round and curved, a study in the voluptuous. And her eyes, though not as striking in color, were enormous, with long, lovely lashes. Her mouth was full. Her soft lips had a slight pouting shape, as though waiting to receive a kiss.

Haydée raised her arms to the heavens. Looking straight up, she began, " 'Hear my voice, O God, in my complaint—' "

"Do you always quote?" Jeannie interrupted. "I mean, I know you do. But why is that, dear? Don't you have anything of your own to say? No original material?"

"You mock me. You do so at the peril of your immortal soul." Haydée turned to Scarlet. "I have given my entire life to The Book," she told her, matter-of-factly. "I know it through and through. Every page. You could not speak a single passage that I could not identify as to chapter and verse."

"Oh," Scarlet said. Haydée waited expectantly. Scarlet searched her mind. "Um, how about, 'The Lord is my shepherd, I shall n—' "

"Psalms, twenty-three, verse one," Haydée pounced, triumphantly.

" 'Many are called but few are—' "

"Matthew, twenty-two, verse fourteen."

" 'Swords into ploughshares.' "

"Isaiah two, verse four."

"Uh . . . let's see." Scarlet came up blank. She never had been good at remembering the Bible.

" 'Call me Ishmael,' " Jeannie suggested.

" 'Call me . . .' ?" A long, incredulous pause.

"Oh, you'll never get it, darling. It's Dick one, verse one."

"She mocks me," Haydée appealed to Scarlet. "And in so

doing, she mocks The Book In Which Every Word Is True."
She spat out the words in anger.

Jeannie smiled again. "You know, The Book In Which
Every Word Is True tells us that 'I am the rose of Sharon, I
am the lily of the valley.' But I can't help wondering . . . Am
I really?"

"Not *you*, you impudent child! That's not what it means."

"Only what it says."

"In the words of Jeremiah, " 'Wash your heart from
wickedness that you may be—' "

"Oh, Jeremiah," Jeannie said, rising from her chair. "I'll
give you Jeremiah." She opened the two doors of Scarlet's
wardrobe. Inside were not the neatly hung dresses that had
been there earlier, but a giant living head, three times the
size of a man's head. It was the head of Jeremiah. It was
Jeremiah, only it looked exactly like Monsignor Leary.

"Doom," the head spoke in a deep, rumbling voice. "Mis-
ery. Bitterness. Rebuke. Pain. Rue. Degradation. Anguish.
Suffering. Woe. Evil. Tribulation."

Haydée stood up and crossed to the wardrobe. "Thank
you," she said.

"What?" Jeremiah was not used to being interrupted.

"Thank you," Haydée said again, very politely. She shut
the doors of the wardrobe and turned back to Scarlet and
Jeannie with a shy smile. "Like all those things that are terribly good for us, I find that a tiny bit of Jeremiah goes such
an awfully long way. Don't you think?"

The light had followed her. She paused to compose herself. Now she started to sway from side to side. Her arms
were down, palms flattened out and parallel to the floor. She
flexed her knees almost imperceptibly to mark a rhythm. By
her side, Jeannie began to chant very softly, "They got, they
got, they got, they got . . ."

Haydée raised her voice in song:

> All God's children got a place in the choir,
> Some sing low and some sing higher.
> Some sing out loud on the telephone wire,
> While others just clap their hands...
>> or paws...
>> or anything they got."

Jeannie sang along, "They got, they got, they got..."

There was a fiddle in the background and something else too, maybe a squeezebox or harmonica. Haydée began the verse:

> Sometimes I sing at even-tide...

And Jeannie picked up,

> Sometimes alone, just me...

Then together in harmony:

> Sometimes we sing out side by side,
> The song of Tra-la-leeee.

Haydée: "Tra-la-leeee...," holding the note.
Jeannie: "Tra-la-leeee...," on a higher note.

The two voices now began to move along the scales in careful progressions—no words, just tones blending prettily. They had done this before, evidently many times. Haydée reached out to take Jeannie's hand in her own. They eyed each other as they sang, smiling slightly. Jeannie's voice seemed to have no upper limit; it went higher and higher, with Haydée's voice right under it, supporting and mixing. Then down together, in complicatedly varying polyphonies to end in a perfect pair of notes, held and held and held.

It was exquisite. Scarlet could not contain herself from clapping. "Bravo!" she called out. "Bravo!" There was other clapping too, for the audience had grown. Liam was there, lying in his bed. His clapping was as loud and enthusiastic as her own. He too called "Bravo!" The wall that separated Gareth from Lancelot was gone, vanished without a trace. Liam was right there, practically at Scarlet's side. She looked around for something to cover herself. But there wasn't a thing. Oh, well.

Now Jeannie and Haydée had locked arms and were dancing, a short chorus line of two, and singing,

> Lilacs and hyacinth,
> Blue forget-me-nots,
> In an English country garden...

They sang and danced back and forth at the foot of Scarlet's bed. The finale was another long-held pair of notes, this time in clear competition. They sang, grinning, challenging each other, goading. Finally they broke off together in a sputter of giggles.

"Oh, Dottie," Jeannie said when she had regained her breath. "We could have been friends. We could almost have been sisters."

Haydée turned on her furiously. "Could have been? Could have been? Were more pitiful words ever spoken? Could have been but for what?" She was choking in anger.

Jeannie sat down, looking resigned.

"But for sin!" Haydée screamed at her. "Sin!"

"Yes, dear, we've heard all this before."

"Sins of the flesh, harlotry, pride, blasphemy, murder... yes, murder."

"Mmm. So you keep saying."

"And theft."

Jeannie raised her brows. "Theft?"

Haydée made the accusation to Scarlet and Liam in their beds, as though to a jury. Her finger was still pointing down at Jeannie. "She stole from me what was rightfully my own. Stole him and then cast him aside."

"Oh, him," Jeannie said, looking bored.

"He gave me his essence, which I received and took into my body, and I gave to him that Ultimate Sacrifice that a woman may—"

"Tell me, Dottie. Did you suck him off? I've always wondered that. He loved it so. But somehow I just couldn't ever see you . . ."

Haydée's face was turning pink, then red, and finally almost purple. She opened her mouth to scream, but no sound came out. These dreams always ended the same way: Haydée mute in rage, her deeply flushing face swelling, growing larger and larger till it filled the room. Then all the dream figures were gone, and Scarlet was alone. After such nights, she would awake tired and depressed.

Through the wall in Lancelot, only a dozen feet away, Liam turned over in his bed with a groan. No more of those heavy desserts, he swore. No more second helpings of anything. On the porch below, a breeze passed through Marjorie's wind chime, producing a series of low, musical tones. Liam smiled slightly to himself, feeling better for the sound. But then an echo of distant thunder rumbled across the Narrows. Usually thunder brought with it a sense of release. This thunder, however, was different, full of frustration and repressed rage.

15

Intra-Structure

The original blueprints for Dark Harbor House indicated a ballroom forming its own small wing to the west. In that era, the room was called Saxony. It had been refitted in the 1890s as a chapel—complete with leaded glass windows, an altar, and a pulpit—and rechristened Bethel. The Colonel had pretensions of making it once again into a ballroom, but the work needed had proved to be too expensive. All he had really accomplished was to remount the original nameplate and get rid of the altar and pews.

Saxony had a soaring ceiling with no bedrooms above. Because it didn't share its roof with any more useful room, the roof had been allowed to deteriorate until finally there were cascades of water coming in on any rainy day. Oddly enough, the room was used only on rainy days. It was here that Colonel Forsythe had installed his elaborate collection of model trains.

"Clark's model trains," the Colonel was explaining to Evan. "Though, now that I think about it, Clark hasn't shown much interest for the past fifteen years. But I do remember, when he was just a little tyke, how much pleasure it gave him to be here. Marjorie would put him over there in his crib under an umbrella, and he would snooze happily while I made various improvements. I don't think he was ever happier really, at least not while asleep. After he got to be a toddler, he toddled off and hasn't been seen in here since."

"But what a collection," Evan enthused. "I mean, look at this. It's a virtual microcosm . . . the towns and this tunnel and the little cemetery on the hill. What a creation."

There were rubberized tablecloths rigged here and there about the room to keep the rain off the tracks and off the miniature villages.

The Colonel pointed with the stem of his pipe to one set of tablecloths formed into connecting troughs to lead the water over to the north wall. "As you see, we make good use of what nature provides us so copiously through the roof."

"The water. Well, it's ingenious. This little waterfall."

"Yes. We made this mountain range, Monsignor Bill and I, expressly to contain the chasm for the waterfall and to give elevation to the river. That was a few summers back. Even then we were taking quite a lot of water through that big crack in the ceiling, and these other cracks, of course."

"I like the way you've led the river across the whole platform"—Evan traced the gurgling flow from the waterfall—"from town to town, then through the farmland and this other little village and finally all the way to the . . . uh . . . end." Two wooden sawhorses and a board formed a barricade where the water poured off the platform and down through the floor. The boards there had long ago rotted away.

Monsignor Leary spoke up from under the platform, where he was wiring track. " 'Even the longest river / winds somewhere safe to sea,' " he quoted, "as the poet Swinburne would have it."

162

"Or in our case," the Colonel amended, "winds somewhere safe to the hole in the floor."

"Quite a job, though."

"Oh, yes. Oh, yes. We laid the riverbed first in papier mâché, as you can see, then set into that a copper insert to carry the water. All the sections of copper had to be brazed together. The Monsignor, as it turns out, is a good man with a gas torch."

"Impressive."

"Managed not to set any fires at all, except in this one place here—"

"Where you have created a miniature burning village. So the charred places fit right in. I like that. Complete with toy fire engines. Very nice."

"One does what one can, you know, to adapt."

"Ready under here, Liam," the Monsignor called up. "Give 'er a test."

Liam stepped over to the control panel to throw the transformer lever. There was a crackling electrical sound accompanied by an acrid odor.

"Mmm." The Colonel looked thoughtfully over the platform. "Under the bridge, I think. Yes, I can see it smoking now. Off switch, Liam. Or we shall need to construct another burning village. All the way over to the far side, Monsignor. Right under the bridge. I think you'll find a spot there requiring the services of your soldering iron." There was a sound under the table of the Monsignor pulling himself along the floor. "Do be careful under there, Bill. Try not to fall through."

Mr. Collyer was on his hands and knees on the platform, molding plaster of paris over a water-damaged section of mountain. Above him, Teddy Ralston was stringing a new complex of waterproof fabric to carry water away from the new leak.

The Colonel carried on. "The original concept was to pattern the model on the island of Islesboro, though of course Islesboro doesn't have a river."

"Or a mountain."

"Or a train, for that matter. But you see we have Pendleton Point there at the south." He pointed to the narrow end of the table. "And Gilkey and the Harbor Ferry landings over there. And here, in the middle, Dark Harbor House."

"Uh-huh."

"I have enlarged the property somewhat, as you can tell."

"Added a few buildings, I see."

"Yes. I think of it as poetic license. A little schoolhouse and a train station and this small stadium. I always did feel it was a shame that we had no stadium on the grounds."

"A stadium? For ... ?"

"Oh, the odd chariot race, perhaps, or maybe lions and Christians, that sort of thing."

Evan was still very serious. "You know, Colonel, what's most impressive here is the quantity of work you have done, the detail. I just wonder whether this kind of creation will ever be done again. Doesn't it seem that American youth has lost the work ethic to some degree? There's going to be no one left to do this kind of thing. I mean, our lot here at Dark Harbor House can't be faulted, but I do wonder about American youth in general."

"Spot on, Evan," Teddy agreed. "Today's youth has got no backbone. They're given over to a virtual orgy of self-indulgence. Kids of this era have no work ethic at all, particularly this younger set just coming along now. The ones in high school."

The Monsignor crawled out from under the platform. "That's the word we hear from the schools, you know. Modern youth can't be got to work for love nor money. Not for love nor money. All they want is for the teachers to amuse them."

"Just what I was saying," Evan went on. "And that's a dead end. School is not supposed to be fun. They have to learn that. I mean, life is not play. The schools are not there to entertain children but to teach them discipline."

"And what better way to teach discipline," Teddy added, "than to put them right to work? The duller the work, the more deadly it is, the better. They have to learn to form that ethic that has made America the greatest country in all history."

"Once," Monsignor Leary corrected. "America was *once* the greatest country. The future, I'm afraid, is going to be quite another story."

"I don't doubt it. What with youngsters the way they are today. No time for work, only for playing records and hanging around and going to films—the Three Stooges and so on—"

"Hold on there," the Colonel stopped him. "I'm a great fan of the Three Stooges."

"For relaxation, though, Colonel. I mean, after a day's work. We labor in here for a full day, building and repairing and creating. Who can fault us if we take in a film in the evening? But not as a raison d'être, don't you see?"

"Not as a raison d'être, no."

"Well, for today's youth, the Three Stooges are a raison d'être. That's what I'm saying."

The Monsignor had completed his repair from the top. "I have a hunch that's the last," he said. "Give us the juice, Liam. Let's see."

"Juice on."

"Mmmmm. Well, Andrew. Looks perfect. What do you think?"

"Just give it another moment . . . yes, I think that's it. Switch off, Liam, and we'll get the locomotives on the track. Mr. Collyer . . . oh, Mr. Collyer!"

"Hmmm?"

The Colonel pointed to a black steam locomotive lying on its side in a cow pasture.

"Oh. Ready, are we?"

"Ready." The Colonel nodded. "Still, we mustn't be too hard on today's youth. Children have always been, well, children, if you get my drift."

The Monsignor could not agree. "But the ignorance, Andrew, that's what I can't swallow. American children today are most appallingly ignorant. Why, I heard that an entire class of seventh graders in Rochester, New York—public schoolers, mind you—thought that the esophagus was a Greek tragedy." He stopped to chuckle. "Imagine that."

"And their geography is even worse," Teddy added. "They can't show you North Dakota on a map, or name any of the state capitals. And if you asked them where Slovenia was—"

"Hmm?" Monsignor Leary raised an eyebrow.

"Slovenia."

"Oh, yes."

"Well, they wouldn't have the foggiest."

The Colonel was hovering over the locomotive, now in place on the track. "If you could hand me one of those little white pills, Liam. From the bottle under the panel. Yes, one of those. Thank you. Now, we just drop the pill into the smokestack...so. That will give us smoke, puffs of smoke."

"Ah, so that's the secret of the smoke."

"One of the many secrets of trains. Takes years, you know, to learn them all."

"Well, it's the ethic that's gone," Teddy went on. "The work ethic. Kids today just can't be serious. Maybe it has to do with the passing of the war. Now, our generation—even those of us who were too young to fight—at least knew of the desperate battles going on. We were hardened by fire. Whereas the younger set—"

"Not just the war, though," the Monsignor interrupted

him. "I can't agree it's just the war. There's also the lack of values. You see, modern children have been raised in a time of moral neglect. Their parents were too busy to instruct them, to provide the basis we all need to go forward. What with the mothers off banging rivets and assembling ships, children were left to fend for themselves. It's not natural. So we have a basically shiftless generation. They'll come to nothing, you mark my words."

The Colonel had the last car in place on the track. "I think we're ready. Caps everyone." He pulled on a gray-and-white-striped engineer's cap. Liam had another. Evan and the Monsignor put on flagman's caps. Mr. Collyer had a conductor's cap.

Teddy was already wearing a Boston Braves baseball cap, which he now turned around back to front. "I'm going to be a fireman this time," he announced.

"Well, fires up, then," Colonel Forsythe instructed him. "Liam, would you do the honors?"

"Fires up. Switch on. Steam building."

The little locomotive lurched forward. "Ready switch," the Colonel called. He pointed toward a switch near Mr. Collyer. "Switch!"

"But I'm a conductor," Mr. Collyer objected.

"Got it," the Monsignor said. He leaned under the platform to pick up a red flag, then hurried forward toward the switch. "Switch . . . in place." He waggled the flag back toward the Colonel.

"Good work, Flagman."

"Next stop, Dark Harbor," Mr. Collyer called out. "Dark Harbor, Dark Harbor."

Liam slowed the train to a stop precisely in front of the station.

"Dark Harbor Station. Everybody off. Everybody off? Okay. Everybody on. Next stop, Harbor Ferry. Board.

Booooooaaaaaaarrrrd!" Mr. Collyer gave the wave to Liam, and the little train started up again.

They watched in silence as it made its way around the platform.

"Now this," Teddy observed, "is men's work. I mean providing basic services like transportation and haulage. Those are the services that let a society exist at all."

Monsignor Leary agreed. "Exactly right, my boy. Exactly right. They are the 'intra-structure,' if I could coin that term. They are what knits a society together."

"Exactly."

"Society, you see, can't really exist, I mean qua society, without this thing I have called intra-structure. Without it, where would we be? Just think. How would people go from Dark Harbor House to the ferry, for example, without our train. How would they go?"

"Well, they could walk, I suppose," the Colonel allowed. "That's what we generally do. I mean, in the absence of a train."

"Precisely my point," said the Monsignor. "Precisely my point. Without this train service that we provide, people are reduced to walking. In other words, they would propel themselves using exactly the same method that the cavemen used." He paused for effect. "Thousands of years of history, all for naught without intra-structure. Yes, Teddy, this is indeed a proper kind of work for real men."

"I agree, sir."

"I don't think you can agree with the Monsignor," Liam pointed out, "since he was only agreeing with you."

"I can too, Liam. I mean, the Monsignor is dead right. This is just what the ethic is urging us toward, this kind of effort. That is the essence of the work ethic. So what if we work our fingers to the bone? So what if we labor long into the night? Don't you see? It will be our labor that allows society to exist as, or qua, society. Without our train, there would be no intra-structure, as the Monsignor calls it. And people would be living just like cavemen."

"Well, I'm with the Monsignor and Teddy on this one," Evan announced. "Just think about the most basic services that simply couldn't exist without intra-structure." He pointed at the little train now wending past him, and its two tanker cars. "We'd be left without petrol, for example."

Colonel Forsythe pursed his lips. "There is, strictly speaking, no petrol on the island."

"Because there is no train." Evan seized triumphantly on the point. "No petrol, no steel, no heavy industry, none whatsoever."

"Hmm. Quite so. Quite so. None of those things."

"With intra-structure, the island could be transformed."

"Factories," Teddy added, "banks, airfields, docks, mines, smelting plants. The sky's the limit."

"And that's just today. Imagine what the future holds. Why, I daresay, with the dedicated efforts of intra-structure workers such as ourselves, we shall live to see trains that go three hundred miles an hour. Well, with such a train," Evan looked around at them, "with such a train, you could go from one end of the island to the other in about—"

"Forty seconds," the Colonel was first to finish the calculation.

Monsignor Leary was nodding. "That, gentlemen, that is the wonder of intra-structure."

"It is," Evan said. "And that's what can make a society grow, what knits us together, as the Monsignor says, into a massive and effective engine for growth. And that's what lets our values survive and persist."

"Of course, it works the other way as well," the Monsignor illustrated by clamping his two hands together. "The intra-structure supports the values while the values enable the intra-structure to function. Interlocked and interdependent: values, society, intra-structure, and growth."

They turned at a sound behind them. The door opened to admit Angela. "Hello, all. Happy rainy day. What's up in here?"

"Philosophy," Evan informed her. "We're waxing philosophical. Talking about the grand, interlocking forces of culture and technology and values and, oh, modern youth as well."

"Too weighty for me," Angela said. She let herself out and closed the door behind her. There was silence but for the rattle of the little train making its way past Dark Harbor Station again.

Evan stared after her for a moment. "That's another thing, you know. We've been deploring the state of American youth. But maybe we should be talking about American womanhood."

Teddy sighed. "Ah, American womanhood. I'm afraid you're right there, Evan."

"Well, I just note that there is not a single woman here to help when there's work to be done. I mean, look around you. Look around." He gestured around the room. "Not a single woman."

"What are they up to, anyway?" Liam asked.

"Sitting around in front of the fire, I imagine. Isn't that what they do on every rainy day? Playing jacks, I would bet." Teddy shook his head. It was true that there was a desultory game of jacks going on in front of the fire in Inverness most rainy days. "Intent on the serious business of play. That's what I mean. That's American womanhood for you."

"Jacks, of course, is not exactly the object of the exercise," the Colonel pointed out. "The object of the exercise is girl talk. Jacks is just something to do with the hands."

Evan nodded. "Sure. But even girl talk, that's a kind of

170

play, isn't it? I mean, what do they talk about? Not the kind of things that we fellows are talking about, I can assure you. We're here discussing deep matters like values and growth and—"

"Transport." The Colonel nodded down toward the platform.

"And transport, but they're in there talking about—"

"Us, I would guess," Teddy said. "Boys."

"Talking about us. Or about fellows in general."

"Or clothes," Liam added. "They go on about clothes quite a lot."

"Girl talk is just play, that's all it is."

"What are we talking about?" Mr. Collyer wanted to know.

"Women," the Colonel told him, raising his voice.

"Oh, women. That's good. I'm in favor."

"Well, we all are," the Monsignor agreed. "Only, one might wish—"

"One might wish for a little help with the task at hand," Evan said. "That's all I'm saying. Instead of just play, play, play."

"I don't know," Liam spoke up. "There's something rather charming about women being made for a life of leisure. Isn't that what civilization is trying to achieve? After all, in caveman times, one supposes, the women were worked to death, carrying rocks and hitting the food with sticks to soften it up and all that. Now, with our intrastructure, women can sit around having a nice game of jacks in front of the fire. That's what gives some purpose to our life of work."

"Islesboro Harbor Ferry is next." Mr. Collyer called out. "Next stop, Harbor Ferry. Look alive there!"

"I think we might sound the whistle, Liam." The Colonel pointed to a red button on the panel. "Give those ferry folks a bit of warning."

171

"Oh, the whistle is shorted out," Liam informed him. "It got dripped on, I guess."

Monsignor Leary filled in for the missing whistle: "Wooo-oooooooooo," he groaned. "Wooooooooo-oooooooooooo." He waved his flag as the train lumbered past.

"Station stop is Islesboro Ferry. Everybody off for the ferry. Everybody off."

16

Haydée

~~~~~~

The steam yacht *Four Square* had been built by Nathanael Herreshoff in the 1890s for Orin Ralston and kept in the family ever since.

"One hundred and twenty feet long—that's L.O.A., mind you," Teddy Ralston told them. "Not counting the bowsprit. A hundred and twelve on the waterline." The combined occupants of Dark Harbor House and North Star were assembled in the main saloon on the upper deck, off for an excursion across the Narrows to Temple Heights.

"Very impressive, very impressive," Compton enthused. "I like all the brightwork. But so much varnishing. It must keep you busy."

"Oh, it does that." Teddy furrowed his brow. "Has to be redone each spring and midsummer, of course, along with the painting. It's a lot of work, but worth it, I think. Then on a daily basis all the brass has to be polished, and there's tons of brass. And the decks washed down morning and afternoon. Keeps us hopping. But we've got nothing against good, hard, honest work. Of course, the crew does the work."

"There are seven in the crew," Louise added. "Captain, cook, engineer, fireman, two deckhands, and Gulliver, here, our steward."

Gulliver, an elderly black man in a white uniform, was passing a silver tray of drinks.

"Why, thank you there, Gulliver. Thank you." Evan helped himself to a tall drink. He tasted and grinned. "Mint juleps to start the day. How perfect." He took a long gulp. "I love to be served by Coloreds," he confided to Liam as soon as Gulliver was out of earshot. "Something about it just seems...I don't know, seems right somehow."

"Think they're made for service, do you?" Liam prodded.

"Well, I do. Not that I'm anti-Colored, mind you. Not in the least. Quite liberal, actually. Old Gulliver there is a regular Uncle Remus. I'm sure he's quite content to serve."

"Dream employment," Liam offered, confident that the irony would be lost.

"It is. Working for a respectable modern family. All the benefits, I'm sure. Why, he's probably almost part of the family. I don't doubt they'll look out for him in his old age."

"I suspect he's already in his old age. Appears to be about eighty."

"And the family is looking out for him, as I said. Keeping him gainfully employed." Evan smiled contentedly. "Yes, there's something that just feels right about being served by the Gullivers of the world."

"Mmm," Liam said.

Evan gestured expansively, taking in the whole saloon and afterdeck. "And going off on steam yachts feels right too. I mean, it's the way things were meant to be. A picnic outing with friends on a summer day."

The Colonel joined in. "Teddy says there's to be caviar as the first course of the picnic. No blinis, of course, as we'll be

174

roughing it, eating on the lawn. But caviar. Would you say that caviar seems right as well?"

"I would," Evan agreed. "A bit on the elegant side, but still right. If you see what I mean."

"Oh, I do. I do."

"'Right' seems to equate with 'rich,' if I get your drift."

"Not at all, Liam. 'Right,' as I'm using the word, has more to do with, well, mannerly behavior. Civilized. It's what separates us from the animals, you see."

There was a long moan of the steam whistle. One of the deckhands rushed forward to cast off the bow line.

Laura squealed girlishly beside Liam. "Ooo. Here we go. Out on the deck everyone." She took Liam's arm and pulled him toward the door. There was a trembling underfoot. Again the long, moaning whistle.

"Oh, dear," Laura said once they were on the deck. "There's no one to wave to." Her arm was half raised in an aborted wave.

"We're all on board, I guess. I mean, everybody's going."

"We should have left someone on the pier to wave to. Or asked the Jervises to come out, or something." She stamped her foot in exasperation. "I mean, honestly, it doesn't feel natural to be steaming away without waving."

"Wave to Dark Harbor House then," Liam proposed.

"Good-bye, Dark Harbor House. Good-bye," Laura called, waving enthusiastically. "Good-bye."

"Don't dismay," Liam called to the house as he waved too. "We'll be back for dinner."

There was a music room amidships with a real steam organ. Bruno sat himself down at the console and tried a note.

"Mmm," he said appreciatively. "Nice tone. Any chance of a bit more volume?"

Teddy nodded. "I'll send word up to the captain to call for full steam." He picked up a kind of telephone apparatus and spoke into it. "That should do it. Give them a minute or so." There was an increased trembling as steam built up.

Bruno pressed another key and produced a much louder tone. "Lovely." Then he pressed the lowest note on the keyboard and held it. Liam could feel the sound vibrating in his chest. "Mmm," Bruno said again. He twiddled a few stops, then arranged himself to play.

He began almost tentatively, sounding a theme in the right hand and answering it with the left. Then that deep, throbbing, low note from the bottom of the keyboard to begin a thundering run up to a long-held chord in the middle. Liam knew the piece vaguely but couldn't think what it might be. He listened on, though, moved in spite of himself. The volume and lovely tone of the organ were impressive enough, but he had to admit that best of all was the playing. Say what you would about Bruno, the man could play divinely.

Liam glanced at Mr. Collyer, beside him. There were tears running down the old gentleman's cheeks. Liam caught his eye and held up his palms in question. Mr. Collyer moved closer.

"Bach's Toccata in D-Minor," he spoke directly into Liam's ear. "I never thought I would hear it again."

☙❧

Liam found Laura and Lizzie and Angela on the afterdeck.

"He's not so much cute as rather dreamy looking. Well, if you ask me." Lizzie looked upward dreamily.

"*Moi?*" Liam inquired.

"No. Teddy. She's talking about Teddy," Angela replied.

"Oh."

"Those eyes of his, couldn't you just drink them in? The color of them. They're almost—what shall I say?—sepia. Yes, they're sepia colored. I have never seen such eyes."

176

"Except on Louise, of course," Liam noted. "Same color."

Laura shrugged. "Well, they're twins, so what would you expect? Yes, Louise too. She has the same sepia-colored eyes. Too bad that color doesn't work so well on Louise. " She paused wickedly. "Too bad she's so flat."

"What?"

"Well, she is," Laura said. "Don't look so startled, Liam. Quite flat. Someone should take her aside and recommend some nice pads. I think it would do her a world of good."

Angela giggled. "Mustn't give away secrets, Laura. I'm sure Liam never noticed that about Louise. He's too gentlemanly to allow his eyes to descend..." She thrust her bosom upward slightly, drawing Liam's eyes. He looked away, blushing.

"I..." he began, then stalled.

"... leave many sentences hanging at the place where they go dot, dot, dot," Angela finished for him. "But we do love you anyway, Liam."

"I..."

"I adore an open-air luncheon," Laura said, sighing, "and this one was utterly perfect. Perfect."

"Nice," Liam agreed.

"Nice and simple—"

"Except for the caviar," he inserted.

"Which was a bit of a flourish," she agreed. "But aside from that, it was the simplicity of the meal that gave it its charm. Simple broiled chicken and boiled eggs, a bit of bread and cheese, and fruit. Really a peasant meal. That's what I mean. Eating out-of-doors, simple, nourishing food, sitting on the ground—why, it takes us straight back to our roots, to prehistoric times, I mean."

"But for the silver—and the freshly whipped cream on strawberries."

"Well, there was silver even in prehistoric times, you

know. It didn't just pop into existence in the modern era. And there were strawberries, and of course there was cream. I'm sure some enterprising cave people had worked out how to whisk their cream. Surely they had discovered that and how to sprinkle in a little sugar. You know, ancient people weren't stupid. I can't believe that the Greeks, for instance, hadn't a bit of whipped cream every now and again. At least for special occasions."

"Perhaps so."

"So often, Liam, it is simplicity that creates moments of great charm. Now, I propose we end this simple meal with a simple walk. Stretch our legs." She held out her arm to be helped to her feet.

Liam jumped up. "May I?"

"Why, thank you." Laura twisted around to examine the seat of her skirt and brushed at it mechanically. But because Gulliver had laid out Oriental rugs on the lawn for them to sit on, she had not even a stray bit of grass to brush away. "Now." She paused. "Down toward the pier, perhaps?"

"Yes." There was a pathway leading from the side of the pier off into a nearby pine woods. If she could be persuaded onto that pathway, he knew there might be kisses in his future. What better complement to a simple luncheon than a few simple kisses in a simple pine woods? Kissing, he thought idly, must have been known to prehistoric people as well. After all, ancient people weren't stupid. They must have discovered kissing. And if kissing was practiced even in the earliest times, by even the simplest people, then Laura might well feel that . . .

"It's so frightfully hot!" Laura exclaimed as they neared the water's edge. "Laura is hot. I think I'm ready for a nice sit in the shade. I'm positively glowing, Liam." She pointed toward the corner of the wooden pier, shaded by a nearby white pine. The wide boards there were clean and dry, but

Liam spread his jacket for her anyway. Laura sat carefully, allowing her legs to dangle over the edge. "Mmmm," she said. "Lovely."

He sat down beside her. This might be a good time to pick up again on the theme of beauty. Since their last, quite unsatisfying, chat on that subject, Liam had prepped a bit on how the conversation might better proceed. He now had his part worked out properly. He would say that beauty was a noble pursuit for even the most unselfish person. Beauty isn't intrinsically selfish at all, really. Rather it is the means by which man eases the burden of others, eases the pain they might otherwise have felt in a world bereft of beauty. Nice, that: "a world bereft of beauty." He would definitely work that in.

He cleared his throat. "B—"

"You mustn't be shocked by this, Liam. I know you are terribly shockable." Laura was folding back the underside of her skirt to push it up underneath her legs. "Modern young ladies wear crinolines under their skirts, you know. Or perhaps you didn't know that, not having a sister to instruct you in such matters. Well, we do. And crinolines can be itchy and scratchy on hot days. So I just fold things a bit, so it's the lovely, fresh cotton against my skin."

Laura lifted herself slightly to push the cotton fabric all the way up under her. Then she proceeded to fold neatly the remaining part of her skirts and crinolines the rest of the way around. Liam felt his jaw dropping. When she was done, her legs were entirely insulated from the crinoline, and her skirt was reduced effectively to half its length.

"There. That's better." She sighed. "Much better in fact. What a relief." She noted his eyes on her bare knees. "And a bit of sun on the knees is always desirable. A bit of tanning." She smiled at him. "You are shocked, aren't you?"

"No!"

"Well, it's nothing you haven't seen before, not half what you see when I'm in my swimming suit. Perfectly proper. Now, you were about to say ...?"

If he went on now about beauty, she would think he was talking about her knees. Which were beautiful, in fact, but...or even about her thighs. He was imagining the lower part of her skirt pressing against her bare thighs all the way up to her, Jesus, up to her underpants.

"Yes?"

Liam could feel himself sweating along the top of his upper lip. He looked into Laura's blue eyes. Then it hit him, all of a sudden. It hit him like a ton of bricks. It was almost impossible to believe, but it was true: Under her clothing, Laura was absolutely, totally nude. Nude! He was sitting only a few inches away from a lovely, nude woman. "Grk," he said.

"What?"

"Beauty is unselfish," Liam covered. "Bereft of—"

"Hey, you two." It was Jody, come up behind them. "We're all going up to see the historic plaque. Want to come?"

"Oh, I love historical things," Laura said. "Let's do go, Liam." She got to her feet, shaking her skirts down as she did.

Liam gawked up at Jody. "Historic plaque," he said.

Jody nodded. "It commemorates the Bentonite settlement here. They used Temple Heights for their summer retreats. They were the ones who built the temple, one supposes, that gave the place its name. Everything they built burned down in the twenties. The whole place burned down. You can still see the foundations, though, farther up the hill. Are you okay, Liam?"

"Oh, yes."

"You look sort of red. Perhaps you should drink something. It's quite a hot day, you know. A regular 'skoa-chah,' as they say in Maine."

"Perhaps I will stop for a drink on the way up."

"Do that. You can't be too careful."

The hilltop at Temple Heights was a circular cleared area, surrounded by the foundations of six small buildings and one large one. In the center was a massive marble gravestone carved into the shape of a coffin overlaid with flowers. The inscription on the side read:

Dorothea Benton

(Haydée)

1860–1905

Gone to Her Maker

"I rather like that last line," Marjorie said. "It ought to be on everybody's gravestone, just so we know the person under the stone is dead. It's rather a comfort not to think of her knocking about down there, trying to get out."

Bruno was faced around, taking in the view. "She's got a nice spot here, anyway. I wouldn't mind having a house with this view." Down below them was the Narrows, sparkling in the afternoon sun. The island of Islesboro was immediately opposite. And behind it were visible Deer Isle and Swans Island and Isle au Haut and North Haven.

"They put her up here, I think, to glower down over the Gideons," Colonel Forsythe suggested. "There was no love lost between the Gideons and the Bentonites."

"Here's the scoop on Haydée," Evan told them. He read out loud from the painted green plaque: "'Haydée, beloved evangelist of the Zion Benton Community. Beloved only child of Horace Benton, who first proclaimed the Zion in 1854. Haydée was an American religious figure and inventor of cereal foods and beverages. She was called the Saint of Soul and Colon. Died of apoplexy at Temple Heights, Maine, on August 19, 1905.'"

"What is apoplexy again?" Sissy wanted to know.

Marjorie told her, "It's what you get when your children are being particularly obstreperous. Your face turns purple, and your veins stand out."

"Oh, dear. We shall have to be good as gold for the foreseeable future so my dear parents don't go apoplectic."

"She had no children, though," Louise put in. "I mention that because there were always rumors about her and grandpa. Dr. Ralston, I mean."

"Rumors and letters," Jody added. "There were some letters from Haydée to your grandfather that suggest—"

Louise nodded impatiently. "Yes, I know all that. Some affectionate letters and some angry ones. Perhaps something was going on between them, but that was earlier. By the time grandpa had come here and begun to build North Star, that was all over. Wasn't it, Teddy?"

"Yes. Quite over. There are always rumors about the old doctor. Some even say that he and Jeannie Isobel had a fling. But you know how people talk. The truth is that they were all friends in their youth and interacted to some degree, then wandered apart. Dr. Ralston was a curiously straitlaced old man. I hardly think he was up for any kind of illicit activity. Or any activity at all. Our father was adopted, you know. I don't doubt that Grandpa went to his grave without ever a single experience of . . . of that sort."

"Still," Bruno said, "it would explain how Jeannie and Haydée came to be enemies. Jody says they came to hate each other. If they were both sweet on the same fellow . . ."

Teddy was shaking his head. "You know, I just don't think people were like that back then. Not like today. They didn't think about such things. Friendship, yes, but not, you know, love affairs. I suspect they differed politely on

182

religious subjects and on nutrition, and that was all. They wandered apart and they each died relatively at peace. At least that's how I think of it."

As the others were collecting their things to start down the hill, Liam and Angela passed behind the stone coffin. There was a second inscription there.

> Shall I not punish them for these things?
> saith the LORD.
> And shall I not avenge myself
> on a nation such as this?
> —Jeremiah 5:29

"Well, I don't know how the others died," Angela whispered, "but I don't think Haydée was particularly at peace."

"No," the Colonel confirmed on the trip back, "not at peace at all. She died in a fury. That much we know. She was whacked over the head by Jeannie with a huge zucchini. That was what people around here call the Great Zucchini War, the final confrontation between the Bentonites and the Gideons. Jeannie picked up a squash the size of a baseball bat—they were standing in the gardens at Dark Harbor House at the time—and brought it down hard on Haydée's head. Haydée said three terrible words, then stalked off. She was all red in the face and seemed confused after that. Less than a week later she was dead."

"What were the three terrible words?" Liam asked.

"Well, no one is too sure. All the written records use the same phrase, 'three terrible words,' without specifying exactly what they were."

"So Teddy was wrong about their just wandering peacefully apart as they got older."

"A bit off the mark." The Colonel was looking out over *Four Square*'s bow rail, where Dark Harbor House was just coming into view. "He might have been off the mark on one other thing too. We don't have a surviving picture of Haydée, certainly not one in color, but there are written descriptions of her. The one thing they all mention is that she had sepia-colored eyes."

17

Wire Nine

AJQC AJQC AJQC AJQC AJQC AJQC AJQC AJQC AJQC AJQC AJQC

The Colonel tapped for attention on the lectern. "Ladies and gentlemen, once again, Dark Harbor's own expert on expertology, Miss Jody Forsythe."

Jody stepped up onto her dictionary and laid a sheaf of notes on the lectern. "Well, everybody's been asking me about Haydée and her feud with Jeannie. So I got together all my stuff on the Bentonites and Gideons . . . by 'stuff' I mean my material, which is the same as stuff but more respectable. So I read it all through, and if you'd like, I'll tell you what I've found."

Murmuring sounds of assent. They were all seated on folding chairs in Navarre, as before. "Yes, please," Liam called out.

"Thank you. Well, where to begin?" She paused. "Back in Battle Creek, Michigan, I think. This would be about 1892. The Zion Benton sanitarium had just reopened a few years before, after reconstruction. Dr. Ralston was in charge. The reopening was the time of Jeannie's theatrical debut in the Cathedral Theater on the sanitarium grounds. As you re-

185

member, she stunned people with her performance and her singing and, of course, the spectacle of everybody getting baptized. I suppose it didn't hurt at all that the Angels were getting dunked in their slinky silver dresses and coming up looking more scrumptious than ever. We know that Jeannie chose only the prettiest girls to be Angels.

"Well, the show just got better and better as time went on. People were coming to Battle Creek in droves to see it and to see Jeannie. In 1891, Elihu Root came and Thomas Edison and William Jennings Bryan. And the next year President Harrison came. He arrived by train with an enormous party of officials and journalists and celebrities, including the Duke of York. By that time, Dr. Ralston had enlarged the sanitarium so that it swallowed them all up and had room for still more. There was a whole cult about the sanitarium. Particularly theater people from New York were coming: Nellie Melba and Eleonora Duse and Lillian Russell and Florenz Ziegfeld. They said it was for their health, but I suspect they were looking to learn some of Jeannie's magic for their own uses.

"Of course, Haydée was miffed at Jeannie's success. It was not just that she felt Jeannie had tricked her into giving away her best secrets on how to speak dramatically and hold a crowd, and had helped her train her voice. The worse thing was that as Jeannie's audience grew larger and larger, a lot of Haydée's audience was beginning to defect. The Bentonite Community was starting to come apart. Finally, in the fall of 1892, Haydée had had enough. She declared the sanitarium closed.

"That was when she found out that she didn't own the place at all. Dr. Ralston did. He had bought the land himself and paid for the building, so it was all totally his. Haydée had missed that. Because it was called the Zion Benton Sanitarium, she had naturally assumed it was hers. But it wasn't. She was rather ethereal in those days anyway. Some would say she was naive.

"The sanitarium was renamed. They called it the Ralston Clinic. People didn't stop coming; in fact, there were more and more visitors—more than two thousand in 1894 and forty-four hundred by 1896. The typical guest stayed on for a month or two. The place was an enormous financial success. Jeannie had started her own religion shortly after the break with Haydée. She knew she needed religion to make the spectacle of all those dripping wet Angels seem respectable. So she invented the Gideon Compact.

"At the beginning, it was just a copy of the religion that Haydée was preaching. But over time, Jeannie made some changes of her own. She wrote in a letter to Norbert that, and here I quote"—Jody picked up a letter from her pile—"'There is really nothing more amusing I can imagine than creating a religion. I dream things up and suggest them to the compact's elders, and the next thing you know we have lovely new ceremonies and robes and songs, all deliciously mystical. I have a positive talent for the mystical. And I honestly think it does no harm.'

"Haydée was furious. She began having terrible visions. In the visions, the sanitarium would be burning to the ground, burning and burning. She told everyone who would listen about her visions. Remember, this was a woman who had a certain theatrical magic of her own; she was the one who had taught Jeannie everything. And she hadn't forgotten how to wrap an audience around her little finger. When Haydée had visions, everybody had visions. Soon everybody in Battle Creek was muttering that the sanitarium would soon burn down, that a just and wrathful God was going to use fire to cleanse the earth of this terrible place. Sure enough, in the summer of 1900, the whole complex burned to the ground. There was nothing left but ashes.

"No one was killed in the fire, but you can imagine that the Gideons were left feeling a bit insecure. The fire was proof that God was not on their side. And if God was not with the Gideons, the people of Battle Creek weren't going to be with them either. Jeannie and Dr. Ralston and the rest of the Gideons fled. They arrived that summer at Dark Harbor House, where Norbert took them in.

"Norbert was the one who had constructed the pools of the Cathedral and contracted all the plumbing for the place. A lot of people made an awful lot of money out of the sanitarium, but, as often happens, the plumber got richest of all. He built a brass foundry in Battle Creek to make fittings for the pools and all, and another foundry in Bridgeport, Connecticut, and then foundries all over the country. That's how the Chance Brass Company was begun. By 1900, Norbert had retired to Maine and was dedicated entirely to counting his money and to building Dark Harbor House and the surrounding structures. The compact was set up here, considerably reduced—in fact they were only active during the summer—and Jeannie picked up where she'd left off. She performed out-of-doors, at the pool. The compact was a big hit with the people of Dark Harbor.

"Well, the story might have ended that way, with Jeannie preaching and singing her way through the rest of her life, summers anyway. The rest of the time she might simply have lived quietly at Dark Harbor House. It might have ended that way, but it didn't.

Haydée, back in Battle Creek, was not yet satisfied. She felt she had to pursue Jeannie and complete her ruin. So she bought land at Temple Heights and built her summer-retreat community there. While at Temple Heights each summer, she preached on only one subject: Jeannie. Her sermons and tracts were thunderous and very dark." Jody picked up a small booklet and read from it: "The title of this one is *Compact with the Devil*. It starts, as usual, with a quote from Jeremiah: 'Be appalled, O heavens, at this. Be shocked, be utterly desolate, Saith the LORD.' Jeremiah two, verse twelve. It goes on to tell you what to be shocked about: the Gideon Compact and their 'unnatural acts,' principally the saltwater baptism. This is where the suggestion comes from that the unnatural act in question was performed au naturel, as Laura puts it.

"At the end, Haydée rails on about the 'corruption of blessed girl children.' What she's talking about there are the Angels. You see, there was a problem with pregnancy among the Gideons during those years. A few of the Angels got pregnant each summer, with the help of the Acolytes, I guess. It was a bit of a black mark for Jeannie.

"Well, the final act: Haydée was eventually getting a bigger crowd in Maine than she did back home. After a while, the people in her local following were all hopping mad about Jeannie. Haydée realized that she was as strong as she ever was going to be. So she planned an attack. She loaded all her followers into boats on the night of August 15, 1905, and they set out toward Islesboro. They were going to burn Dark Harbor House to the ground. That was the plan."

"Only Jeannie was way ahead of them. One of Haydée's 'disciples' was really an ex-Angel, a spy. She rowed over to Dark Harbor House ahead of the fleet of small boats to tell Jeannie what was about to happen. So the Gideons were ready. By the time the boats began to arrive, the Gideons were lined up on the shore. The Acolytes waded out into the water and upset the boats, one by one, dunking everybody. Fortunately for Jeannie, it was a cold night, as Maine can sometimes produce in August. So after their Gideon saltwater baptism, the Bentonites were freezing cold. It took all the fight out of them. They didn't stay around to argue. They just righted their boats and rowed back miserably to the other side.

"Haydée and the people in her boat were the only ones

to make it ashore. She came up to confront Jeannie. They met in the main garden. Haydée was soaking wet. She started to say something, but Jeannie wasn't inclined to listen. Instead, she picked up a big zucchini and cracked it over Haydée's head. Haydée was stunned. She said three terrible words to Jeannie. Then she got back in her boat, absolutely fuming. Supposedly she fumed all the way back. Finally, from so much fury, she dropped dead, as the plaque said, apoplectic. And that was the famous Great Zucchini War that we celebrate every August 15. It had only that one fatality, but nobody was really the same after it."

Jody looked up for her notes. "That's the end, I guess. I mean, I don't have an ending for my talk. There's really no high note to finish on. But that's how the war ended." She stepped down.

"Hear, hear!" Angela said, and began clapping. The others joined in.

"Oh, here's our ending," Jody said. "Tyndall has got some punch for us. Thank you, Mr. Tyndall, for your perfect timing." Mr. Tyndall was setting down a tray of punch cups.

Once they were all served, Laura proposed a toast. "To our wonderful historian, Jody. Well done, Jody." She raised her cup.

"Thank you."

"Yes, well done, darling," Marjorie said. "A splendid job. And you all don't know how much work she's put in to be able to tell us these things."

"Well, it was a good deal of work," Jody admitted.

"It was a ton of work," Sissy chimed in. "She wrote letters to everyone she could think of who knew Jeannie or Norbert or any of them, and collected materials from all over. Didn't you?"

"I wrote a good number of letters, yes."

"Her greatest triumph was some wire recordings made

by a reporter from the *Portland Free Press.* They have Jeannie's own voice on them."

"No," Liam said. "Is it true?"

Jody nodded. "A Mr. Thomas E. McLaughlin interviewed Jeannie in the twenties for a piece in his paper. He visited at her home in Canada. Mr. McLaughlin is retired now, living in Winthrop, Massachusetts. When I wrote to him, he sent the wire recordings he had made. They're very brittle, but you can hear her voice. It plays for a minute or two, then it breaks. Mostly I just listen to them and write as fast as I can to make a transcript."

"You mean there are recordings we could listen to right in this very house and hear Jeannie's voice? Her actual voice?"

"Yes. Would you like that, Liam?"

"Yes! Would I ever!"

"Why not?" said Jody. "We could play a segment that has already been transcribed. Then, even if it broke, it wouldn't be a total loss. Come along then; we've got all the wires and apparatus right across the corridor in Biscay."

Jody led the entire troop into the library. Colonel Forsythe lifted a gray metal box out of one of the cabinets and plugged it in. "A vanishing technology, the wire player," he told them. "It's vanishing for good reason. The damn thing destroys each wire as it plays it. Well, it doesn't *always* destroy it, only usually. We'll be lucky to get two minutes."

Sissy was helping Jody with a tray of spools. "Of course, as the pieces break the lengths get shorter and shorter, till they can't be wrapped onto the spindles. So what you're about to hear may never be heard again. I'm glad that at least we have a crowd. Seems a particular shame when it's only Jody and me, and a piece breaks off that can never be played again."

Jody squinted at the fine print on one of the boxes. "This

is a good one," she said. The sound isn't as scratchy as on some of the others. You can hear Jeannie's voice quite well. Of course she was an old lady by this time, but she still sounds wonderful. You can imagine how she could enchant. Mr. McLaughlin is clearly enchanted."

The Colonel put the wire in place and switched on the machine. There was a hum, then a deep male voice.

"Thomas E. McLaughlin. Wire Three. Continuation of interview with Jeannie... with the very *lovely* Jeannie Isobel."

"Aren't you sweet? And I, an old lady." A magical giggle.

"You were saying...? About the early years, I believe."

"Oh, yes. That I took my role as fashioner of the Gideon religion as seriously as I have ever taken anything in my life. I felt like an architect, responsible not only for the functional aspects of my creation but also for the aesthetic." Jeannie's voice was clear and sweet—not the voice of an old lady at all but that of a woman in her prime. Liam and the others were leaning toward the machine so as not to lose a word.

Jeannie paused, and there was only the hiss of the wire. Then, "I looked back at my own early religious life—I was brought up Bentonite along with my three brothers—and thought of it as depressingly arid of all things aesthetic. Sister Haydée, and her father before her, had no use for the aesthetic. To carry on with the architectural image, they were structuralists. I, on the other hand, was a romantic, even an ornamentalist. They wanted their religion to be spare, uncompromising, unembellished. But I wanted mine to be a delight to the eye and to the spirit. They thought only of heaven and personal subjugation, while I was thinking more of charm, and of fun.

"The costumes we wore were my first concern. They had to be delicious, things of beauty in themselves and enhancers of the beauty that lay beneath them. And I was not, as some have suggested, entirely surprised by how they looked when wetted. In fact, we had tried them out beforehand, and liked what we saw.

"The various Gideon rituals were also my doing. Why shouldn't a ritual have some amusement value? I wondered. And so mine did. The evening spiritual ceremony, for example, the one that we performed on so many lovely summer evenings in the woods around Dark Harbor House, was supposed to be as enjoyable as it was. In fact, I based that ceremony on a game that I had always loved as a child. The game was called Capture the Flag. Perhaps you know it?"

"Oh, yes," Mr. McLaughlin said.

The magical giggle again. "Well, then you know all about the evening spiritual ceremony. In place of a flag, we used a—" There was a slight click and then silence.

"Broken," Jody said after a moment.

Liam breathed in. He realized he'd been holding his breath to hear.

"We could do another, I suppose," Jody said, but her face was dismayed at the thought.

"No need for that," the Colonel came to her rescue. "I think the one little bit was just perfect, my dear. Just to give us all a taste of who she was. Those wires that have been transcribed and remain unbroken might be passed along to future historians, perhaps some who are clever enough to invent a wire machine that doesn't break the wire. Just as evolution eventually hit upon animals who didn't eat their young. It's called progress."

Bruno had his hand up. "Questions for the professor?" he asked.

"Oh, sure."

"You've told us that Jeannie left 'in disgrace' after the Zucchini War. But what was the disgrace? It seems as if Haydée died from her own temper, not from a little tap with an oversized squash. So it couldn't have been that that disgraced Jeannie."

"No," Jody allowed. "Not that. Of course when Haydée died, it did take some of the spirit out of Jeannie. There's nothing like having a real enemy to give you spirit. But Jeannie stayed on that fall, preaching and putting on her show, as before. The compact usually stuck it out in Maine till the end of fall, or as long as the good weather lasted. Then they would break up for the winter. That year there was a particularly long Indian summer, lasting through most of November. By the time it was over, Jeannie knew that Haydée had won after all. She knew that the compact could never come together again." Jody flushed slightly. She looked up at Marjorie. "You tell them, Mummy."

"The little problem of pregnancy," Marjorie picked up. "As you know, in each of the other years a few of the Angels got pregnant. Haydée, you see, had got her facts pretty straight. But 1905 was a particular disaster. There were twenty-one Angels that year, and by the end of November it was obvious to everyone that the pregnancy rate was appalling." She stopped.

"How appalling?" Bruno asked after a moment.

"They were all pregnant," Marjorie told them. "Every single one."

Liam hung back as the others left to dress for dinner. When he was alone with Jody, he put his question to her.

"So what were the three terrible words, Jody? Surely you must know."

"I don't, actually. I never did learn that. Everyone is so coy about saying what the actual words were."

"Oh."

"'Cause I'm a child. They're all protecting me." She smiled slightly. "But I will know eventually. Mr. McLaughlin

194

wrote me a letter along with the wires. And in the letter he mentions that Jeannie repeats the words on one of the spools."

"She does?"

"On wire nine. Nothing coy about Jeannie. He specifically warns me about that section. Says I may be shocked by the language. He suggests, in fact, that I skip wire nine entirely. Says there is nothing on that spool but the very end of the interview, which in his mind was spoiled by those words. So I might just as well give it a by." A pause.

"Only you're not going to."

"No." Jody snickered. "Well, I have my duties as historian, don't I? And anyway, I'm curious."

"Me, too."

Jody hesitated. "Well, we could, I suppose. Couldn't we?"

"We could."

She considered another moment. "Let's do it, Liam."

"Let's."

"You won't tell?"

"Not a word."

"Wire nine, then. Here it is. You just wrap the end around the empty spindle and put on the rubber band to hold it firmly." She watched while he followed her instructions. "Good."

Liam switched on the machine, and there was an answering hum.

"This wire hasn't yet been transcribed," Jody noted. "So we need to copy down exactly what they say in case it breaks. It goes quite fast, so we've figured out a scheme, Sissy and I, to use two people. I'll show you how it works."

She handed Liam a pencil and writing tablet and took another for herself. "Now, we sit side by side and copy down alternate sentences or little groups of talk. You take the first one and I take the second and so forth. I coordinate with my foot. When I press down on your foot, you listen and write. When I lift up, it means I'm taking the next one, so you have a moment to catch up. You'll need it. Do you understand?"

"I guess so. I write down whatever they're saying while you've got your foot pressed on mine. I don't have to worry about the sentences in between."

"Right. Then we copy over the alternate sections to make a complete transcript. It usually works pretty well."

"Okay."

"Have you got it?"

"Yup."

She sat down and slid her chair over tight against his. "Are you ready, Liam?"

"Ready."

Jody released the clutch. "You're first." She pressed her foot down on top of his.

"Thomas E. McLaughlin," the machine said after a moment. "Wire nine: Isobel interview." A silence. Jody lifted her foot. Liam was writing. "So you hit her over the head with a squash? Did you really?" Jody began writing, too. Her foot pressed down on his again.

Jeannie's voice: "I did. Just a tap. I am not a violent woman."

"A tap. And what was her reaction?"

"She turned beet red, almost purple." A laugh. "It was quite comical, really. I've never seen anyone so upset."

"Purple?"

"Quite purple."

"And she said something, I believe?"

"She did."

"The three terrible words?"

"The three terrible words."

"Which were . . . ?"

A low, soft laugh. "I'll shock you, Mr. McLaughlin, if I say

196

them. You are a very proper gentleman, I believe. I'm not often wrong about such things."

"Still. Just for the sake of posterity."

Jeannie paused. "Since you insist. When Sister Haydée finally stopped sputtering and caught her voice, she stood up tall and put her face directly into mine. She positively spit out those words at me. She screeched, 'Odious ... diabolical ... cunt!' Then she turned on her heel and left."

There was a long silence from the machine. The two writers caught up with their portions. Finally the male voice again: "Thomas E. McLaughlin, Charlottetown, Prince Edward Island. End of interview." Liam wrote down his words.

There was nothing more on the wire. Jody shut off the machine. "Well," she said.

"Well."

Jody looked down at her pad. "I think we got it all. Don't you?"

"I think so, yes."

"Yes." She ran her pencil lightly along underneath her scrawled lines. "Almost all of it. The actual three terrible words..."

"Yes?"

"I was doing that part." Jody stared down at her pad. "Um, I have a question about the third one, the third of the three terrible ones, that is."

"Yes. Hmm. Well, it means—"

"Oh, I know what it means." She frowned again at the transcript. "I know what it means. Only, you know, I don't believe I have ever seen it written, actually. I was wondering...?" Jody looked up at him.

"Um...With a C, I think. Yes, I'm practically sure of that."

"Thank you, Liam."

18

Aunt Grace

⚜⚜⚜⚜⚜⚜⚜⚜⚜⚜⚜⚜

Mr. Collyer was down early for breakfast. Liam came upon him first thing, before Tyndall had even put out the coffee.

"Why, Mr. Collyer. Up so early. This is a surprise. You're looking very smart this morning, I must say."

"Thank you, Liam. Thank you. In the mood, I suppose, to dress up a bit. Nothing special." Mr. Collyer had on a blue blazer, powder gray slacks, a white shirt, and a black-and-red striped silk tie. "No excuse for slouching about in old corduroys and tweeds all the time the way I have. No excuse at all." His hair was slicked down too.

"And that's cologne, I believe. Or is it an aftershave?" Liam sniffed appreciatively.

"*Kölnische Frischen Wasser*. I get it through the mail. From a specialty importer. Do you like it, Liam? Do you?"

"Very much."

"Gives one the air of a go-ahead man, don't you think? At least that's what I think."

"Definitely a go-ahead sort of scent."

"And what have *you* got planned for today, my boy? Anything special?"

"Well, yes. A wildflower expedition with Laura. She has asked me especially. It's to be just the two of us." Liam colored slightly. "I mean, just Laura and myself. As it happens. Picking some flowers."

"Won't that be nice. A wonderful girl, Laura. Ah, here's coffee."

Liam stared after him as the little man moved toward the breakfront, where Tyndall was setting out the early service. Something odd there, but what was it? Something decidedly different about old Mr. C. this morning. Liam stepped up behind him and said, very softly, "Mr. Collyer?"

"Yes, Liam." Mr. Collyer turned about, smiling, cup in hand.

"Oh, nothing, sir. Got your coffee, have you? Well, that's good. Here, I may have some myself." Mr. Collyer had his hearing aid in, that was it. The little receiver was pinned prominently onto his lapel.

When the Colonel came down a few minutes later, Liam asked him, "What's up with our Mr. Collyer today? He's a veritable fashion plate. Even got some sort of cologne on. Told me it gave him a 'go-ahead' air."

"Love, my young friend. That's love."

"Love? Mr. Collyer?"

"Oh, yes. Aunt Grace is coming in today, arriving on the afternoon ferry. And Mr. Collyer, as it turns out, has got rather a soft spot for my Aunt Grace."

Scarlet had nodded off to sleep before lunch in one of Inverness's overstuffed chairs. Laura got out her sketch pad to make a portrait. She was not quick, and she did erase a good deal, but before long a credible likeness began to emerge. Liam watched over her shoulder, marveling. First she drew the mouth open—it was in fact wide open, snoring. But then, as the portrait neared completion, she went back to close the mouth properly and even added a slight smile.

Was this artistic license, Liam wondered, or just tact? Was it permissible to capture someone's likeness like that, then use that likeness to create an image that never had existed? Was that proper? It was an ethical conundrum.

Compton and Sissy had come up behind them. "Pretty good," Compton whispered.

Soon the rest of the young moderns had assembled to look over Laura's shoulder. She frowned in slight annoyance as Scarlet stirred. Holding one finger to her lips to indicate silence, Laura stood slowly and led the group quietly out toward the porch, leaving Scarlet to snore on alone.

"I didn't know you could draw," Bruno said. "I'm impressed."

"Yes," Liam told him stiffly. "She draws all the time."

"Just something to do in a drawing room." Laura laughed. "I don't so much draw, really, as dabble in drawing." She batted her eyes at Bruno.

Bruno's expression dripped admiration and deep, thick sincerity. "But such talent. And you've got this thick drawing pad, now almost full up. Do show us some of your past efforts, Laura. If they're only half as good as the one of Scarlet, they're worth showing off. Really."

"Well, if you like. I don't mind." She pulled one of the benches away from the rail so she could seat herself on it and the others could arrange themselves behind her. Liam seized the part of the bench by her side for himself. The others dutifully moved around to Laura's back—all except Bruno, who knelt down on one knee at Laura's other side.

"Well, there's this one," Laura said, paging backward. It was a portrait of Mr. Collyer, also asleep. "And this one...," a sketch of Monsignor Leary with his eyes closed. "And this one...," Marjorie asleep on the veranda.

"They're marvelous," Bruno said heavily. "They really are marvelous."

"This was supposed to be Jody, but it didn't really come out."

"Still, though...," Bruno said.

"Show them the old bum in Cambridge," Sissy suggested.

"Oh, yes. That's an interesting one. Laura paged back some more. She found a pencil sketch of an elderly man sprawled on a park bench asleep.

"Now that!" Bruno exclaimed. "That is not just a drawing. That is beginning to be art."

Laura shook her head modestly. "I suppose art is what you think it is."

"Yes," Liam said. "Art is—"

Laura pressed on. "I mean it's in the eye of the beholder, don't you think? Although I might think of it as nothing more than a simple pencil sketch, Bruno sees something more. Who's to say which of us is right? Is that what you were about to say, Liam?"

"Um, more or less."

"Well, I agree with you then. Entirely." She looked up brightly at the others. "Now, people, do you think we're sophisticated enough to look at a few nudes?"

A squeal from Lizzie. "Oh, yes. Do show us your nudes, Laura. Do."

"Well. If you like." She opened the pad enough to slide a thumb in at one of the paper markers placed along the binding. "Now, no snickering. Among the boys, I mean." She looked severely at Liam and at Evan and Compton. "We all need to be terribly grown up about this. Well, here." She opened the book to the selected page and showed them.

A slightly overweight young woman in the buff looked out at them from the page. Bruno grunted appreciatively.

"Why, you certainly have caught her, I must say. I mean, look at this. And the composition."

"Yes," Laura said. She found the next marker. "And this one." This one was a seated nude, slimmer than the first. The face was left undeveloped.

"Oh, Laura," Lizzie said. "You've caught her too."

"And *this* one." The third was of a middle-aged man, wiry and well muscled. He was nude but for a narrow cloth covering his crotch.

"Did you have a course?" Gabriella asked.

"Yes, at Radcliffe. Not really a course, though. I mean, not so much instruction as just drawing. With models, you see. A different model each night. The models were both women *and* men."

"All nude." Lizzie seemed enchanted by the thought.

"But of course. Of course."

"Lovely," Bruno said. He stood. Then, looking down at Laura: "It must be...fulfilling to draw nudes," he said.

"Yes," Laura said simply. "It is."

"For someone of talent, it must be the ultimate drawing experience."

"It is. The ultimate."

"Too bad the opportunity to draw in the nude comes so seldom."

"It is too bad."

"Only in the classroom, only behind its closed doors. There must never be enough chance to draw nudes."

"Never." Laura sighed. "I think I could draw nudes forever."

Bruno looked off over the water, his eyes unfocused. "So what is the young artist to do to exercise this god-given talent she has—the ability to draw the human body in all its glory—when people insist on keeping their bodies covered up and out of her sight?"

"Um..." Laura looked slightly uncomfortable.

"Well, here's a thought," Bruno said, as if he were suddenly struck. "If she were herself not only talented but extremely lovely..."

Laura closed the pad and looked down at it.

"She might be inclined to—at least one might suspect this—to—"

"Bruno!" Liam said.

"Well, why not? In the privacy of the girls' dorm, with all the shades drawn, the door locked, just herself alone...and a mirror."

"Really!" Liam objected.

Bruno ignored him, his eyes boring into Laura. "She might be the model herself." He paused significantly. "And such a model. How could one resist the opportunity to draw such a lovely nude model? There would not even be a modeling fee to pay. It would be quite free. A lovely nude model, whenever the need arose."

"Well, what of it?" Laura said. But her voice broke slightly at the end.

"Is that what you do, Laura?"

"Well, what of it?" Laura said again, almost inaudibly.

"And perhaps in this very sketch pad, there may even be a few of these very special nudes..."

Liam stood up. "Now, that is just enough."

Gabriella put one hand on Liam's arm, restraining him. "She's a big girl, Liam. She can take care of herself."

Laura seemed to take courage from that. "Yes," she said. "I do. Why not? I do whenever I want."

"And in this pad...?"

Laura looked down again at the pad in her lap somewhat glumly. "Yes, if you must know."

Bruno, wickedly: "Any that we could see?"

"I—"

"I mean, we're being terribly sophisticated here, aren't

we? As you keep telling us. Nothing to be shy about with the human body. Is there even one, Laura, that you might be willing to show?"

Laura bit her lip. "To all of you?" Her voice broke again on the word "all."

"Would you let me see one, Laura?"

Laura fiddled with the edge of the pad. Then, after a moment, she opened it a crack at the corner and thumbed through several pages. She hunched over slightly to confirm the page without the others seeing.

"There!" she said, opening the pad, turning it, and thrusting it into Bruno's hands all in one motion. "There, that one."

Bruno looked down at the image appreciatively, shaking his head in wonder. Then he closed his eyes, remaining motionless for a long moment. Before opening his eyes again, he shut the pad with reverence.

"My friends," he said at last, handing the pad back to Laura. "We have among us one who is not only extremely talented . . . but exquisitely, exquisitely lovely."

Liam tagged along with the party that set out to meet Aunt Grace's ferry. They were Mr. Collyer, the Colonel and Marjorie, Sissy, Jody, and Compton.

"Quite a woman, my Aunt Grace," the Colonel told Liam. "If you like that sort, I mean. Not an easy woman to be with, mind you. But still—"

"I'm sure I'll like her."

"Of course. Of course." Colonel Forsythe walked on awhile. "Though no one has, that I can think of."

Marjorie felt that some explanation was required. "It's just that Grace has been afflicted all her life—"

"I am sorry to hear that," Liam said, thinking of psoriasis or gout.

"...with a great deal of money."

"Oh."

"And it has affected her outlook."

"Oh."

"Never had any children, either," the Colonel added. "Children are more than a match for that problem."

"Outlook?"

"No, money."

The ferry was quite close by the time they arrived at the dock. Marjorie lined them up next to the ramp. She pushed a wayward lock back from her husband's forehead. "Andrew, you look lovely, as usual." She brushed the front of his blazer. "And Sissy...no rouge. How prescient, dear. Oh, my, Jody, those fingernails."

"Sorry, Mummy."

"Best keep your hands behind your back, darling." Marjorie took out her handkerchief and wet it on her tongue. She scrubbed a moment at the corner of Jody's mouth. "Oreo cookies?"

"Oops."

Compton was next. Marjorie looked down at his shoes. "Mmm, Compton." He rubbed them against the backs of his trouser legs. "That's better."

"Liam, always impeccable." She tugged the back of Liam's collar into place over his tie. "Now, I think we're all ready." Marjorie took her place beside the Colonel. The passengers were already beginning to come down the ramp. "Won't it be nice to see Grace again?"

There was no doubt which one would turn out to be Aunt Grace. She was a stout woman in black with walking stick and scowl.

"Hello, Grace." Mr. Collyer stepped up to her, beaming. He reached out to embrace her, but instead she took his hand.

"Langley." She looked him over. "Not too much decline, then?"

"No, Grace. Bearing up. I—" Grace had moved on to the Colonel.

"Andrew." She reached up to reshape the knot of his tie. "Any success keeping that roof together?"

"Um, some success. But for a few places."

"Keep after it. Water is man's great enemy. Water that leaks in through the roof, that is."

"Yes, Aunt Grace."

"Good day, Marjorie. Nice to see you." She looked down at Marjorie's stomach without comment. Marjorie drew her breath in slightly.

"Welcome to Dark Harbor, Grace. We—"

"Yes." She raised a hand until Marjorie went silent, then moved on.

"Sissy." She leaned forward into Sissy's face to look closely. Finding nothing to fault there, she moved back a step, appraising. "Shoulders back."

Sissy squared her shoulders. "Nice to have you again, Aunt Grace."

"Mm." She stepped along. "Jody." Aunt Grace held out her hand as if to shake hands. Jody automatically offered hers. Grace looked down at the nails and rolled her eyes.

"Welcome, Aunt Grace," Jody said weakly.

"Welcome to Dark Harbor, Aunt Grace," Compton said.

"Compton."

"Looking forward to one of our chats, Aunt."

"And who is this young fellow?" She indicated Liam with her nose.

"That's Liam Dwyer, Aunt Grace. Liam, this is Mrs. Grace Hollerith."

"Yes. Welcome, Mrs.—" Liam began. His hand was left dangling.

Grace was staring fixedly at him. Liam tried to smile. She was staring at his face. After a moment she turned to Compton. "Good teeth," she said. "It is impossible to over-emphasize the importance of good teeth in the young."

She looked back at the Colonel. "You'll see to the bags, Andrew?"

"Oh, yes, Aunt. We've had Mr. Jervis bring the launch along." He gestured down to the gas dock, where Arthur Jervis was standing beside the *Nellie B.* Mr. Jervis tipped his hat up toward Aunt Grace.

"Pff," she said. Then, turning toward Mr. Collyer. "Come along, then, Langley. You could use a good, brisk walk, I think."

"Yes, Grace." Langley hurried up to take her arm.

"We'll have you huffing and puffing in two minutes," she said grimly. "Come along." She half led, half dragged Mr. Collyer up the road, leaving the family still standing in line.

"What a terrifying woman," Liam said.

Remarkably, the others were looking rather cheerful. No one had yet moved to start back toward Dark Harbor House.

"Aunt Grace's visits can be daunting," Jody said, "but there are offsetting advantages. At least, sometimes there are."

"Indeed there are," the Colonel said, smiling. "Some-times."

"And she stays only a few weeks," Compton added.

They were staring expectantly toward the ramp, where the dock men were beginning to carry down luggage. One of the men came up to the Forsythes.

"Luggage for Dark Harbor House, Colonel." He had two carpet bags.

"Oh, yes, Mr. Abbott. Thank you. Mr. Jervis will take it." He gestured down toward the *Nellie B.* "Was there more, by the way?"

"Not that I saw, Colonel."

"Oh, dear." The Colonel turned back worriedly.

Jody was at Liam's side. "Sometimes, inexplicably, the 'offsetting advantages' are left behind. And that is too bad."

"Um, just what are the 'offsetting'—"

"Now this could be promising." Colonel Forsythe was pointing toward a heavy case coming down. "Is that one for Dark Harbor House, Mr. Gates?"

"It is, Colonel. Some kind of refrigerator box, I'd say."

"Excellent. Down to the *Nellie B.*, then." Everyone looked relieved.

"And these too, Colonel." Another dock man approached with a pile of various-sized boxes on a dolly.

"Oh, yes. Good. Set them all down on the dock by Mr. Jervis."

There was a high-voiced call from up the ramp. "Oooay, Zhoa-deeee!" Liam looked up to see a short, portly man in a striped suit. He had on an old-fashioned boater. He called again, waving and pointing at Jody: "Zhoa-deee." He took off the boater and waved that too.

"He's here!" Jody gushed. "*Ici*, Monsieur, *ici!*" She ran up to the round little man and hugged him. He lifted her off her feet. The others crowded up to him.

When all the hugs and backslapping were done, Jody pulled the fellow down the ramp to present him to Liam. "This is our good friend Liam Dwyer. Liam, I want you to meet Monsieur Cartefigue, from Nice."

He took Liam's hand, still keeping his left arm around Jody. A wide smile. "Monsieur," he said through the smile.

"Monsieur. A pleasure."

M. Cartefigue had a waxed mustache that extended beyond the sides of his well-rounded face. He was quite pink. Now he lifted both arms dramatically to take in the surroundings. "Hello, Dark Harbor," he said, his accent thick and French. "Hello again." The Forsythes clapped enthusi-astically.

On the walk back toward Dark Harbor House, Liam caught up to the Colonel. "I take it Monsieur Cartefigue is the 'offsetting advantage.'"

"Aunt Grace's cook," Colonel Forsythe filled him in. "Some years she leaves him behind—out of pique, I believe. But when he does come, he takes over the kitchen. We give the Jervises a bit of well-deserved vacation. And then," the Colonel looked heavenward, "then we have a bit less chow-der and a bit less fried chop, and a bit more *saumon en croute* with *sauce béarnaise.*"

"And bouillabaisse," Marjorie said, "and what a bouill-abaisse."

"And *gigot au feneuille,*" Sissy added, rolling her eyes happily.

"And a *granité au chocolat,*" the Colonel put in, "that re-ally does have to be experienced, my young friend, before one can be said to have lived at all."

19

The Beastie

A mong the treasures left behind from Norbert's time was a mysterious wooden and brass apparatus sealed inside a glass display case. The case had been on exhibit just inside the entrance of East House for as long as any of the Forsythes could remember. Most guests of Dark Harbor House traipsed past it at least twice a week, once on the way in and again on the way out after the movies. There was a polished brass plate under the case that read:

"Theatrical Engine"
1912
Norbert Chance, Inventor
Ephram Whittier, Engineer
Construction Work: Evander N. Hopkins

"It is, quite simply, an abstraction," Laura told them. "It represents theater just as the dramatic masks do, the tragic and comic ones."

"Still, it does look as though it might almost be ready to roll onto the stage on its little wheels. Maybe take a bow and begin declaiming." Liam was peering under the framework, looking for clues.

"Well, the wheels are symbols, Liam." Laura spoke with great authority. "They stand for motion, just as the hornlike thing on the side stands for noise, or maybe music. It is all quite symbolic. You can't have a thing representing theater if it doesn't look as though it's prepared to act. But that doesn't mean it really can do anything. Beyond just sitting there, I mean."

"Mmmm." The Colonel was noncommittal. "There is that winder-upper-like thing on the back. You could imagine it being cranked up like a mechanical toy with some kind of a giant key. I don't doubt there's a spring inside that might give it power."

"The spring would be a symbol of tension," Laura observed. "Dramatic tension."

Gabriella shook her head. "You wouldn't call it an engine, though, would you Laura, if it just sat there? You'd be more inclined to call it theater, or drama, if you really intended it as static allegory. I think it's got some kind of dynamic potential."

"Do you suppose it could put on a show?" Jody asked.

"Something like that."

"The glass case I can understand," Liam said. "It's probably just to keep the dust off. But what is the significance of the scale the thing sits on?"

"I never figured that out either." Colonel Forsythe reached over to balance the scale. "And quite a precise scale too. Here we see that the theatrical engine and its case together weigh some...four hundred twelve pounds, three and a half ounces. But so what?"

"The scale could represent the weightier side of drama," Laura suggested. "That would be the tragic. Or, as well, the lighter side, the comic. It all works perfectly as a symbol."

"I can't see how its weight would ever change," the Monsignor observed. "So what need would it have for a scale? It's not as though the thing expected to lose weight."

Scarlet hadn't said anything yet. "Maybe it expects to gain," she offered.

"Like the rest of us." Angela patted her tummy.

"Maybe it expects to gain," Scarlet said again.

The Colonel looked at her curiously. "Why would it gain weight, Scarlet?"

"If it leaked."

"What would it leak?"

"Gas."

"Ah. A lighter-than-air gas. Yes, that would explain gaining weight. Or, if it leaked a heavier-than-air gas, I suppose, it would lose weight. But what would the gas be there for?"

"That's easy enough," Liam suggested. "The case might be filled with a protective gas of some sort."

"One of the noble gasses." Monsignor Leary nodded ponderously. "Neon, helium, argon, krypton, xenon—they are all quite inert. A mechanism sealed in with neon, for example, would be preserved perfectly. It could neither rust nor mold nor decay. Even its lubricant would be kept fresh. It is one of the wonders of science."

"But again," Gabriella said, "why the scale?"

Liam tapped on the case. "Well, to tell us when to put in more neon, perhaps."

"Of course, Liam. That must be it," the Colonel exclaimed. "To warn us that the case is leaking."

"That's what I said," Scarlet reminded them.

"And quite right you were, my dear. Quite right."

"No use protecting the mechanism of an abstraction, though," Gabriella pointed out. "I'll bet the theatrical engine does do something."

"Evander Senior was my father," Mr. Hopkins told them after the film. "Tim's grandfather. And it was he who built the engine, or the 'Beastie,' as he called it. I can remember him saying it would put on the very hell of a show. Excuse me, ladies."

"But what on earth kind of a show?" the Colonel asked.

"Damned if I know. Excuse me. I asked him, when he was working on it, if the Beastie could juggle. I thought of juggling, then, as the ultimate form of theater. This was before the film, or at least before talkies. I was just a boy. 'No, Andy,' he said, 'twon't juggle as it stands now, but perhaps it ought to.'"

"So it was to perform an act, then?"

"I guess. I never saw it do anything."

"And your father built the Beastie?" Liam asked him.

"More than that. He collaborated with Mr. Whittier at the beginning on how the mechanisms would work. Mr. Chance, of course, was the inventor, as the plate says. He decided what the engine had to do. Then Ephram and Father worked out the details, the how-to's. They were joint designers, you could say. Only Ephram Whittier was gone from here before 1912, and it was my dad who finished the project."

Jody thought there might be some mention of the engine in Norbert's diaries. She pulled down the volumes for 1900 through 1912 later in the evening and piled them on the reading table in Biscay. She enlisted Liam and Gabriella to help.

"We know that Ephram was still here in 1903, as that was the time of the wager," Jody told them. "I propose we divide up the years and just look for mention of the theatrical engine; it should go quickly. Gabriella, if you could look into 1912 and 1911, that's when the work would be nearing completion. There's sure to be some mention there. I'll take 1906 through 1910, which are relatively short diaries, since Norbert was here only during the summer months. The project was almost certainly started in 1903 or 1904. See what you can find in those years, Liam."

They set to work at Jody's direction. The sounds around the table were mostly the noises of pages turning, plus an occasional giggle from Liam. "It was like a house party," he told them. "Like a big, silly, extended party." The others were strangely quiet, he thought.

There were sporadic references to "work on S.D.M. Engine with Whittier and Hopkins," or "S.D.M. progress," or "testing Beastie," through 1904 and 1905. The middle years produced nothing. And there was no indication at all of when the project came to completion. Both Jody and Gabriella came up blank in the diaries for their years. Liam started back into 1903. There he found a page made up into a kind of post bill, with an ornate, hand-drawn border. The lettering was done in block capitals.

ANNOUNCING . . .
THE GREAT THEATRICAL ENGINE!
(S.D.M.)
APPEARING SOON AT A THEATER NEAR YOU
SORRY FOLKS, ONE SHOW ONLY

The stage at East House was brightly lit with a spotlight picking out Colonel Forsythe in the center. Jody played a trumpet fanfare to quiet the crowd. When she was done, Mr. Collyer hit the Chinese gong.

"Ahem," the Colonel began as the gong hummed into silence. "Ahem. Yes. Welcome, ladies and gentlemen. Welcome." He held up his hands for quiet. "Thank you. Thank you. Welcome to another East House extravaganza. Tonight we have, for your amazement and amusement, something entirely out of the ordinary. Tonight is to be a theatrical happening presented entirely by a . . . machine!"

Another fanfare on the trumpet. Cheerful applause.

East House was full. Most of the regular cinema crowd was there plus a number of strangers. There was even a reporter from the *Camden Herald*.

"This evening you are going to experience something never experienced before. We think. Or perhaps we are about to experience a nonexperience. Who knows? There is a certain tension in the unknown. What could be more theatrical?"

Liam and Compton were rolling the engine out from the wings. It moved easily on its wheels, but each rotation caused a ratchet to click inside. Compton thought it meant that a mechanism on the inside was connected to the wheels and might even be able to move the engine around under its own power. Even if it did move, though, they thought it might not have much idea where to go. Accordingly, they placed the Beastie in the exact middle of the stage, facing toward the audience. That way it would have the most room to maneuver in all directions.

The Colonel waited for them to step away. Then he swept an arm toward the Beastie. "Ladies and gentlemen, the fabulous Chance-Whittier-Hopkins theatrical engine." More applause.

Colonel Forsythe waited again for silence. "Well. This is one of those glad occasions of local boy makes good. The local boy in this case is the theatrical engine, what Mr. Hopkins calls the Beastie. Many of you have known the engine all your lives. It has been a constant of life in Dark Harbor. Who has not walked past its case and wondered, Now, what on earth is that thing supposed to do? Well, tonight we're going to find out. This is the Beastie's big night, its theatrical debut.

"Let me tell you what we know about the theatrical engine, and some things we don't know. We know it was the brainchild of Mr. Norbert Chance, Esquire, and that he had some important help building it. The principal builder was the scion of Dark Harbor's own Hopkins family"—cheers and applause—"yes, the Hopkinses of Pitcher Point. Mr. and Mrs. Evander Hopkins, Jr., and son, Tim, down here in front." More applause. "Thank you. Thank you.

"As a result of extensive research at the National Institute of Institutionalization, also known as the Biscay library at Dark Harbor House, we have managed to unearth the original plan for the engine. That is, my daughter, Jody, managed to find the plan. And we have it here to show you. Sissy, if you please."

Sissy passed the end of a long, rolled blueprint up to the Colonel on the stage. Then she walked along the front of the stage, unrolling the blueprint as she went. When it was entirely unrolled, she handed the far end up to Compton. The blueprint was thus displayed in its full length between Compton and the Colonel.

"The plan is a work of art in itself," Colonel Forsythe told them. "I think we might take a few moments for people to file up and look closely at the draftsmanship. If we could just begin with the front row . . . yes, and then row two and so forth. That's it. Just come along up and have a look.

"The plan was originally drawn by a Mr. Ephram Whittier. Mr. Whittier is no longer with us, but he was, at the time, a noted builder and boatsman. He ran a line of traps out on this side of Six Hundred Acre Island, where Mr. Gates and his son have their traps today. In fact, some of their traps, Mr. Gates told me this evening, were built by Ephram. And he says they are very beautiful traps indeed. Mr. Gates has offered to bring one of them up here to East House and leave it for a while to show off Ephram's skills. But I doubt that Ephram did anything more skilled, more

217

wonderful than this drawing. Note the fine detail work of the mechanisms. And note too the very wonderful printing. A work of art."

When everyone who wanted to had looked at the blueprint, Compton and Liam rolled it up again.

The Colonel turned back to the audience. "Now, having said all that about Mr. Whittier, we also need to note that the Beastie you see before you is not exactly what Mr. Whittier called for in his plan. I mention this because it is clear that Evander Hopkins Senior has also taken part in the shaping of the engine. I mean, he didn't just build it as designed, but he made some improvements of his own. The workmanship on the Beastie is also wonderful to behold. Look, for example, at the mechanical hands. Liam, if you would, please."

Liam pulled open a door on the Beastie's side. Very gently, he extracted a mechanical arm with an oversized wood and metal hand on its end. The fingers were mahogany cylinders, hinged together with brass. The audience oooed.

"Construction, design, and concept: each was wonderful in its way," continued the Colonel. "I say that so that the full credit for this remarkable invention will go to all three of its creators: Messrs. Chance, Whittier, and Hopkins." Liam put the hand back in place and closed its door.

Jody handed the Colonel a water glass and he paused for a drink. "Now, on to what we don't know about the engine," he said. "We don't know what it does, if anything. If it turns out to do nothing at all, we have got a rather wonderful dessert planned for everyone, another of Monsieur Cartefigue's creations, his famous *bombe alaskienne*." He indicated Mr. Cartefigue in the audience. Applause. "The dessert will be a high point of the evening, whether the engine performs or not. The question for now is whether Cartefigue's dessert will be the evening's *only* high point." Nervous laughter.

"So, we don't know what the Beastie does, we don't know how long it takes to do it, and we don't know if it will even work. After all, it has been in storage for nearly four decades. Finally, we don't know why the engine is often referred to as S.D.M., as you saw written across the top of the plan."

The Colonel looked back at Liam to be sure all was in readiness. "Well, on with the show. There's a switch on top of the engine, and I propose that we now throw it into the on position and see what happens. We have asked Mr. Bruno Nougat, a guest at Dark Harbor House, to provide musical accompaniment. Bruno..." An expert run up and down the keyboard from Bruno. "Thank you, Bruno. Curtain... No, actually the curtain is open already. Well, then, Liam, switch it on." The Colonel stepped hurriedly down from the stage to take his place in the front row next to Marjorie. "Ladies and gentlemen, the S.D.M."

Bruno played a tentative opening and nodded to Liam. Liam pushed the lever on top of the engine to its opposite extreme. Then he retreated to watch from the wings.

The engine shuddered a moment. A hand emerged slowly from the side panel and reached up to the top of the frame. It went straight to the switch, flipped it off, then retreated to its paneled opening, pulling the door closed behind it. Nothing more. Bruno's accompaniment trailed off. The audience was silent.

"Is that it?" Aunt Grace asked.

"Um...," Colonel Forsythe said.

More silence.

"I think it's a joke," Gabriella offered. "I think we were supposed to laugh." The audience dutifully laughed.

"Um...," the Colonel said again.

Scarlet spoke up from the second row. "Just Act One," she suggested.

The Colonel brightened. "Of course. Thank you, Scarlet.

That was Act One, ladies and gentlemen. Evidently just the warm-up act. Liam, the switch again, I think. Presenting S.D.M., Act Two. Bruno..."

Again the piano roll. Liam threw the switch a second time.

Very slowly, the engine rolled down to the edge of the stage and stopped. With a creak, part of its upper structure opened and a cylindrical projection screwed itself up to form a head. It even had a pair of button eyes.

"Go, Engine!" Evan called out from the back.

A crack appeared in the Beastie's midsection as the upper half of the structure wound itself up an inch above its lower parts to form an articulated torso. Both hands were out now. The engine placed one hand over its midsection and the other at its back, then performed a stiff bow. Bruno played some appropriate bowing music. Cheers and loud applause.

The machine reached inside one of its panels and came out with a hammer, which it showed to the audience. Then it began hammering at its own front panel.

"Ouch," Marjorie said.

The second hand emerged with a kind of crowbar, which it now began to use on the underpart of the panel, wrenching as the other hand hammered. Within a minute it had the wooden panel reduced to pieces, which it shoved under its lower frame. The wide band spring was now clearly visible inside, along with a clockwork mechanism of moving gears.

Now the hammer began pounding on the head, quickly breaking the button eyes as well as the brittle Bakelite frame that held the head together.

Jody winced. "This is awful!" she said. "The poor thing!"

The Beastie put down its tools and used both hands to wrench off the head. It pushed the ruined pieces under its frame with the wood shards from its front. Then it took out a black metal blow torch from its interior and made it light up. There was an acrid smell of burning.

"Oh, dear," said the Colonel. "I don't like this!"

The engine played the torch on the pile of rubble under itself. The wood and fabric pieces burst quickly into flame. The opposite hand suddenly emerged with what looked like an enormous red firecracker.

"Oh, my," Marjorie breathed. "You don't suppose, do you, that S.D.M. stands for—"

"Self-destroying machine," the Colonel finished for her. He was on his feet. "Ladies and gentlemen, don't hurry now, but I do think we should begin to move quietly toward the exits. No one panic. That's it. We have plenty of time, I think." He looked over his shoulder, where the machine was just lighting the fuse. He was glad to see that it was a longish fuse and that it wasn't burning too quickly. "Move along there. That's it. Plenty of time, but do move along."

The group reassembled on the lawn in front of East House. Colonel Forsythe was the last one down. "Everyone accounted for, I think. There was no one left inside." He turned with the others to look at the end of East House, where a thin trail of smoke was coming up from under the eaves. After a moment there was a flash and a heavy, dull thud. The sound of glass breaking somewhere. Then silence.

"Well," Marjorie said.

"Well, indeed," her husband agreed. He turned back toward East House. "Ladies and gentlemen," he said. "The management of East House is pleased to have presented, the one and only performance of . . . the theatrical engine." He began clapping slowly. The rest of the audience joined in.

20

Polka Dots

"What is essential here," Liam was explaining, "is not just the great subtlety of flavors, but rather the way they interact to form a harmonious whole." He shoveled another large portion of Cartefigue's *ragoût provençal* onto his plate. "Yes, I think the analogy of music works well in this case: almost, I might say, that of the symphony. We have the heavy brasses present in the *lapin,* and the woodwinds suggested by the chicken, an altogether lighter theme, don't you see? Then a rhythmic counterpoint is provided by the combination of tomato, onion, and fines herbes, set off, as they are, against the woody notes of thyme and rosemary." He paused to chew thoughtfully. He had stopped by the kitchen that morning to chat with M. Cartefigue and to jot down the names of the ingredients, just to be sure. "And then, finally, there is the surprise element—always a surprise somewhere in a symphony, you know—provided by the capers and the little *cornichons.* They give us—oh, I don't know—perhaps a touch of humor. Yes, humor. Don't you think, Monsignor?"

"Peeree goob," the Monsignor said through his mouthful.

"That is how I view the *cornichons,* in this case," Liam went on. "There to provide an element of humor to the symphony."

"Not to mention flavor," the Colonel put in.

"That's what I was saying. A symphony of flavor."

"Oh, quite, quite," Colonel Forsythe agreed.

The ragout was settling into Liam's stomach on top of a generous layer of pâté made of dilled shrimp mousse in a puff pastry crust, another little symphony of its own, or perhaps a sonata. Liam had had two helpings. He and the Monsignor were somewhat behind due to extra servings. The rest of the table was already pressing on toward dessert, a caramel gâteau, except for Marjorie, who had arrived late, back on the noon ferry from shopping in Camden.

By the time Liam was finishing his gâteau—he had been tempted to pass entirely on dessert but didn't want to appear rude—Marjorie was just beginning hers. "Don't wait for me, people," she told the company. "I am so slow. Don't miss this lovely afternoon." She waved them off.

There was a general commotion of chairs being pushed back, and talk of swims and strolls along the beach. Bruno had his guitar out and was strumming and playing difficult, entirely unnecessary little runs on it. Liam stayed behind to keep his hostess company. Just to be mannerly, he took on an additional small slice of gâteau.

"Now this too," he observed, "has a certain musical character. Sensed on the palate rather than heard."

When there was finally nothing at all left to eat, he accompanied Marjorie out of the dining room. With so much lunch under his belt, Liam was thinking of a nap. But Lizzie was waiting for him in front of the fireplace in Inverness. She was all done up in lederhosen and leather hat.

"Another great birding day, Liam! I've got the scope and our logbook. Off in pursuit of the crested grebe."

"Grebe," Liam repeated dully.

"What a day." She had zinc oxide smeared over her nose.

"Actually, I was thinking of settling in with a book."

"Nonsense," Lizzie told him. "Nonsense. Can't think of spending such a day as this indoors. What would our mothers say? Right, Marjorie?"

Marjorie nodded in agreement. "I think I can speak for mothers on that score. Any mother worth her salt would have you outdoors on such a day."

"Won't you come along, Marjorie?"

"Thank you, Lizzie. But not today. I thought I might just take the littlest nap. But do have a lovely time."

Lizzie handed the birding scope to Liam. "Well, we're off. I expect great things of us, Liam. A dozen new spottings or more. The sky's the limit."

"Rose-breasted grosbeak!" Lizzie cried in triumph. She had her eye glued to the scope. "Write it down, Liam. Write it down. Oh, we're hot today."

"Right. Grosbeak. Hot. Got it." He tried not to yawn.

"Isn't this just heaven? I mean, look at us. Out and about in clean, clear air, communing with nature, after a good tromp over hill and dale." She gave him a manly clap across the shoulders. "Hidden away here on our little elevation, and master of all we survey. I mean, really!"

"Really."

She was back to her scope, twisting it around to focus on an edge of woods by Ames Pond, down beneath them. "Let's see, let's see."

Liam leaned back and closed his eyes.

"Now here's something we haven't seen before."

"Oh, rapture."

"At least something I've never seen. How interesting."

"Colors?" he asked sleepily.

"Um . . . well, black and white . . . polka dots."

"Probably a wood thrush again." As if anybody cared. How would the world somehow be worse off if wood thrushes got to go about their business unobserved? He looked around for something to cushion his head.

"Not a wood thrush."

"Hmm." He put the logbook under his head. There. Not too bad.

"Not black polka dots on white, but white on black."

"Mm. Interesting."

"You might want to have a look." She pulled him up. "I've got it set."

"Oh. Right." He applied his eye to the eyepiece.

"You see the guitar?"

"Guitar?" There was indeed a guitar in the center of the magnified field. It was leaning against a bit of stone wall in full sun. Just visible next to the guitar was a bare foot.

"Just slide a little right from the guitar, and you'll see."

Liam moved the scope slightly to the right. "Oh!" He felt the need to look away quickly. But fascination kept him frozen in place. "Oh, my."

"Oh, my, indeed," Lizzie said. She lowered herself heavily onto the rock where Liam had been sitting.

"Bruno." Bruno, damn his eyes.

"Definitely Bruno."

Liam stared in disgust at the bare buttocks, moving rhythmically in the scope. And the black hirsute covering of the shoulders. All that was visible of the second participant, underneath, was one long, bare leg. Just beside her ankle was a frilly undergarment, black with white polka dots.

Liam looked up from the scope. "Do you suppose that's Louise?" he asked. Louise was the only unattached female he could think of beside Lizzie.

"Laura, I'm afraid."

Liam sputtered, "Of course it's not Laura!"

"Sorry."

"I don't see how you could even suggest...I mean, all you can really make out is her—"

"Panties. They're Laura's. I know because I saw them in Cleopatra."

"Oh, really."

"I mean, in her wash, you know. Not when she was—"

"Please."

"I showed her mine, as well. Mine are just regular white, though."

"Please. Spare me the details."

"She was quite proud of the polka-dotted ones. Said she got them at Bergdorf's. Paid five dollars a pair for them."

Liam sat down numbly.

Lizzie was shaking her head. "I was thinking at the time that this is what passes for sex in our repressed age. A couple of girls showing each other their undies in the wash. That would be the entire erotic content of our summer. Just that." She paused thoughtfully. "Turns out I was wrong on that score."

Liam was feeling shattered. His whole belief system was based on, he now realized, a childish faith that things like this just couldn't happen. His sense of propriety, his ethics, his entire notion of right and wrong were all in a jumble. Not to mention his feel for reasonable pricing. "Did you really say five dollars a pair?"

"Five dollars. She was quite definite about that."

"My god."

"Five dollars a pair. And when I say 'pair,' I mean just the one—"

"I know that!"

"Sorry."

They sat in subdued silence, each thinking private thoughts.

Finally Lizzie spoke. "You know, Liam, I'm twenty-one this summer."

"Oh."

"I made a kind of vow to myself. I decided that this summer would be the occasion of . . . well, of a kind of passage."

"Passage."

She stared at him earnestly. "Passage. Becoming a woman, I mean. I decided . . . don't you see?" She put a hand on his arm.

How could Laura have done this to him?

"Do you get my drift at all, Liam?"

"Drift?"

"In order to complete this passage, I need a bit of help."

"Help."

"A fellow. I've been thinking of just who that fellow ought to be. The one to receive my favor, I mean."

"Favor."

"And I thought of you," she pressed on.

"Me?"

"You seem very clean."

"'Clean?!'"

"Yes, well, one can't be too careful."

"Really, Lizzie, I hardly think—"

"Well, now just suppose, just suppose that you were inclined to take part in this passage."

"I—"

"To share it with a certain young lady who happens to be staying in the room called Lamorak, by the way. She could just leave the window open tonight with a little ribbon on the latch so you could see which one it was. And you would know that I—that is she—would be welcoming should you happen to be passing by along the roof walk . . ." She looked back down at her lap, suddenly shy. "Just think about it, Liam."

There was, it went without saying, no acceptable course of action now but to depart Dark Harbor House. Liam had his honor to consider, after all. He would pack his bags that evening and be off on the noon ferry tomorrow. That's what he would do.

Not to leave now was unthinkable. He was prepared to destroy his holiday and ruin the rest of his summer just to establish, for one and all to understand, that there were certain standards he held absolute. When those standards were sullied, demeaned—well, the others might put up with it, but Liam Dwyer would not. He would withdraw. He would vanish manfully without ever even saying why. Of course, they would all know. Laura would know. She would understand. If you want to maintain the respect of a Liam Dwyer, you don't pass off your favors lightly to a cad like Bruno Nougat.

The noon ferry, then. What other option did he have, really? Well, one possible alternative came to mind: he could catch the three o'clock and not miss tomorrow's lunch. Who could say what wonders Cartefigue might produce for another lunch? A few extra hours at Dark Harbor House would hardly spoil the effect of Liam's departure.

Yes, that might be an even better plan. A too precipitous departure, he now realized, might risk offending his hosts.

On his way up to dress for dinner, he encountered the one person he least wanted to see.

"Liam, old man."

"Bruno." He hoped his voice was properly chilly.

"Thought we might have a talk."

"Really, I was just headed—"

"Step right in here, why don't we? A nice private talk." He put an arm around Liam's shoulders to guide him into the little Coventry sitting room. Bruno pulled the glass doors shut behind them.

"I'll get right to the point. I was hoping for a bit of a loan."

"Not bloody likely."

"To see me off tomorrow. Just got word that there's a casting call for one of those little off-Broadway numbers down in New York. Appears there may be a part in it for me. I thought I'd give it a fling. Sad thing is, though, I'm a bit short for the train fare. I thought ten dollars—"

"You do have your nerve."

"Yes. Well, let's call a spade a spade here. You wouldn't be too inconvenienced, would you, if I pushed on? Just between us? And for the paltry sum of ten dollars..."

Liam was outraged. "I would not even consider..."

Bruno held up his hands, placating. "No, of course not. Matter of principle and all that."

"I should think so."

Bruno smiled slightly. "You're at Cornell, aren't you, Liam?"

"Right."

"Studying fine arts, wasn't that it?"

"Fine arts, yes."

"Funny, I heard a somewhat different story, though, about a Liam Dwyer at Cornell. Possibly another Liam Dwyer. Man I know at Cornell says there is a Liam Dwyer there, but not in the college of arts."

Liam stared at him.

"No, this Liam Dwyer is in the Ag school. In the state school of agriculture and animal husbandry."

"It's all the same school."

"Well, they are close to each other, I'll grant you that. But the one is a university, don't you see, while the other is a kind of trade school."

"Hardly a trade school!"

"Free tuition, cows and mucking out, and that sort of thing. Not exactly the Cornell that one thinks of. What do you study there, Liam? Home Ec.?"

"Veterinary medicine," Liam said, choking. "With a minor in fine arts."

230

"Ah. Veterinary medicine. How admirable. Admirable. My friend at Cornell had another little tidbit about this Liam Dwyer that might amuse you. Told me the fellow's name wasn't Liam at all."

"Wha—"

"At least, not when he first arrived. No, when he first got to campus, it appears his name was . . . Chuck. Chuck Dwyer." Bruno smiled nastily.

"Charles Liam Dwyer, if you must know."

"Chuck. I like that. Well, Chuck, I get the feeling that you and I are a bit of the old oil and water. Don't you agree? We'd really both be ever so much better off each going his own way. I could be gone first thing tomorrow morning without ever getting a chance to share these oh-so-amusing discoveries with the others. Beginning to catch my meaning?"

Liam took out his wallet. Inside was a five-dollar bill. "Five is all I've got." He held it out to Bruno.

"Thank you, Liam. I'll just hold onto this while you go get the other five. I trust you implicitly, by the way. I saw Mr. Tyndall earlier in the pantry. He will be able to open the safe for you. I'll wait for you right here."

21

The Spectator

He was a horrid, horrid man." Aunt Grace glared around the table that evening, daring to be contradicted. "Simply horrid."

"Our Norbert? Horrid? I wouldn't have said that," Jody protested. "Sad, maybe. He seems to have been left out of so much. No family, no children, no love that we know of, and no work to do, at least not after he became so rich. That does seem sad."

Marjorie agreed. "Life was something that happened around Norbert; he didn't really participate in it very much. I have always thought of him as rather a spectator."

"Spectator!" Aunt Grace choked on the word.

"Yes. He was one of life's spectators. And that is sad, as Jody says."

Aunt Grace was still sputtering. She turned to the Colonel. "When your father bought Dark Harbor House in the autumn of 1914, I came here with him to take possession. Your Norbert Chance had just died the winter before. I am still shocked at what we found that fall. Shocked. It was the state of the house."

"Ah, yes." The Colonel nodded knowingly. "It's always been a bit of a faller-downer."

"Not at all. In impeccable repair it was. The falling down has all happened on your watch." She leveled a long white finger at him.

"Too true, too true," Colonel Forsythe allowed. "But you said the state of the house—"

"What we found upstairs. There were hidden passages. For spying."

"Passages? I never noticed any passages."

"We had them blocked in. I insisted. Your father had the work done that winter. Filled in all the damnable things."

"But where did they go, these passages?"

"From Norbert's dressing room in Charlemagne through the walls into the east wing, ending up in Cleopatra."

"Cleopatra?" The Colonel looked perplexed.

"Oh, my," Jody said. "Norbert was watching the Angels in their bath!"

"He was," Aunt Grace confirmed. "Through a viewing port, a tiny slit in the wall where the linen closet is today."

There was an uncomfortable silence around the dinner table.

"It does explain one thing, though, that has always puzzled me," Jody told them. "Norbert used to write a cryptic little code in the margins of his diary. Usually something like 'Cleo: 3h 20m.' There is such an entry almost every day during some summers."

"Hours?" Marjorie raised her eyebrows. "He actually watched for hours?"

"Two or three or four hours. One day he wrote: 'Cleo: all afternoon and evening.'"

Compton was shaking his head. "What on earth was there to watch all that time?" he asked. "I mean, I might understand sneaking a peek during bath night. That could have been a great temptation for a dirty old man, maybe even enough to justify constructing secret passages. But to spend all day and evening crouched in there? There must have been no one to watch during most of that time."

"A lonely vigil," Liam observed. "People of that era were not famous for taking many baths. Not even the young ladies. I'll bet Cleopatra was empty most of the time that Norbert was hiding in his secret passage."

"You're forgetting one thing, Liam," Sissy said after a moment. "All the water he was running through the girls. Remember, they were drinking seven quarts a day each."

A deadly silence.

"Oh," Liam said at last.

"Oh, indeed."

"Hydrolism for women. Puts something of a different light on it, I guess."

"I guess."

"That would explain all the hours, though." Colonel Forsythe nodded thoughtfully. "We could calculate: What would be the 'flow time,' if I could use so delicate a term, for seven quarts of water?"

"Well," Liam thought, "about the same as the time to drink that amount of water, more or less. Perhaps a bit more."

Many eyes unfocused as they worked it out.

Compton used the time to drink a glass of water. "Say twenty to thirty seconds a glass. One glass is about a cup. Four cups to the quart; two minutes a quart. About fourteen minutes for seven quarts. Probably a bit more. Let's say twenty minutes."

"Twenty minutes," the Colonel picked up. "Times twenty-five Angels . . . comes to approximately eight Angel hours per day. There was at least one of them in there most of the day."

"Poor Norbert." Jody looked away in disappointment.

Time for a change of subject, Liam thought. Turning to Laura: "Well—"

"It's monstrous," Laura cut him off. "It's simply monstrous. He was a rich man. He could have had almost anything he wanted. And they were just poor girls. Jody says they had no education, most of them. They had nothing. Nothing more than their modesty. And he stole that from them. I think that's just . . . monstrous." She looked as though she might be about to cry.

Evan shrugged. "Well, I don't see what the great harm of it was. Of course it was ungentlemanly of Norbert. But I don't see that the Angels were hurt in any way."

Groans and protests from around the table.

"Well? Well, tell me. What was the great harm done to those girls? Since they didn't know they were being watched, they were really none the worse for it."

"Oh, Evan!" Angela said in disgust.

Mr. Collyer, with hearing aid in place, had been following the conversation closely. "Your logic may be correct on this, Evan, or it may be wrong," he said. "We can never say for sure. One thing we can say, however, is that the opinion you have just expressed is not likely to win you much agreement in this company."

"I should say not!" Laura declared.

"Nope," Sissy seconded.

"Uh-uh," Marjorie added.

"Not in this company," Angela said.

"No," Lizzie said.

"Not likely," Gabriella concurred.

The others just shook their heads.

Aunt Grace liked to play a few rubbers of bridge after dinner. Since the Colonel had made good his escape, Marjorie was looking for someone to partner her against Mr. Collyer and the formidable aunt.

"I seem to remember you played quite a respectable hand of bridge, Liam." Marjorie had intercepted him on the way out of Xanadu.

"Oh, please," he said miserably. "I really can't." All he wanted was to be alone with his troubles.

Marjorie took pity on him and seized upon Gabriella instead.

Liam was looking forward to an evening of pure melancholy. He would be a tragic figure, lost in contemplation of Laura's betrayal with Bruno and, in general, of life's colossal mean streak. He would place himself prominently in one of the big easy chairs by the fire in Inverness. The others would tiptoe around quietly, awed by the depths of his depression. He intended to cast a deep gloom onto everyone's evening.

As it happened, though, there was no one to appreciate his melancholy. No tiptoers. Inverness was deserted. He sat there until he was thoroughly bored. This was not at all what he had had in mind. If he was going to cast a gloom onto anyone rather than just out onto the ether, he realized he was going to have to find where they'd all gone.

He got up and made a tour of the downstairs. Biscay was empty, as was Aragon. There was no one on any of the porches. The little card party of four was alone in Savoy. Liam went back to his lonely seat by the fire and gave it another half hour.

He had the expression right—the abiding sadness of disappointment. His sigh was perfect. He was dressed appropriately in muted tones. A cashmere scarf draped around his neck was a symbol of the chill imparted by betrayal. Only the most churlish observer could fail to grasp the symbol. He practiced a tiny shiver. But without observers, churlish or other, it was all for naught. Finally he gave up and headed to his room. He would spend the evening reading in bed. They'd be bound to notice his absence, and understand from that how he was feeling. If there was anyone to notice, that is.

At the top of the stairs, he stepped up to the little alcove window where he'd sometimes seen the Monsignor taking in the stars. Someone might encounter him there, he supposed, staring off in sadness. He went to the window and stared off in sadness.

Instead of stars, he found himself looking at a brightly lit interior. And presented there, to his amazement, was a certain polka-dotted undergarment that he had never expected to see at all, and now was looking at for the second time today. Laura was standing with her back to him, nude but for the polka dots. How could he be looking into Laura's room from here? he wondered. He was facing east, and her room looked out to the south. He paused to consider the puzzle. What he was looking at, he realized, was a reflection on a pane of glass: Laura's casement window. The window happened to be open at an angle that made it possible to see into her room. Laura put her hands to the waistband of her underpants and slid them down.

Liam stumbled away from the window, blushing. How could he have looked? That was no way to treat his friend, to take advantage of her privacy. But then he stopped halfway down the corridor. Laura, his friend? She had hardly been a friend to him today. A fat lot she had cared about his delicate feelings, so why should he care about hers? He hurried back to the window to see what more he could see.

What he saw was an entirely nude backside, but this time not Laura's. There was thick, dark hair on the shoulders, and heavy muscles. It was goddamned Bruno. The man was cavorting about in his birthday suit in Laura's room. Cavorting!

Liam left the window in disgust. He went back to his room and threw himself down on the bed. How could she? How could she be doing this to him? He moaned. It was not a moan produced for consumption by others, but an honest-to-god moan of pain. He let out another one. How could she?

Revenge. Revenge. There must be some revenge for this. Some way to strike back. What would it be? Something he could do that would be as devastating to her as her actions were to him. But what? He rolled over and stared up at the ceiling. What could it be? Well, for one thing, he could . . . Ooooo! How appropriate that would be. And it would serve her right. He never would have considered it before, but now . . . why not?

He popped up and into his bathroom to brush his teeth. Then he combed his hair carefully, adding water to press down the cowlick. Mr. Collyer, in a moment of generosity, had given him a little vial of *Kölnische Frischen Wasser*, which he'd dropped into his toilet kit a few days back. Liam dumped the contents of the kit onto the bed. There was the vial. He splashed a little onto his hand. Put some . . . where? He had no idea. He opened his shirt with the other hand and applied the scent under his left arm. He sprinkled a bit more down the front of his chest. There was still half the vial remaining. He stepped out of his loafers and emptied the rest of the cologne onto his socks.

Enough of the somber tones, he thought. He threw off his tweed jacket and put on instead the dark blue velvet one. This required that he change his pants as well. Maybe a silk scarf, the purple paisley. He folded it over twice at his neck, hoping for the elegant effect of an ascot. What he got instead of elegant was dumb. He took off the scarf, folded it, and put it into his jacket pocket, the top corner flopping out. He pulled at it a few times to increase the flop. Yes.

He had only the vaguest idea which room was Lamorak. But that's where Lizzie's charming idea of the ribbon on the window came in. He would just make his way around the rampart walk until he happened upon a beribboned window, and that would be Lizzie's. She would be waiting, he supposed, hoping. "I have come," he would say. And she would reply, "Oh, Liam. Darling." Liam opened his window and stepped out.

Most of the windows were open on this balmy August night. Most of the rooms had someone in them too; he could hear whispering voices. But the lights were out. Voices? Why were these people whispering to themselves in the dark? Oh. He had passed Angela's room and Sissy's room, both occupied. All the rooms were well occupied. So that's where the rascals were. The only room with a light on was Childeric. He saw Jody through the corner of his eye in her bed with a book. She at least seemed to be behaving herself. She would be the only one this evening.

As he came to the next gable, he saw the ribbon fluttering from the top of an open window. Lamorak at last. He took a breath and opened his mouth to announce his presence.

"I have come," a deep male voice said. Only it wasn't Liam's voice. He stopped dead, mouth still open. Ahead of him he saw the back of a crouched form in the window. "I have come," the deep voice repeated.

"Oh, Evan. Darling," Lizzie replied.

Oh, shit. Liam turned in his tracks and scurried back around to his own window.

22

Casper and Lupine

G enerations to come would think back on Liam Dwyer and say, Life was something that happened around Liam. He didn't really participate in it very much. He stared at his reflection in the bathroom mirror. He was just a spectator, a member of the audience, watching other people on life's big stage. Watching, but not playing any part at all. That was Liam Dwyer for you: nonparticipant. All promise and no delivery. He looked critically into the mirror for signs of nonparticipation. There were plenty: sallow color; a hint of weakness in the chin, a dead giveaway, that. He turned sideways to check the partial profile. What he saw in the mirror was the partial profile of a nonparticipant. He stared at it accusingly.

He glared at the reflection. Undoubtedly a failure, but not a bad-looking one, all in all, in his velvet jacket. He brushed mechanically at the neck and shoulders where any bit of dust or dandruff might accumulate. He leaned forward to check the little nose hairs that sometimes grew out disgustingly. Sure enough, there they were. He rummaged through his toilet kit looking for the nose scissors.

Trouble with being a member of the audience tonight was that the show was out early. The performances going on around him were strictly private. He could hardly peep again into Laura's window, or creep around to spy on the others. He didn't even want to. But what did he want? He sat down on the divan. While others were making love all around him, he would be here alone in Lancelot, doing what? Reading H. Ryder Haggard? How grim.

He switched his velvet jacket for a sweater and headed downstairs.

A partly completed chess game had been left set up in the library. The Colonel and Scarlet, he remembered, had been playing before dinner. Liam contemplated the board, trying to make sense of the positions. It didn't help that he never could remember just how the knights did their curious little two-step.

There was a dull thump on the porch outside, and a scrabbling noise. Liam looked up. He listened for more. No, nothing. Wait. Yes, there it was, a light chirring sound. He smiled to himself. He left the chess game to grope his way in the darkness into the main dining room.

Mrs. Jervis always left a bowl of fruit on the breakfront in Xanadu. Liam turned on the lights there and found what he needed: a banana and a bunch of grapes. Back through Biscay and out through its French doors to the open porch, trying not to make too much noise. He stopped just outside the door. There were three raccoons in the shadows at the end of the porch. "Hello," he said softly. "Hello, raccoons. Only me. You remember me. Nothing to be frightened of." He kept his voice low. Not just low, but deep. Raccoons are threatened by high-pitched sounds. It was a mother and two kits. "Hello, babies. Hello. Hello, Momma."

The larger of the two babies was probably female, he

thought. The males tend to lag behind in early growth. He had decided on another evening that her name was Lupine. "Hello, little Lupine. What a pretty girl." Liam crouched down and offered her a grape. "Oh, you like grapes, do you?" The little raccoon approached confidently. Liam held out some grapes as well to the mother, who was coming up from the other side.

The male came up too but ignored the grapes. "Ah. He wants his banana, doesn't he? Don't you ... um, let's see ... Casper. Don't you, Casper?" Casper and Lupine, those were their names. And the mother's name, he was practically sure of this, was Sugar. Liam sat down on the porch floor and Casper crawled onto his lap. "Now, where ever did you learn to like bananas? Hm? Are there banana trees out there in the woods?"

A slight sound behind him: the door opening. "Oh, my," a voice said, a soft, gravelly voice.

Liam didn't turn. "Just move very slowly," he told her. "Keep talking as you move. Keep your voice nice and low."

"Why, aren't you beautiful?" she said. "What beautiful little creatures. I've never seen them so close." She hadn't moved very much from the door.

"You can come closer," Liam told her. "If you move slowly and talk as you move, you can come right up."

"Is that true, little raccoons? Would you let me come closer? Would you?" She was right behind him. Sugar stared at her.

"Lower yourself all the way down. You don't want to tower too much above her. Sugar, this is Gabriella. Gabriella, Sugar. Gabriella is a very good person, Sugar. You can trust her." He looked back at Gabriella. "Now, hold out your hand," he told her, "very slowly. Keep it low near the floor, palm up. Offer it to her."

Gabriella crouched down, offering her hand. The mother

raccoon considered the hand for a moment, then put her paw into it. She looked up into Gabriella's eyes.

"Ohhhh." Gabriella melted beside him. "Ohhhh. Sugar, I am so...honored."

"This is Casper. Casper, meet Gabriella." He held the rest of the banana over Gabriella's lap, and Casper accommodatingly scrambled over.

"Ohhhh," she said again. "Casper. Casper, would you let me—"

"If you go very slowly, and coo a bit."

Gabriella, cooing softly, wrapped her free arm loosely around Casper. "Casper. Do you like that? Do you like to be cuddled? You do, don't you?" Casper studied her face from only a few inches away as he chewed the banana.

When the bananas and grapes were gone, the three raccoons waddled off. Gabriella sighed deeply, staring away into the dark.

⚜

"I have this maddening sense of being a member of the audience, when what I really want is to be in the show."

Gabriella nodded gravely.

"Just to play a part. Any part." He couldn't believe he was telling her this.

"Of course you'll play parts, many parts. You're just feeling blue because the music has stopped and you've been left without a chair. That's what's happened, isn't it, Liam? All the Angels and Acolytes have paired up, and on this round you've missed out. But there will be other chances."

"Is it so apparent that they've all paired up?"

"Oh, yes. Pretty apparent. Laura and Bruno..."

He looked away.

"She might have done better, I think. For all his talents, Bruno lacks a bit of soul. Oh, aren't I terrible? Poor Bruno started with nothing: no money, no prominent family, no education, and what he's made of himself he's done all on his own. Seems a quibble to complain if he lacks a bit of soul."

"He does, though. I agree." Liam nodded up at the ceiling. "They are, as we speak—"

"Of course. It was in the cards." She smiled gently.

"And Evan and Lizzie—"

"As we speak. Yes, you could see the arrangements being made for that over dinner. They could barely wait for the meal to be over."

"As obvious as that?"

"There is little on Earth more obvious than young lust."

"Then there's Angela and Tim."

"Now that's a better match. They seem to have found kindred souls in each other. I'm very fond of both of them."

"And Sissy and Compton," he added, sure that this one at least would be news to Gabriella.

"Uh-huh. As we speak."

"You knew?"

"For weeks."

"But they're cousins! First cousins."

"Uh-huh."

"Aren't you shocked?"

Gabriella laughed. "The object of the exercise, Liam, is to make love, not babies. I'm sure they're competent to do the one and not the other. If they aren't, then the fact that they're cousins is dwarfed by their other problems."

"But it's incest."

"Oh, Liam." She shifted her eyes back out to the darkness of the yard. "Oh, Liam."

"I just think that propriety requires—"

"Yes, propriety." She paused, smiling slightly. "Tell me, if propriety is offended by cousins, wouldn't it be even more offended by siblings?"

"Well? Wouldn't it? I mean, there do have to be some standards."

She was silent a long moment. "You don't have a sister, do you, Liam?"

"No."

"But imagine you did. Perhaps you have already imagined one."

He didn't reply.

"Pretend for a moment that you have a sister. Let's give her a name, just so we can talk about Liam's sister. I think we might call her..."

"Well, let's call her Candace," he said.

"Ah. Candace. And Candace, if she existed, would be, let me think, a bit older than you, or perhaps a bit younger?"

"Maybe older. Just a year. But in some ways younger."

"Uh-huh. Now, tell me about Liam and Candace. Are they close?"

Liam shrugged. "Yes."

"Affectionate?"

"Quite."

"Do they hug? Do they kiss sometimes? Do they hold hands while they walk along the beach, discussing life and all its meanings?"

"Yes, but that doesn't mean—"

"No, of course not. But now consider: Candace is troubled by the feelings she's starting to have. Her body has a will of its own. She can barely sleep sometimes. Would she tell these troubles to her brother Liam?"

"I hope she would. I hope I would be someone a sister could talk to."

"And as she talks to you, you come to realize that she is frightened. She's worried that in the rough-and-tumble of relationships, she may be hurt by the very sensuality that in the long run is her great treasure."

"Um..."

"She's particularly frightened about 'the first time.' I can tell you firsthand that I was."

"Well, I'd be there for her to talk to."

"But suppose she wanted more than just talk? Suppose she wanted the first time to be with someone she knew she could trust, someone she knew—absolutely knew—loved her. And loved her for herself, not just for a moment's pleasure."

"Mm."

Gabriella was unfocused again, staring out into the yard. "All this is academic for you, Liam. You don't have a sibling. It's not academic for me."

"Oh. You have a brother?"

"Yes."

"Older or younger?"

"Older. But in some ways younger."

"Ah." He waited for her to go on, but she didn't. He thought a little help might be called for. "And did you ever feel—"

She nodded. "There was the war, always the war to confuse things. He was called up in 1942, toward the end of the year. Just a boy, and he was about to be sent off into battle."

"Mm."

"Even now it's hard for me to believe that we send our sons and brothers into war."

"Yes. Hard to believe."

"That autumn we were together at our parents' summer house, closing it up. Just the two of us for a long, leisurely week."

"I see."

"And I suddenly realized during that week that he was never going to come back from the war. He was going to be killed. I knew it."

247

"Oh."

"He was a virgin. We both were. We talked about these things, you see, so I knew. And I thought, as I considered his imminent death, that somehow the worst of it was that he would die with so little of his life lived."

Liam nodded. "I see. I think I understand what you were getting at before. I never thought of it quite this way. And did you—"

"No." She shook her head sadly. "I didn't. I was a coward. I have always hated myself for that."

"And was he killed?" Liam asked softly.

Gabriella laughed her low, masculine laugh. "No. He spent the war in Washington. Came home fit as a fiddle. He's married now to a woman I think of as a sister and has two lovely daughters, whom I adore."

"Well then, it all worked out for the best, didn't it?"

She rounded on him, eyes flashing. "It certainly did not! It was wrong, what I did. What I didn't do. It doesn't matter that it worked out acceptably. The only thing that matters is that I let myself down."

23

Drunk on Butter

The evening had turned chilly, and they moved back into the library. There was always a fire laid there; all it took was a match to start it. They sat together on the red Chesterfield couch, their faces lit only by the flames.

Gabriella put her hand up to her mouth in feigned shock. "Oh, I must not have said that." She giggled. "Not what you thought I said. Not that. I couldn't have."

He stared at her, stunned. What she had said was "Will you sleep in my bed tonight, Liam?" She had turned to him, looked him right in the eye and said, softly, "Will you sleep in my bed tonight, Liam?" She really had.

"What *did* you think I said?"

He had no idea what to answer.

"I certainly couldn't have said *that.* Not a well-brought-up young lady such as I. No, I must have said something that rhymed with that. That must have been what it was." She giggled again.

"I—"

"You fellows do have active imaginations, I'll give you

249

that. And an active imagination can play tricks on you. On the other hand..."

"On the other hand?"

"On the other hand..." She made herself suddenly serious, or mock serious. "On the other hand, you never can tell. If I were you, Liam, and a certain person were to yawn elaborately and say she thought it might just be time for bed, well—"

"Yes?"

"Well, I think I'd accompany her up the stairs. And see what might happen."

"Oh." He checked to be sure his mouth was closed.

Gabriella yawned elaborately. It was a lovely, languorous yawn. What a performer she was. "I think it's this girl's bedtime," she announced.

Liam jumped to his feet. "Yes! I mean, yes." He checked his watch. "Oh, it is that time, isn't it? Where has the evening gone? Well, um, me too. I mean, my bedtime too. I think. Not that I'm tired."

She offered him her arm. "Would you walk me up the stairs, Liam?"

"I would." He felt himself shiver on contact. It was possible he'd never touched her before. His head was swimming.

Halfway up the stairs, Gabriella had a fit of the giggles and had to stop.

"What?"

"I just thought, what if anyone should see us? It would be so obvious. 'There is little on Earth more obvious than young lust,' you know."

"Well, it might help if you wouldn't giggle."

"It might, but I'm helpless."

"Some actress."

"Suppose it were...Aunt Grace who saw us?" She sputtered again. "Or the Monsignor." She leaned back against the paneling.

"Come on." Liam pulled her up the stairs.

At the door to Gawaine, he stopped, suddenly shy. He could hardly go barging in.

"It was Jeannie's room, you know," Gabriella said easily, opening the door for him. "Come have a look. Jeannie's room, almost the way it was in her time." She shut the door behind them. "Jeannie's room, and Jeannie's bed."

"Oh. Jeannie's bed."

"This is where she brought her lover, Liam. They made love in that bed, in what is going to be our love bed."

"Lover. Jeannie had a lover?"

"Oh, yes."

"But who? It couldn't have been Norbert."

"Goodness, no." Gabriella laughed. "Norbert liked to watch the girls go tinkle, but I think that was as far as his sex life ever ran. And Jeannie wasn't much for spectators, anyway."

"Dr. Ralston, then?"

"That old stuffed shirt? No. No, Jeannie was chock-full of life, full of love to give, and sexy as any woman has ever been." Gabriella slipped her cardigan off her shoulders casually. "She needed a real man to be her match."

The front of her was full and soft as she moved inside her silk blouse. Liam struggled to remember what the subject was. It was...oh, yes, Jeannie's lover. "Who, then? Who was he?"

"A man of great passions, a man so beautiful as to take her breath away, a man of the sea, a master builder..."

"Ephram!"

"Ephram Whittier. Ephram was her lover." Gabriella sat down on the edge of the bed. She patted beside her with her hand for him to come too. "He proposed to let her taste the forbidden food, the dreaded lobster. Dared her to try it. Jeannie was always a sucker for a dare."

"Their first date?" Liam sat down.

251

"It was. They had a lobster binge. They built a fire on the beach and ate oysters while the lobster steamed. Then they ate a four-pounder each, drenched in butter. Jeannie said afterward that she was 'drunk on butter.' She brought him back here that very night, and they consummated their love in this bed."

"How do you know all this?"

"Oh, from old stories, rumors, hearsay."

"No hard fact?"

"The hard fact is that she departed with Ephram that November in his lobster boat when she had to leave in disgrace. They made their way down the coast to Calais, where he had family. And then on to Prince Edward Island the next spring."

"Why does everyone say she left in disgrace? How was she disgraced if a few Angels got pregnant?"

"*All* the Angels got pregnant."

"Still. How was *she* disgraced by that?"

"All the Angels got pregnant, Liam, including Jeannie herself."

⚜

He had no idea how to begin.

"I think you might begin...here." Gabriella looked down at the front of her blouse and pointed, almost shyly, to the top button. "Here. Yes, this would be a nice beginning."

Liam reached out to undo the button. His heart was thumping. Gabriella pressed her two hands onto his chest. "The first time, Liam? I think so."

"Well, like any fellow, of course, I've done a bit of—"

She put a finger to his lips. "Let's not tell any untruths to each other, Liam. Not any. Not in this love bed. Not on this night for love."

He nodded. "The first time, yes." He bit his lip.

"How lucky for me. Thank you, Liam."

"And it's not Liam, it's Chuck," he blurted out. "Since we're telling the truth. Chuck Dwyer. Or Charles Liam Dwyer. I changed it to Liam because I thought that Chuck was just so vulgar. I could never be a poet with a name like Chuck. And I'm not really in the school of fine arts at Cornell, but in the state school of agriculture and animal husbandry."

Gabriella's low laugh again, "I suggested we tell no untruths, Liam. I didn't suggest we go back and set the record straight on every single subject. It might take us all night."

"Oh."

"You're Liam. You've made a good change. Lots of people change their names. Dorothea became Haydée; Jane Isadore became Jeannie Isobel. Who would say that wasn't their right? Even I—"

"*You* changed your name?"

"I did. I needed a lovely name for the stage."

"You weren't born a Lake?"

"I was. It's the first name I changed, Gabriella."

"What was your first name?"

"Veronica."

"But that's a lovely name. Veronica Lake."

"Unfortunately taken."

"Oh."

"And there can't be two actresses with the same name. Those are the rules."

Liam hadn't known that. "Makes sense, I guess. The other Veronica Lake, though . . . that might not even have been her real name."

"It wasn't."

"She probably had some awful name."

"Constance Ockleman."

"Oh, the poor thing."

"She made an improvement, yes. And so did I. You see,

253

I took the name of my brother, Gabe. It was when I thought he would be killed. I thought I would take his name and make it live on. And everything I did with that name would reflect honor on him. I hope it always will.

He woke with the first light. Gabriella's body, her delicious, nude body, was pressed against him. He had made love to the most beautiful woman he'd ever encountered in his life. The most beautiful person imaginable, body and heart and soul.

"Mmmm," she murmured beside him, sensing him awake.

"I was just thinking—"

"What a lovely thought." Her eyes were still closed.

How did she do that?

"How do you—"

"Easy."

He looked down at her face, childlike and sleepy. "May I?"

"Uh-huh."

He lifted the sheet slightly to let the morning light fall on her bosom.

"Touch too," she said, eyes still unopened.

He laid the back of his hand ever so gently on her breast.

"Thank you."

"Thank *you*."

"Do you think we could?"

"Liam!" She opened one eye. "What does a girl need to do to satisfy you?"

"I am so satisfied. So deeply satisfied."

Gabriella sat up, pulling the sheet to cover herself, or to partly cover herself. She adjusted it thoughtfully, smiling at him as she did. "I'm afraid our time of play has to be over, my lovely Liam. We need to be discreet, to respect the con-

254

ventions of our host and hostess. You, I'm afraid, have to go back to your own bed before anyone else is awake."

"Of course, the traffic of people going back to their own beds before anyone else is awake is likely to be substantial."

"It is. But those people are all very careful not to notice."

She was right. He would have to go soon. He could hear sounds from the kitchen, a door being opened, and the muted tones of Cartefigue's kitchen Victrola playing one of his early-morning opera records. "I'll get my things." He reached for his shirt to cover himself as he stood up.

"Oh, no." Gabriella took it away from him.

"Oh. Oh." He stood quite nude in front of her.

"Nice." She twirled her finger in the air, smiling happily. Liam turned slowly for her.

"Did anyone ever tell you that you have a very cute bottom?"

"Um, no. Actually not."

"You do."

He found his pants and sweater and socks on the floor. "Uh, I don't suppose you've seen—"

"I have."

"I'm missing my—"

"Boxer shorts. Light blue."

"Those are the ones. Where are they?"

She lifted her pillow to reveal a corner of light blue fabric. "I'm keeping them," she announced.

"Oh."

She held out her hands to take his, to stop him from dressing. She managed to do that and still keep herself mostly covered, though she could not have been a more entrancing vision no matter how much more naked she was. "Liam?"

"Yes."

"Are you going to tell?"

The right answer was, of course not. It's what a gentleman would say. But for the rule of truth. The truth was, mightn't he, someday?

Gabriella laughed. "What a silly question, Gabriella, to ask of a young man who is not allowed to tell any untruth. Of course you're going to tell," she said. "I want you to. I want you to tell simply anyone you wish. Only, I want you to wait until after noon today, when I fly back to New York. Till then it will be our secret only."

"I just thought that, years from now, I might want to share something of this night with someone. But only years in the future. Before that, I would never think to—"

"Oh, but I want you to. I do."

"You do?" he asked.

"I do."

"Whom would I tell?"

"I don't know. Tell someone who would be charmed to share our happiness. Marjorie, perhaps. Maybe Jody. Andrew. You decide. Tell someone. Tell them I wanted them to know."

Liam looked befuddled.

"But not before my departure. Not a word, not a look. You must be quite the perfect actor until then. I require it."

"As you say."

"Now, off with you."

24

"I Think I Knew That"

orry about Bruno, everybody," Sissy announced at breakfast. "He appears to have left like a thief in the night. Or a thief in the morning, actually. Looks like he slipped off on the six o'clock ferry."

"Oh, well," Liam said.

"Never even said good-bye. And that's not even the worst."

"What's the worst, dear?" the Colonel asked.

"He borrowed ten dollars from me last night."

"Oh, no."

"He did. Said he needed it for train fare to New York. Said he's going to try out for one of those off-Broadway reviews. I've been kicking myself for giving it to him."

"Mm. Well, the truth is," Colonel Forsythe admitted, "he borrowed five from me as well. Yesterday afternoon."

"No."

"Mmm."

"Ooops," Jody said.

"Oh, no. You too, darling?"

"Uh-huh. Three dollars."

"Ten dollars from me," Liam acknowledged.

"Ten from me," Gabriella said promptly. "Seemed like a good investment at the time. He was worried he might not be able to go without it. I didn't think we'd miss him too terribly much."

Aunt Grace had a sour look.

"Not you too, Grace?"

"Three dollars," she sputtered.

"Oh, dear."

"Ten," Laura said sadly.

"Oh, dear."

"Five," said Evan.

"Anyone else? No, not you, Tyndall?"

"Sorry, sir."

"How much?"

"Five dollars."

"Angela too," Sissy said. "I passed her on the way into her shower. Ten dollars. I'll bet he got that much from Lizzie too. Lizzie was always a sucker for Bruno."

The Colonel shook his head. "Well, he seems to have done rather well by us."

There was a sad silence as they all contemplated how much better the money might have been used.

Marjorie breezed in, fresh from her morning walk. "Morning, everybody. Heard about Bruno? He looks to have left without saying good-bye."

"Yes, Sissy was just telling us."

"That boy had a good deal of cheek, I must say. Tried to borrow ten dollars from me." She shook her head in wonder.

"No, really? And did you give it to him?" the Colonel asked.

"I should say not!"

"You didn't?"

"Of course not. Fat chance. I never would. Would you?"

"Well—"

"Of course not," Gabriella interrupted. "The Colonel sent him off with a good lecture."

"You mean he asked you too, Andrew?"

"He did. Tried to put the touch on each of us, matter of fact."

"And you all disappointed him?" She looked around the table.

"Of course," Liam said.

"Of course," Gabriella said.

"All he got from me was 'what for?' " Sissy said.

"He had no chance with me," Evan said.

"Money doesn't grow on trees," Jody said.

"Sent him packing," Aunt Grace said.

"As did I," Tyndall said.

"I told him he had his nerve," Laura said brightly. "He did have his nerve. I'm not sorry to see the back of him."

Marjorie had a thoughtful expression. "All the same, though, I do worry how he will make do. Hate to think of him not being able to get lunch."

"Oh, I wouldn't worry too much about Bruno," the Colonel assured her. "Seems a resourceful chap."

❧❦

Colonel Forsythe was fiddling with the knobs of the big Emerson, trying to tune in the weather from Bangor.

"We've had pretty good luck on the weather each year for the celebration," he told Liam. The next day was August 15, the date of the annual reenactment of the Great Zucchini War. The Forsythes had sponsored the event for each of the last ten years. "The essential is that it not rain."

"Oh, I daresay we'd still have a wonderful time even if it did rain," Liam said. "We're all looking forward to it."

"We'll have the food under tents, and some of the games as well. But the war itself, the reenactment, does require dry weather."

"Now, why is that again?" Liam was none too sure of the mechanics of the reenactment, having missed last year's event.

There was a loud burst of static from the Emerson and a distant voice: "Fzzzsdrbrzzz zaaaat sssseszzerbezers.... zz aaakk aaakkk szerzerbwrek grewsdazzerblk zatt akk aak."

"Oh, good." Colonel Forsythe breathed a sigh of relief. "Fine weather expected all day. That is a piece of luck." He switched off the set. "Rain would wipe us out, you see. The way we conduct the war is by keeping track of who gets wet. The last dry ones are the winners."

"You mean the defenders, the Gideons, don't always win?"

"Oh, goodness no. Where would be the amusement in that? No, in fact the attackers usually come out on top, at least these last few years. That Tim Hopkins and his two brothers make ferocious Bentonites. We poor Gideons have all we can do to keep dry for even a few minutes. I'm afraid they usually wipe us up rather quickly. Now, I say 'us,' but I really mean you, as we elders don't actually take part in the war. It's the young contingent from Dark Harbor House that has to defend. You are the Gideons. All the others, the townies and the North Stars and the rest, are Bentonites."

"Oh, dear."

"Oh, dear, indeed."

They passed through the French doors onto the porch and down to the front yard where Marjorie was standing.

"What *were* you thinking, Andrew? What on earth is this for?" She pointed to a boat trailer that had just been delivered from the ferry. It was stacked high with cartons of eggs."

"For the egg toss, my dear. I thought we might add an egg toss to this year's events."

"For an egg toss we might expect to use three or four dozen eggs. You must have a hundred dozen here."

"Yes, well . . ." The Colonel smiled mysteriously. "Got a particularly good price on them by buying a few extra. I don't think they'll go to waste. We can always hard-boil any that are left over. Nothing better for us than eggs."

Gabriella had to miss the reenactment, as her rehearsals began in New York on the same day. She was fetched in a seaplane, piloted by a tall, young man with the approximate appearance of a Greek god. She said he was a producer. He buzzed once over the house just at noon before landing on the calm water in front. Gabriella was ready. All the others made a line on the pier for hugs and handshakes. She had a nice word for each one.

"Liam," she said, taking his hand. "Good luck at school this year. I know you'll do well."

"Very nice to have met you," Liam said casually. Casual was the key. He had been casual, the consummate actor all morning.

"Likewise." She went on to give Jody a squeeze, and a big hug to the Colonel and Marjorie. She turned before stepping up onto the plane's pontoon. "Good-bye, everybody." She waved. Then she paused.

She handed her shoulder bag to the Greek god producer and ran back up the pier, directly to Liam. She stopped in front of him, her eyes laughing.

"Oh, darling Liam," she said.

He stared at her.

She threw her arms around him and kissed him deeply. "You were . . . just *wonderful*." She ruffled his hair with her hand. A faraway, dreamy look. "Wonderful . . ."

"But I thought you said we weren't going to—"

"That only applied to you, silly. Not to me."

She kissed him again. "Good-bye, my darling." Then she ran back down the pier and hopped into the plane.

As the little craft pulled away, Jody slipped a hand into Liam's. "Isn't she just splendid?"

"She is. Splendid. Just splendid." He used his other arm to wave.

The little plane banked low over Six Hundred Acre Island and zoomed back over Dark Harbor House, tipping its wings in good-bye.

When the noise of the takeoff was past, Jody leaned close to tell him, "She is Jeannie's grandchild, you know."

He thought about that a moment. "Yes, I think I knew that," he said. "I mean, no one ever said it in just so many words. But I think I knew."

25

The Great Zucchini War

Blue for the defenders, for the Gideons," Colonel Forsythe explained, holding up a light blue bib with ribbons. There was a large dark blue G on its front.

All of Dark Harbor was assembled on the front lawn on
a perfect Maine summer day. The wind was gentle and
warm, just enough to make the bay sparkle prettily down
below them. It was the most peaceful of days, but all their
minds were on one subject only: war.

"Yay, blue!" Laura shouted.

"Gideons, get your blue bibs. Gideons over to this side.
Come along now," said the Colonel. Marjorie, at his side,
was handing out the blue bibs.

Liam got his and one for Laura. He took his position with
the other Gideons: Jody, Sissy, Laura, Evan, Angela, Compton, and Lizzie.

"And Bentonites in green," the Colonel said next. He
waved a green bib emblazoned with a white B.

Boos from the Gideons as Tim Hopkins and his brothers
and the other townies came forward to get their green bibs.
Special boos for Teddy and Louise Ralston.

The Colonel held up his zucchini for attention. It was as big as a baseball bat. "Now, you all know the rules. If your bib gets wet, you're out. I said 'rules,' but actually that's the only rule. Anything goes, anything at all. No bodily violence, I hope, but more or less anything goes. The last side to have any dry participant is the winner. All disputes will be subject to judgment by our referee. Today's referee is, ladies and gentlemen, our own . . . Mr. Collyer."

Cheers for Mr. Collyer as he took off his jacket to reveal a black-and-white striped referee's shirt. He had a black whistle around his neck on a lanyard. "If I say you're out, you're out," he said. "If I blow my whistle, it means I felt the whistle needed blowing." He blew his whistle and they all cheered again.

"Pouring water on nonparticipants is discouraged"—he looked around severely at the Bentonites and Gideons—"discouraged, but not illegal."

The participants all cheered. Nonparticipants stepped back slightly, thinking of their fine clothes.

"Pouring water on the referee is a capital offense," Mr. Collyer told them.

"But not discouraged," the Colonel added. "All right, now, Bentonites to your boats."

Mr. Collyer blew his whistle. "The Great Zucchini War is begun," he shouted.

Tim and his team ran back over toward the float at North Star House, where the three little Bentonite rowboats had been set out.

"Okay, everybody," Laura said as soon as the greens were out of earshot. "Everybody up to the hose. We've got a little surprise for those Bentonites."

She got all the Gideons assembled by the hose at the corner of the front porch. Angela had disappeared for a moment into the house and came back carrying something in her skirts.

"Our secret weapons," Laura told them. "Water balloons." Angela dumped the empty balloons onto the ground. "Jillions of them. Quick, get them filled up. We haven't got much time."

The Bentonites were now just distant figures with green bibs, racing down the lawn at North Star. They would be in their boats in another minute or two.

"Compton and Sissy, take these to the back hose." Laura shoved a handful of balloons toward Compton.

Liam had one balloon already pulled onto the nozzle. Angela was on the faucet.

"Careful now, don't get yourselves wet," Laura cautioned. "Jody, take these into the kitchen. Evan, find a bathroom and get these filled. Hurry. Fill a dozen each. Lizzie, here are yours. Take the downstairs powder room." She gave them each a handful of balloons. "Hurry."

They scurried off.

"You there." Laura pointed to the Monsignor, who was watching them with a grin. "Get us a wheelbarrow from the garden shed, pronto."

"I'm a nonparticipant," the Monsignor protested.

"You'll be a wet nonparticipant if you don't do what I say." Laura looked at him sharply. "Now, hop to it." Monsignor Leary rushed off toward the shed. Laura looked toward North Star, where the three little boats were just pulling away. "Five minutes," she estimated. "Five minutes to H-hour."

The others were rushing up with armfuls of filled balloons. The Monsignor was there with the wheelbarrow, looking a bit red in the face.

"Balloons in the wheelbarrow," Laura told them. "Okay, here's the plan. Angela, Sissy, Jody, and Lizzie, you're going to wade out into the water—"

"What!" they protested.

"Just do as I tell you. Only up to your thighs. Raise your

skirts. Obviously you won't go in far enough to get your bibs wet. You're the decoys. The boats will come ashore right where you are. You'll be shouting at them and daring them on. That's the plan. I want you in the water right beside the pier. That's where we want them to pull up. Go. Go!"

She pushed Sissy. The four girls hurried off toward the shore.

"Liam," Laura gathered the others in, "get the wheelbarrow down to the pier. Just leave it there. Then come right back and stand with us on the shore behind the girls. We'll all be shouting at the Bentonites and daring them to come. Draw them in. Then when I give you the word, you boys rush out onto the pier and let them have it with the balloons. Try to get Tim Hopkins. He's our main worry. Let's go!"

She led them at a run down to the shore. The boats were less than a hundred yards away. "Two minutes," Laura called to her Gideons.

Liam pushed the wheelbarrow full of water balloons onto the pier and rushed back to Laura's side.

Angela and Sissy and Jody and Lizzie were in the water, squealing. "It's icy!" Angela wailed.

"Stay where you are," Laura said severely. "Don't budge till you can see the whites of their eyes. Remember, they'll try to splash you with their oars. When I give the word to the boys, you girls turn and wade back to the shore. Don't run, or you'll splash yourselves. A nice orderly retreat. But not till I say so. Here they come. Now taunt them. Booooooo, Bentonites!" she shouted. "Come on, cowards. Come and get your medicine."

The front line of girls booed and shouted, waving their fists at the attackers.

Some of the greens were standing in the front of their boats, ready with oars to splash the Gideons.

"Boooooooo, Bentonites," Laura screamed. "You're all going to be soaking wet soon. Come and get it."

Liam stared at her, amazed. Lovely Laura, doubly lovely now with her blue bib tied down over her sundress, but this was a Laura he had never seen before. "Booooooo, Tim Hopkins," she shouted. "We'll get you!" She was hopping up and down, pointing at Tim.

Mr. Collyer was wading out beside the Gideon girls to see the action close at hand.

Laura timed the moment with perfect cool. "Wait . . . wait . . . wait," she told them. "Not yet. . . . Now! Now! Run boys, run! Girls, back you come. Come along. Don't panic."

Liam and the others raced up to the wheelbarrow.

"Fire!" Laura shouted, dancing in excitement. "Fire! Let them have it."

Compton and Liam and Evan grabbed the balloons and rained them down on the lead boat.

"Whoaaaaa," Tim shouted at the oarsman of his boat. "Back away, back away. They've got water balloons."

"You're out!" Mr. Collyer screamed at one of the greens whose bib had been soaked with a balloon.

"First blood!" Laura shouted triumphantly.

"Out of the boat," Mr. Collyer told the boy. "Into the water with you. You're out."

The boy shook his head sadly and jumped out of the boat. More balloons were landing on the others around him.

"You're out!" Mr. Collyer was pointing at Louise Ralston. She was soaked. "Out of the boat."

A great cry from the pier. The second boat had upset itself trying to get away. All three of its Bentonites were drenched.

"Out! All out!" Mr. Collyer declared.

Tim's boat and the other pulled back and headed for shore farther down from the pier.

"Blue. Blooooooooooo. Blues to me," Laura shouted. She was up on the lawn. "All blues to me."

They rushed up to her. She was standing by the little trailer with its stacks of egg cartons. There were only about ninety cartons left after the egg toss.

"All's fair," she announced. "Get them open." She was handing out cartons. "Let them have it. Go! Attack!"

Liam had his carton open and was rushing down toward the Bentonites. He could see that they were filling buckets with water. Laura was right beside him with an armful of cartons. "Stop here," she shouted. "Let them come to us. "Boys throw, girls fetch more eggs. Go. Run. More eggs." She turned back to the Bentonites, approaching menacingly with their buckets. There were five of them.

"Fire!" she shouted.

Liam and Compton and Evan and Laura began throwing eggs as fast as they could.

The attackers scattered, many suffering direct hits.

A whistle. "Eggs don't count!" Mr. Collyer shouted. "They do no harm, though. Carry on."

"Jody, on the front hose." Laura pushed her. "We'll drive them up toward you. Drive them up toward the hose, everybody. More eggs, girls."

Jody made it to the hose just in time to spray Teddy Ralston and to receive a full bucket of water in the face.

"Both out!" Mr. Collyer pointed at them. "Both out."

One of the town boys, covered with eggs, reached the hose.

"Fall back," Laura instructed. "Get out of range of the hose. Liam, quick, fetch the wheelbarrow."

Liam ran.

By the time he got back, there were eggs raining down on Laura and her Gideons. Three of the greens had seized the trailer.

"Stand your ground," Laura said coolly. "Ignore the

eggs." One caught her full on the shoulder, and she didn't even flinch. "Everybody around the wheelbarrow. Get your water balloons." She looked off toward the town boy at the hose. "We'll need to retake the hose, that's the plan." She considered her options.

"Angela." Laura took her by the arm. "Angela, you are to receive the greatest honor of all."

"Oh, my."

"You're going to be a sacrifice for the cause."

"Little me? So much honor?"

"Little you. They'd get you anyway sooner or later, Angela. I'm sorry to say that you run like a girl. It's just a matter of time before that Tim catches you. This is your chance to go down in style."

Angela saluted. "I only regret that I have but one bib to give up for the Gideon cause."

Laura kissed her on both cheeks. "Take these two water balloons and run all the way around the house. We'll start shouting and throwing balloons at him. When you hear us, jump around the corner and let him have it. Of course, you'll be squirted to death."

"Of course," Angela said bravely.

"Good girl." Laura pushed her off. "Now, Lizzie and Sissy, stay by the balloons. Don't let them get to you. Let's go, boys, to the attack. Stay just out of range. When I give the word, we'll race up a little bit and throw, then fall back. Don't forget to shout. Ready?"

She waited for Angela to peek around the corner. "Go! Attack!"

They raced forward, shouting, and let the balloons go.

"You're out!" Mr. Collyer pointed at Evan, who had been sprinkled with the hose.

Angela stepped around the corner and clobbered the boy with both balloons. As he fell to the ground, he squirted her liberally.

269

"Out, and Out!" Mr. Collyer screamed.

"Where is Tim?" Laura said worriedly. "Uh-oh." There were screams behind them as Lizzie and Sissy were attacked by Tim and his two brothers. They lifted the girls onto their shoulders and dragged them, squealing, down to the tidal pool, where they were unceremoniously dunked. "Uh-oh," Laura said again. "Compton and Liam, quick. Get those two last balloons from the wheelbarrow." Laura was absolutely covered with egg. "Go!" She pushed them. "Get them."

They raced down toward the three Hopkins brothers. They stopped just short of the pool and let fly their balloons. Both balloons hit the same brother—unfortunately, not Tim.

"You're out!" Mr. Collyer announced. "Out."

"Back to me!" Laura shouted. "Back to me."

Liam and Compton raced back up the hill toward her. Tim and his remaining brother ran for their buckets, which they filled at the pool and then set out in pursuit.

"To the hose?" Compton suggested.

"No, we'll be pinned down," Laura said. "I've got an idea. Let them think they've caught us with no water at all. Draw them up the hill."

She turned to the two Bentonites advancing on them with their buckets. "Oh, no!" she cried. "Whatever shall we do? All is lost. Run for our lives."

"This way," she said under her voice, leading up the hill. "Not too fast," she panted. "Let them gain on us."

They ran up where Laura directed them, toward the folly.

"Up the slide," Laura told them. They scrambled up behind her.

"Oh, no," Laura wailed again. "They've got us, boys. I'm afraid all is lost."

Tim and his brother were at the foot of the slide. They

started up, each with his bucket. Laura judged her time to the split second.

"Now!" she shouted. Liam and Compton threw themselves off the two sides of the slide. Laura launched herself through the air and caught the flush line. There was a huge rush of water down the slide.

"You're out!" Mr. Collyer was pointing at Tim's brother, who was completely drenched. "And you're out." He pointed at Compton. Tim's bucket had caught him in midair.

Mr. Collyer looked around. Tim had jumped clear at the last moment. Liam and Laura were picking themselves up. "The rest of you are just eggy," Mr. Collyer announced, something of an understatement. "Carry on."

"Quick, the hose," Laura said. "Run, Liam. Don't let him catch us."

Liam and Laura dashed for the hose at the corner of the porch, with Tim in hot pursuit. "Run, Liam," Laura said, puffing. "Don't wait for me." She pushed him ahead. He put his head down and ran.

There was a squeal behind him just as he reached the hose. "Noooo," Laura cried out. "Tim, don't you dare!"

Tim had Laura over his shoulder. "Noooo," she cried again, beating on his back with her fists. "I won't have it. I won't. You terrible brute. Tim, I'll get you for this. I will."

Liam got the hose on and turned around. He lifted the stream of water for maximum distance, but it wouldn't quite reach. Tim was striding down the hill, carrying Laura like a sack of potatoes. Liam stared in awe. Could I carry her like that? he wondered. Could I? Oops, wars to win here, maidens to rescue. He turned off the hose and dashed down after them.

"Noooooooooo . . . . Tim, don't you dare!" Tim stood on the edge of the pool and calmly launched Laura out over the water. She flailed in midair. A great splash.

"You're out!" Mr. Collyer shouted, pointing at her.

Laura came up spitting water and swimming hard back toward Tim. Liam had one chance, he thought: throw himself through the air and push Tim and himself both into the water, but Tim first. Now here was the key matter: Because his bib would arguably be the last to be wetted, wouldn't a reasonable man conclude that he had prevailed? Or would it simply be a tie? Could Mr. Collyer be counted on to realize that even the merest quarter-of-a-second difference in the wetting of bibs could be construed...?

Tim squared around to face him, and the chance was lost.

"Hey," Tim said, looking down at his foot. "Hey, no fair."

Laura had his ankle. She was trying to pull him in.

"No fair." Tim looked to Mr. Collyer for help.

"All's fair." Mr. Collyer shrugged.

"Leggo."

Laura had Tim's foot in both hands and was pushing back with her feet against the side of the pool to pull him in.

Liam picked up the Colonel's zucchini and whomped Tim across the chest with it. Tim looked stunned. Laura switched her tactic to push on his ankle instead of pull, and Tim toppled slowly down on top of her.

Liam jumped back to avoid the splash. He looked around for more Bentonites, but there weren't any.

"The winner!" Mr. Collyer screamed. "The winner." He held Liam's hand up in the air. "I declare the Gideons have triumphed!"

A great cheer went up from all.

Laura surfaced again, sputtering. "Hurrah!" she shouted as soon as she had her breath. "Hurrah for Liam. Hurrah for the Gideons."

Liam pulled Laura out of the pool and got a wet and eggy

kiss. Then he pulled Tim out. "No hard feelings, old man? Ooooops..."

Tim lifted him off his feet and pretended he was about to pitch him in.

"Hey!"

Mr. Collyer blew his whistle again and Tim paused, then set Liam down on the edge of the pool. "No," he said. "No hard feelings." And he offered his hand with a grin. More cheers.

Laura was jumping up and down, still squealing. She hugged Angela and Jody and Compton. "We won, we won!" she kept shouting.

How could anyone be so delicious soaking wet and still covered with egg, Liam wondered. "Here. Let's get you washed up," he said manfully, taking her by the hand.

"We won, Liam. We won!"

"We did."

"You were wonderful."

"*You* were wonderful." He got her up to the hose and got the water turned back on.

"Squirt me everywhere," she said. "Everywhere."

He started with her hair, flushing the water over it and scrubbing a bit to wash away the egg. Laura was still hopping with excitement. She let the water run over her face, didn't even put a hand up to clear her eyes. She was holding onto Liam's arm with both hands. "Oh, Liam."

Liam adjusted the stream to squirt the egg off her dress.

"Do here too," Laura told him, leaning forward and opening the throat of her dress. She pulled the collars back wide to show where the egg had gone in.

Liam squirted as instructed until she was clean and pink, then went on to wash down the rest of her dress and her legs.

"Ooooooo," she exclaimed as he stood up. "Ooooooo. I have never had so much fun in my life. Never. Never!"

Liam squirted the odd bit of egg left in her bangs.

"Never," she said, ignoring the water. "Liam, this changes everything."

"It does?"

"It does." She was grinning even more. "I mean about my life. About what I want to do. Don't you see? Everything is changed."

"It is?"

"Yes. Before I was going to be an artist or a teacher, or something like that. That's what I've always thought. And now—"

"And now?"

She looked at him happily, water still streaming down her face. "Now I think I shall be a general."

26

Summer's End

***

Old Mr. Collyer was never quite the same after the Great Zucchini War. He seemed cheerful, but he didn't speak much. In fact, he didn't speak at all.

"Langley? Feeling okay, are you?" the Colonel shouted to him. Mr. Collyer looked up, smiling. Just the smile. He was seated by the fire in Inverness. He was spending most of his days there now.

"I don't doubt he's had a little spell," Colonel Forsythe told Liam worriedly. "Something in his brain." They had stepped out of earshot.

"Oh, dear."

"I don't think he *can* speak."

"Oh, dear."

Liam went back and took Mr. Collyer's hand, which was warm enough. "Mr. Collyer?" he asked. Mr. Collyer turned his smile onto Liam.

Something familiar about that smile, Liam thought. Something he had seen before. It seemed so sweet, as though there were nothing on Earth to be concerned about.

A child's smile. It was the smile, Liam thought, that a baby gives you in exchange for a tickle: charmed, but utterly uncomprehending.

☘

Though Mr. Collyer managed to dress himself and take his meals, it was clear that he ought not to be left on his own for the journey home. The Colonel didn't think he was *copis mentis* enough to switch trains, might not even know what to do when he arrived.

Liam changed his plans to leave a day early to accompany the old man to New York. He would deliver him by cab directly to the uptown house that Mr. Collyer shared with his brother. The brother had been called long distance.

So it was summer's end for Liam. In another few hours, after one last Cartefigue luncheon, they would leave for Rockland and the afternoon train. He found he wanted nothing more to make his summer a total success than to spend the last morning in his own company.

He walked up the hill after breakfast. There was a lovely view from there out over East Penobscot Bay. He settled in to see what the morning would offer. The pretty village of Castine was visible across the bay, and just south of it Little Deer Isle and Eggemoggin Reach. By now he knew all the seascape by heart.

Although it was only the end of August, the leaves were already starting to turn. There was a chill to the nights, at least here on the island. He had noticed the starlings this morning, swirling around and flocking, obviously getting ready. They would take off in a sudden flurry, circle about, then falter and come back down again. It was just a matter of time.

He could see that the Canada geese had already begun their migration. He remembered a rhyme from his school days: "Something told the wild geese that it was time to go

/ And though the fields were golden...something whispered snow."

He watched distant lines of geese beginning their way south: the tug of nature. He checked inside himself for the migrator's urge. Could he share the birds' rising uneasiness, the pull? He thought he could. Something pulling him...south? Well, no, not exactly south. But pulling him, at any rate. Pulling him toward his life, whatever that would be. He thought he could feel the tug.

He was not the only watcher over the sea that morning. Below him on the rocks was another solitary figure, a rather stout one in a skirt and green blazer and Tyrolian hat, with a walking stick. It was Aunt Grace. She hadn't seen him. Liam watched her, along with the rest of the sparkling morning. She stood quietly, her back to him, looking out over the water.

From the north, another wide vee of geese was approaching. Where had these come from? Maybe from the Bagaduce River, he thought; that was what lay directly behind them. Or maybe they had come farther, from Canada, or even beyond. These were headed directly over Hewes Point. When they were still a quarter mile away he could hear their honking. Honk, honk, honk. It was a wonderful sound. Liam got to his feet for them, respectfully; he stood as he would for a woman entering the room. He raised his arm in a wave.

Down below him on the rocks, Aunt Grace was waving up to the geese too. "Good luck," she shouted to them. "Good luck."

"There can be no regrets. Ever," Laura told him. "Life is too short. What happens is best, I firmly believe that." She was holding Liam's hand in both of hers. "Only this summer, I might have wished for a tiny difference."

"Oh?"

"I shall wish that difference forward to next summer."
She brightened. "I shall hope that *that* one might be our
summer, Liam."

"I would like that."

She leaned forward to give him a generous, sisterly kiss.
Then she stepped back, smiling. Her eyes locked firmly onto
his. "I would like that too," she said.

Sissy, Jody, Marjorie, Aunt Grace, Colonel Forsythe,
Compton, Cartefigue, Angela: hugs, handshakes, thanks,
bon voyages, reminders to come back again next year.

"You must come again, Liam," Marjorie told him. "Come
always. We won't know how to have a summer without you."

"Or a Fourth of July or a Great Zucchini War," Jody
added.

"Thank you, thank you," Liam told them. "I will. I'll come
back. I always will."

"Well, my boy." Another affectionate hug from the Colonel. "My boy." There was a low toot from the *Nellie B.* "Well,
must be on your way. Train won't wait, you know."

Liam took Mr. Collyer's arm (again that sweet smile) and
led him down the pier. He helped him into his place on
Nepenthe's red leather banquette seat. Then he climbed in
beside him.

Another toot from the *Nellie B.* Mr. Jervis engaged the
gears. The lobster boat gathered way, taking up the slack in
the tow line. And *Nepenthe* lurched forward, out into the
Narrows behind her tow.

Liam turned back to wave. He waved and waved till Dark
Harbor House, all but her tower roofs, was lost from view,
waved until nothing was left to wave to but one tiny figure
on the end of the pier. He waved a last time, and Laura
waved back.

AUTHOR'S NOTE

THE REAL VILLAGE OF DARK HARBOR is on the lovely island of Islesboro in Maine's Penobscot Bay. Islesboro lies just a few miles off the coast, in full view of the Camden Hills and the little towns of Lincolnville and Northport. On the mainland, to the west and slightly to the north of Islesboro's Grindle Point, is the settlement called Temple Heights, scene of frequent spiritualist and revival camps in the late 1800s and early 1900s.

Jeannie Isobel and Haydée are characters of my own invention. However, the evangelists Aimee Semple McPherson (1890–1944) and Ellen G. White (1827–1915), on whom they were based, were very real. They traveled around the country, dispensing their unique blends of religion, music, and dietary advice. There were persistent rumors about Aimee that were no less shocking than those about Jeannie. Jeannie's theory about "religion as theater" would have struck a responsive chord in Aimee. And the choleric irritation that Haydée felt toward Jeannie was very like Ellen White's outrage at the new generation of female preachers, as much for their nutritional heresies as for the occasional indiscretions of their personal lives.

W. K. Kellogg (1860–1951) and C. W. Post (1854–1914) are real figures, but Dr. Ralston is not. He is purely a work of fiction, only it wasn't I who invented him. He was conceived as an advertising gimmick by the Ralston Clinic, now part of the Ralston Purina Company. The clinic felt it needed a doctor's credentials to buoy its image, so it concocted Dr. Ralston.

Portland Free Press reporter Thomas E. McLaughlin, who made his reputation with extended interviews of early twentieth-century evangelists, was my grandfather. He went on to cover sports for the *Boston Post* and eventually became advertising editor of the *Saturday Evening Post.*

There is a real Dark Harbor House—not the elaborate, tumble-down mansion I have portrayed, but a pleasant country inn by the shore of Gilkey Narrows on the island of Islesboro. It was on the lawn of the real Dark Harbor House, one summer afternoon, that I began to think about the events that would take place in that bygone Dark Harbor House of my own imagining.

ACKNOWLEDGMENTS

Thanks to my editor, Karin Womer, at Down East Books, for her thoughtful guidance in organizing and assembling the final work. Thanks, too, to Chris Cornell and Alice Devine and Neale Sweet of Down East for their help, and to Barbara Feller-Roth for her careful line-by-line editing. For his deep involvement in the project and for his lovely cover painting, my thanks to the artist, Anthony Bacon Venti, of Cushing, Maine.

For encouragement and suggestions on specific scenes, I am indebted to Aleta Daley, Nellie Hart, Bruce Taylor, Justin Kodner, and Sally O. Smyth.

—Tom DeMarco
Camden, Maine